IT COULDN'T MATTER LESS

Peter Cheyney

IT COULDN'T MATTER LESS

A Slim Callaghan Mystery

COLLIER BOOKS

Macmillan Publishing Company

New York

Copyright © 1941 by Peter Cheyney Limited
First published in 1941 by William Collins Sons & Co. Ltd.

Collier Books
Macmillan Publishing Company
866 Third Avenue, New York, NY 10022

Library of Congress Cataloging-in-Publication Data
Cheyney, Peter, d. 1951.
    It couldn't matter less/Peter Cheyney.—1st Collier Books ed.
    p.   cm.—(A Slim Callaghan mystery)
  "First published in 1941 by William Collins Sons & Co. Ltd."
  —T.p. verso.
    ISBN 0-02-031040-4
    I. Title.   II. Series: Cheyney, Peter, d. 1951. Slim Callaghan
  mystery.
  PR6005.H4818   1989   89-9794   CIP
  823'.912—dc20

First Collier Books Edition 1989

10 9 8 7 6 5 4 3 2 1

PRINTED IN THE UNITED STATES OF AMERICA

Contents

To
Peggy ('It Couldn't Matter Less') Martineau

At the tender age of fourteen, **Peter Cheyney** (1896–1951) persuaded his parents to let him drop out of school so that he could become a writer. His first published story followed within the year. Between that auspicious beginning and his untimely death, Cheyney went on to publish 150 more short stories, thirty-five novels, and a host of radio dramas. His series characters included Lemmy Caution, an American G-man stationed in Europe during World War II; Sean Aloysius O'Mara, a smooth-talking secret agent; Alonzo McTavish, gentleman jewel thief; and Slim Callaghan, the wise-cracking Sam Spade of London's criminally laden East End. Slim is the only British private eye, from the hard-boiled school of hard knocks, still surviving in print from the golden age of detective writing. Cheyney was an inveterate storyteller, which is suggested by his favorite working method: He preferred to *tell* his books, rather than write them—dictating to his faithful secretary, Miss Sprague. Devoted readers of Peter Cheyney will be long in her debt as they relish the spontaneous, tough quality of her boss's delicious prose.

1

Birthday Night

Callaghan – sole occupant of the downstairs bar at the
Green Paroquet Club – tilted his chair back against the
wall, put his hands in his pockets, gazed solemnly, with
eyes that were a trifle glazed, at the chromium fittings of
the bar-counter at the other end of the room. The bartender, wearily polishing glasses, wondered when he would
go.

Callaghan was wearing a well-cut double-breasted din-
ner-jacket, a white silk shirt with a soft collar, a black
watered-silk bow. His face was inclined to thinness and
his jaw-bones stood out. His hair was black and unruly.
His shoulders were broad, tapering down to a thin waist
and slim hips.

He tilted the chair forward, felt in the breast pocket of
his jacket and produced a thin red and white gold cigarette case. He flipped it open, took out a cigarette, lit it
and sat, his shoulders hunched up, looking at the inside of
the open case. Inset on the red gold in silver were the
words: 'To Slim Callaghan from Audrey Vendayne.'

Callaghan began to think about the Vendayne case and
Audrey Vendayne. After a bit he tilted his chair back
against the wall again and began to whistle softly. He was
whistling a tune called: *It Was Good While It Lasted.*

The bartender rested his elbow on the bar, his head on
his hand, and yawned. Callaghan put the case back in his
pocket, got up. He put on a black soft hat and walked
slowly towards the exit.

The bartender said lugubriously: 'There's another
bleedin' air raid on, it's rainin' an' it's no good lookin' on
the rank outside for a cab becos there ain't none.'

Callaghan looked at him. For some unknown reason the gloom of the bartender made him feel better. He said, almost cheerfully:

'That's too bad. But why be depressed?'

'Why not?' asked the man. 'What 'ave I got to be pleased about. Look at this bleedin' war . . .'

'All right,' said Callaghan. 'Look at it.'

The bartender took down a bottle from the shelf behind him and poured a small brandy. He drank slowly. He hiccupped. He said:

'My missus 'as joined the A.T.S. Every time I see 'er she's always beefin' orf about the sergeant. My missus don't like the sergeant becos the sergeant is a blonde – a natural one I mean, an' my missus can't get the same effec' with peroxide. Las' week I find out that the sergeant is a girl I 'ad a bit of trouble with a year ago. It's a lousy situation. . . .'

Callaghan nodded. He said:

'It's pretty bad. Practically anything can happen. . . . I know what I'd do if I were you.'

The bartender asked: 'What would you do?'

'I'd cut my throat,' said Callaghan. 'Do that. You'll feel happier. . . .'

He pushed the door open and went out.

Chief Detective-Inspector Gringall, his overcoat collar turned up, his hands in his pockets, his bowler hat tilted slightly forward, turned off Bond Street and began to walk towards 'Ferdie's Place.' When he arrived he went down the area steps, knocked on the door and waited. After a minute the door opened. Framed in the dim light from within was a short figure in a dinner jacket.

Gringall said: 'Hallo, how are you, Ferdie?'

Ferdie grinned.

'All right, thanks, Mr Gringall,' he said. He grinned again. 'We've got a new turn tonight,' he said. 'I think you'll like her. She'll be on in five minutes.'

Gringall said: 'Think I'll come in out of the rain.'

He followed Ferdie along the passage, left his coat and hat in the cloakroom, went up the stairs to the Club Room Floor. There were a lot of people sitting round at the tables, making the most of their one-course meals. Gringall sat down, ordered a sandwich and a bottle of Worthington.

Five minutes later the band wandered on to their platform and began to play a haunting tune. People got up and danced. Half-way through the refrain the lights went out. The curtains at the far end of the room parted and a spotlight fell on the figure of a woman who had begun to sing. The dancers went back to their tables.

Gringall looked at the woman appreciatively. She was about five feet eight inches in height, slim but curved in the right places. As she sang she moved her hips slightly in a quiet unexaggerated way that was very effective. Her face was surprising. It was quite beautiful, very intelligent. Her big eyes, extraordinarily blue, looked at you with an expression that denoted a vague surprise. She sang very quietly, very effectively. You could have heard a pin drop.

Towards the end of the number Gringall stubbed out the cigarette he had lit, got up very quietly and went to the telephone box in the passage.

Windemere Nikolls, his arms hanging over the sides of Callaghan's best arm-chair, his feet on Callaghan's desk, lit a Lucky Strike from the stub end of the last one. Nikolls was wide in the shoulder, running to a little fat. His eyes were bright and penetrating, his face round and good-humoured.

He got up, switched off the light, went across to the window, drew aside the black-out curtain and looked out. A shaft of moonlight was trying to illuminate the corner of Berkeley Square. Nikolls dropped the curtain back into place, switched on the light. He stood leaning against the wall looking through the half-open door of the outer office, appreciating the side view of Effie Thompson.

Effie, in a smart fur coat over a blue suit, a little hat on one side of her head, sat before her desk with her gloved hands clasped in an attitude of patient resignation.

Nikolls heaved himself away from the wall and walked into the doorway. He said:

'Effie, has anybody ever told you you've got one helluva figure?'

She said yes without looking at him.

'You don't say,' said Nikolls. 'Who?'

'You have,' she said, 'a thousand times. Don't you ever think about anything else except my figure?' Her voice was slightly acid.

Nikolls considered.

'Sometimes I do,' he said, 'but not often.'

Effie said: 'I'm about sick of this. He said he'd be back at five, that I was to stay till he came back. He wanted to dictate a report on that Malling case. I suppose it's some woman.' Her voice was sarcastic.

'I wouldn't be surprised,' said Nikolls. He opened his mouth and exuded a large mouthful of smoke. 'Another thing,' he said, 'I just remembered something. It's his birthday.'

'My God!' said Effie. 'I suppose that means he won't be back at all.'

The telephone jangled. Nikolls lounged over to Callaghan's desk and took the call. After he had hung up, he said:

'That was Gringall. I wonder what the hell he wants.'

Effie said: 'I hope nobody's going to start something at this time of night. I'm fed up. I had a date to go to the cinema.'

'There'll be other dates, honey,' said Nikolls. 'I remember a dame I knew when I was in Chicago . . .'

'I know . . .,' said Effie. 'The one with the different coloured eyes. . . .'

She cocked her head on one side as the sound of a footstep came from the corridor outside. They both listened. They heard the lift gates clang and the noise of the lift ascending.

'That's him,' said Nikolls. 'He's forgot all about us. He's just gone straight up to bed.' He grinned. 'Ain't he the heartless guy?' he concluded.

Effie said: 'I'm going to ring through and tell him what I think about this. I wonder if he realizes it's nearly twelve o'clock.'

Nikolls said: 'He probably don't realize anything. But if I was you I wouldn't use the telephone. Sometimes he's sorta acid at this time of night. Why don't you go up, honey?'

Effie said: 'Why should I?'

'Go on,' said Nikolls. 'You know you're curious. You wanta see if he's really cock-eyed or only half stewed. I know you. Another thing, there's always the hope he might even kiss you.'

Effie said: 'You damned Canadian. Sometimes I hate you.'

Nikolls' grin was broad and benevolent.

'Sure you do,' he said. 'I sympathize with you. But stick around long enough and he might – who knows!'

He went back to the arm-chair as Effie walked towards the office door. As she turned the handle he called out:

'You might tell him that Gringall was on the line just now. He wanted Slim to go over to some dump called "Ferdie's Place," off Bruton Street. He wanted to see him there.'

'I see,' said Effie. 'Anything else?'

'Yes,' said Nikolls. 'I told him it was Slim's birthday today. I told him that I thought he'd been out on a jag with somebody, that he probably wouldn't be comin' over. Gringall said to tell him that there's a woman over there doing a torch act that would make a dead man sit up and blink. He said he thought she was the real Callaghan type.'

Effie said bitterly: 'I suppose he thought that would do the trick.'

Nikolls shrugged his shoulders.

When Effie Thompson walked into the sitting-room of Callaghan's flat on the floor above the office, he was lying back in a big leather arm-chair blowing smoke rings.

She said icily: 'Can I go. You've probably forgotten that I've been waiting since five o'clock. You said I was to wait till you came back. I suppose you did forget?'

Callaghan said: 'Correct – I forgot. Do you want to resign or something?'

Effie flushed. Her green eyes gleamed.

'That was uncalled for,' she said.

Callaghan nodded.

'That's what I thought,' he said. 'Anything else?'

She said: 'Chief Detective-Inspector Gringall came through six or seven minutes ago. He was speaking from a Club called "Ferdie's Place," off Bruton Street. He wanted to know if you would go over there and meet him. He didn't say what it was about. Nikolls told him it was improbable, that it was your birthday and that you were out – probably with somebody. I suppose you won't go?'

Callaghan said: 'Your supposition is correct. I'm not going. Anything else?'

'Yes,' said Effie. 'Mr Gringall said also that there was some woman at Ferdie's Place, a singer I believe. He said she was a most wonderful person; that she was a Callaghan type. I suppose,' she concluded acidly, 'he thought that might get you over there.'

Callaghan said: 'You don't say?'

She said: 'If he comes through again is Nikolls to tell him you're *not* going over there?'

He looked at her.

'I wouldn't know,' he said. 'I think not. Good-night, Effie.'

She walked to the door of the sitting-room. When she got there, Callaghan said:

'Effie!'

'Good-night,' she said.

She turned round.

'You've got very nice ankles, Effie,' said Callaghan.

'That gets me somewhere, doesn't it?' she said caustically. 'Nikolls told me a few minutes ago that I'd got a good figure. I'm doing well today.'

Callaghan grinned at her. He said amiably:

'I'm glad you're pleased. Goodnight, Effie. . . .'

She paused with her hand on the door-knob. She said:

'I wanted to wish you many happy returns of the day. I haven't had a chance before. . . .'

'Too bad,' said Callaghan. 'Are you going to?'

She asked: 'Am I going to what . . .?'

Callaghan smiled patiently at her.

'Wish me many happy returns of the day?' he asked.

'But I've just done it,' she said.

He shook his head.

'You haven't. You said you *wanted* to do it. Always do what you want, Effie. It's a good habit.' His grin was maddening.

She opened the door. Over her shoulder she said:

'Many happy returns of the day.' Her voice was like an icicle.

Callaghan said: 'The same to you, Effie. . . .'

She opened her mouth to say something. Then she shut it with a snap of her white teeth. She drew the door slowly to behind her, and when it was almost closed, slammed it viciously. She walked along the passage, entered the lift, crashed the gate and descended.

On the way to the ground floor she thought of some of the things she would like to do to Callaghan.

Callaghan got up from the arm-chair and began to undress. As he took off his clothes he threw them on to the floor. When he had stripped to his underwear he went into the bathroom, filled the wash-basin with cold water and dipped his head into it. He kept it there until it began to ache.

Then he dried his face and began to rub eau-de-cologne from a quart bottle into his thick black hair.

Still rubbing, carrying the bottle in his hand, he went back into the sitting-room. He picked up the inter-communication telephone and waited. After a while Nikolls' voice came over the wire from the office.

Callaghan said: 'Come up here, Windy.'

He put the bottle on the floor, went into the bedroom, selected a shirt, collar, tie and lounge suit, and began to dress.

Nikolls came in. He was smoking a cigar. He said: 'Happy birthday. Are you finishin' it or startin' another one?'

Callaghan put on his trousers. Then he walked into the sitting-room, went over to the sideboard and poured himself out four fingers of Canadian Club. He drank it neat, lit a cigarette, indulged in a fit of coughing. When it was over he asked:

'What did Gringall want?'

Nikolls shrugged his shoulders.

'Search me,' he said. 'I think he wanted you to go over to the dump he was at – Ferdie's Place, off Bruton Street – an' see him. I told him you wasn't in. He said it didn't matter.'

Callaghan said: 'All right. . . . Look in about eleven o'clock tomorrow morning, Windy.'

Nikolls exuded a large mouthful of cigar smoke.

He said: 'O.K. I hope you had a nice birthday an' everything.'

He went out. Callaghan heard the lift gates close.

He stood leaning up against the sideboard. He drew a mouthful of smoke down into his lungs and sent it out in a thin stream through one nostril. He finished dressing, put on a thin overcoat, a black soft hat, and went down the stairs to the office. He unlocked the outer office door, switched on the light, opened the telephone directory. He looked up the address of Ferdie's Place.

Three minutes afterwards he was crossing Berkeley Square in the direction of Bruton Street. The moon had come out from behind the clouds – the thin sleeting rain had stopped. Somewhere above a German bomber droned.

At the Berkeley Square end of Bruton Street he stopped to light a cigarette. He was thinking about Audrey Vendayne. After a while he began to think of Mrs Riverton and some other women whose faces flashed across his mind.

He turned off Bruton Street, found the address he sought, went down the basement steps, knocked on the door. After a few minutes Ferdie opened it.

Callaghan said: 'My name's Callaghan. Mr Gringall telephoned me from here some time ago. Is he still here?'

Ferdie said: 'No, Mr Callaghan. He's gone.' He was smiling amiably.

'I'm not a member,' said Callaghan. 'But I'd like a drink. . . .'

'That's perfectly all right,' said Ferdie. 'Any friend of the Chief Inspector's . . .'

He led the way along the passage.

When Callaghan had left his coat and hat he went up the stairs and into the main room. There were a lot of people there dancing or eating and drinking. They were the usual sort of people that you find in a place like Ferdie's at times like this.

Ferdie said: 'Order anything you want, Mr Callaghan. It's on the house. I'll have your name put on the invitation list tomorrow. There's a turn on in a few minutes . . . a good one . . . I hope we'll see a lot of you.'

Callaghan sat down on a gold chair at a small gold table. He picked up the menu and read it. Printed on the back in silver lettering were the words, 'Ferdie's Place . . . London's Most Famous Bottle Party . . . with Doria . . .'

A waiter came to the table. Callaghan ordered a double Canadian Club. He asked the waiter who Doria was. The man said she was Miss Doria Varette; that she sang. He went away.

Callaghan sat looking at the people around him. He thought they were not fearfully interesting. He wondered what they did – or did not do – when they weren't at Ferdie's Place.

The band stopped playing and the people on the floor went to their tables. Ferdie went on to the band platform and the house lights went out. A spot lime was put on Ferdie. He said:

'Ladies and gentlemen, I present with great pleasure . . . Doria. . . .'

The band started an *ad lib*. The spot lime was switched off Ferdie on to the opening between the curtains, which parted slowly. Callaghan looked at Doria.

She was wearing a tight-fitting frock of silver lamé with a little train. Over it she wore a three-quarter length cloak of the same material, lined with scarlet crêpe-de-chine. There was a high black fox roll collar on the cloak.

She began to sing. She sang in a peculiarly effortless manner and rather as if she were bored with the process. She sang a number called 'I Could Learn,' but by the way she sang it she indicated that even if she could it would be too much trouble. She created an extraordinary atmosphere while she sang. Callaghan noticed the complete and utter silence in the room.

Occasionally she moved. Merely a suggestion of movement, but it was so graceful a movement, so alluring, that one waited expectantly for a repetition.

Callaghan drank his whisky and then a little water.

The woman finished singing. There was applause and the curtains came together. The house lights went up. A young man sitting at the next table leaned over and said to a subaltern in battle dress: 'Christ . . . what a hell of a woman . . . Oh, boy . . . !'

Callaghan signalled the waiter who was hovering.

He tore off one half of the menu and wrote on the blank part: *'I want to talk to you. It might be urgent.'* He signed the note, gave it to the waiter. He said:

'Put that in an envelope and see that Miss Varette gets it immediately. And bring some more whisky.'

He gave the man a pound note.

The band began to play a tango. After a while the waiter came back with the whisky. He brought the bottle. Callaghan wondered whether Ferdie was always so generous to prospective customers. He watched the dancers, drinking whisky when the sight bored him.

He waited a long time. Eventually a lanky page-boy appeared and quietly asked Callaghan to follow him. They went out of the room, downstairs and along a passage that ran parallel with the room above. At the end was a door. The page-boy opened the door and went away.

Callaghan stood in the doorway looking into the dressing-room. He inhaled the scent of face powder and perfume that clings to such places.

Doria Varette was sitting in front of the large wing mirrors on her dressing-table. She was wearing a black suit and a fox fur. Beneath the fur Callaghan could see a suggestion of a lace ruffle.

He thought that the young man upstairs was right. She *was* a hell of a woman. Her beauty was heightened by the incongruity of her raven black hair and the almost icy blueness of her eyes. The whiteness of her skin was accentuated by her hair, and the sensitiveness of her nostrils was matched by that of her mouth.

When she moved to look at Callaghan she imbued the slight movement with the same peculiar grace that he had noticed when she was singing.

She said: 'It was nice of you to want to meet me, Mr Callaghan. I don't often meet members of this place. But you said it might be urgent. *Why* is it urgent?'

She did not smile. While she spoke she held the piece of menu on which Callaghan had written his note between the forefinger and thumb of her right hand. She opened her fingers and the piece of cardboard fell on to the table.

Callaghan thought that the gesture was as effortless as her singing. He said:

'I didn't say it was urgent. I said it *might* be urgent.'

He grinned at her. He was leaning against the doorpost. She noticed the strength of his narrow jaw and his strong even teeth. Suddenly she smiled.

She picked up a cigarette case from the dressing-table and opened it. She offered it to him. Callaghan took a cigarette and produced his lighter.

She inhaled deeply. After a minute she said:

'Why *might* it be urgent?'

He shrugged.

'I wouldn't know,' he said. 'I've never been in this place

before. Earlier a friend rang me up and asked me to meet him here. He also said that you were singing here and that you were my type.' His grin became mischievous. 'He was right . . .'

She got up suddenly. She stood facing him. She was still smiling. Callaghan was looking at her mouth. He thought she had a hell of a mouth. It was superbly carved, mobile, sensitive.

'Well . . .' she said softly. 'And where do we go from there?'

Callaghan said: 'I don't mind. I've got a flat in Berkeley Square. There's a good fire, two bottles of Goulay, a dozen Canadian rye and bourbon, some brandy and a little gin . . . if that's of interest. . . .'

She turned back towards the mirror, picked up a small tailor-made hat and began to put it on. Callaghan thought that putting on a hat was a good test for any woman's figure. A woman either looked very good or she didn't. This one did.

She said suddenly: 'You're a detective, aren't you – a private detective?'

Callaghan nodded.

'How did you know?' he asked.

'Ferdinand told me. He said you had quite a reputation.'

'It just shows you,' said Callaghan, 'doesn't it . . .?' He inhaled and began to blow smoke rings. 'Incidentally, it's my birthday.'

'That makes it *quite* different,' she said. She turned away from the mirror. She was still smiling. She said:

'Well . . . what about the Goulay, the Canadian rye, the bourbon, the brandy and the gin . . .?'

Callaghan smiled at her and pushed the door open. As she was about to pass him she turned towards him. She began to say something, stopped suddenly as if she had changed her mind.

Callaghan put his arm round her shoulder. He noticed the odd look of surprise that came into her eyes for a split second. Then they softened. Quite naturally she put up her mouth for him to kiss.

18

After a moment she said: 'You *are* having a birthday, aren't you?'

He grinned at her. He said:

'We'll see. . . .'

Callaghan unlocked the outside door of his apartment, went inside, switched on the hall and sitting-room lights and waited for her to come in. As she walked across the hall into the sitting-room he swept a practised eye over her.

Her clothes were good, her shoes and stockings expensive. He hung up his overcoat and hat and followed her. She was standing in front of the fireplace looking into the fire.

Callaghan went across to the sideboard, took out a bottle of Goulay and two champagne glasses, and began to open the bottle. He said:

'If you want to powder your nose you go through the bedroom and you find the bathroom on the other side.'

She said: 'Thank you. I think I'll do my face. I can never do it properly in that dressing-room at Ferdie's.'

She opened her handbag, took out a small leather make-up case, put down the handbag on a small table by the fireside and went into the bedroom.

Callaghan put the bottle down and crossed the room very quickly, very quietly. He snapped open her handbag and looked inside. The bag was a fair-sized crocodile bag and it held a lot. Inside were the usual things – a small flask of perfume, a lace handkerchief, a lipstick. At the bottom of the bag was a .28 Spanish automatic marked 'Guernica' and three small ampoules with Japanese lettering on the outside. He recognized the markings. Two of the ampoules contained morphine and the third cocaine.

Callaghan closed the bag, put it back on the table and went back to the sideboard. He poured out two glasses of champagne and pushed the big arm-chairs into place in front of the fire.

When she came back he was standing with his back to

the fire. He passed her a glass and indicated an arm-chair. He said 'Happy Days' and drank off the glass of champagne. He went to the sideboard, brought back the bottle, refilled his glass.

She said: 'I suppose you're a very expensive detective . . .?'

Callaghan nodded solemnly.

'Very,' he said. He began to drink his second glass of champagne.

She went on: 'I haven't a great deal of money, but I've *some* money. I want to find someone. Nobody seems to know where he is.'

Callaghan finished his second glass of champagne.

'That's too bad,' he said.

He watched her drink her own drink. He refilled her glass.

She looked up at him. He could see that her blue eyes were misty.

'I'm fearfully serious about this,' she said. 'That's why I came here. . . .'

He grinned.

'I knew there was a catch somewhere,' he said. 'Tell me about your boyfriend. Maybe he's joined the Army . . . or something. . . .'

She shook her head.

'He hasn't done that,' she said. 'He couldn't. He couldn't pass the doctors.'

Callaghan went to the sideboard and poured out some bourbon. He came back with the glass in his hand. He said:

'I'd like to hear *all* about it. I'm very interested.'

She threw him a quick glance. She said:

'I'm not quite certain as to whether you're taking me absolutely seriously, but I'll tell you about it and then you can tell me how much you'll want to help.'

She drank some champagne. She said:

'His name is Lionel Wilbery. He's a poet. He's one of those young men, very good-looking, very well-dressed.

The sort of young man who pays a guinea for a tie and isn't quite certain where the money to pay for it is coming from. I should think Lionel owed rather a lot of money.'

Callaghan nodded sympathetically.

'He sounds as if he might,' he said. 'Does he drink a lot too . . .?'

'No,' she said. 'Lionel doesn't drink much. He used to, but he gave it up. He gave up drinking when he began to take drugs. . . .'

'Yes,' said Callaghan. 'They usually do. . . .'

'He was fearfully interested in writing poetry,' she went on. 'He was quite keen about it and, I believe, not at all bad. He used to write verse mainly about the sea. He was very fond of the sea. . . .'

Callaghan cocked an eyebrow.

'Perhaps he's drowned himself in it,' he said.

'Oh, no,' she went on. 'I'm certain he hasn't done that. I'm certain that he is about somewhere, but I've got to find out where.' She looked at Callaghan. 'You see,' she said quietly, 'I'm terribly in love with Lionel. I've *got* to know about him.'

Callaghan said: 'What about the police? They's not half bad at finding people. If I wanted to find somebody I'd probably go to the police. And they don't charge anything.'

She shook her head.

'That would be quite useless,' she said. 'I'll tell you why. Lionel got into rather an odd crowd . . . a not very nice set of people. I'd just got him to stop drinking and then he met these people, and I'm certain they introduced him to drugs. He's rather a weak type.'

'D'you know who these people are?' Callaghan asked.

'No,' she replied. 'I only know about them from Lionel. He told me about them after he'd first met them. He thought they were very clever and amusing and smart. And there was an attractive woman, I believe. . . . They are the sort of people who don't do anything and have enough money to be comfortable on and spent quite a lot on drink and things like that.'

Callaghan took the Goulay bottle from the mantelpiece and filled her glass. She sipped the wine absently.

'I don't know why,' she said. 'But I believe they've got Lionel somewhere. I believe they've got some scheme about him. Probably something that they would consider amusing. . . . Do you think you can do anything?'

Callaghan grinned.

'I can try,' he said. He walked across to the writing desk in the far corner and came back with a sheet of notepaper and a fountain-pen. 'Write down his name and address – the last address you knew,' he said. 'I'll get in touch with you in a day or so and let you know what I think about it.'

She rested the notepaper on the arm of the chair and wrote on it. Then she handed the pen and paper to Callaghan. He put them on the mantelpiece.

She got up. She said:

'I'll send you a cheque for a hundred pounds tomorrow. Will that do?'

'It's a good start,' said Callaghan. He stood looking at her, grinning.

'I think I'll go home now,' she said. 'You won't forget to let me know about things, will you?'

Callaghan said he wouldn't. He finished his bourbon. She began to walk towards the hall. She looked at Callaghan when he took his hat and overcoat. He grinned at her.

'I'll drop you,' he said. 'Where are you going?'

'I have a tiny house off Wilton Place, in Knightsbridge,' she said. 'Is that too far . . .?'

Callaghan picked up a late cab in Berkeley Square. The moon had gone in and the black-out was very black. His head ached a little. He wondered vaguely just how much he had drunk during the day.

Doria Varette sat back in the corner of the cab and said nothing at all. Callaghan, looking at her out of the corner of his eye, saw she had regained the cold self-control which, in spite of the dressing-room episode, seemed characteristic.

He paid off the cab on the corner of Knightsbridge and Wilton Street. They walked a little way down the street and turned into a tiny *cul-de-sac*. At the end a blue door showed dimly in the light of his electric flash. She pushed it open. Inside a little flight of four or five stairs curved up to another doorway.

She went inside. Callaghan heard her keys jangle. Standing on the doorstep of the outer door he flashed the torch so that she might find the keyhole.

She opened the door and stepped inside. She said: 'Good-night, Mr Callaghan. Thank you very much.'

He said good-night. He pulled the outer door to, walked down the alleyway into the main road. As he turned towards Knightsbridge a car crossed the road and braked by the pavement.

Callaghan stopped. He leaned up against the wall and waited. The car stopped and someone got out. Callaghan could see the tiny disc of light from an electric torch moving along towards the *cul-de-sac*.

He moved quietly after it. It stopped for a moment in front of the outer door of Doria Varette's house and then disappeared.

Callaghan waited for a moment. Then he moved silently towards the outer door, found it, pushed it open a little way, inserted his head and looked round the corner, up the little stairway.

Doria Varette was framed in the open doorway at the top of the stairs. The light from behind her silhouetted the man who stood to one side of the door.

The man wore no overcoat. His lounge suit was exquisitely cut. He looked as if he had been poured into it. The shoulders were squared and descended into an ultra-slim waistline. The rather wide trousers were draped beautifully over well-polished, tiny shoes. He wore a white silk shirt with diagonal blue stripes and a stiff double collar with long points to match. His tie was made of plain, white matt silk. Stuck in the middle of it was a ruby heart surrounded with splinter diamonds.

He began to speak in a low voice. Callaghan could not hear the words. Doria Varette looked at him with no expression on her face. She stood quite still. In the middle of a sentence she slammed the door in the face of her visitor.

The man began to laugh softly. It was not a very nice laugh.

Callaghan walked down the *cul-de-sac* and stood leaning against the wall, on the corner. After a minute the man appeared, his torch picking out a tiny circle of light on the pavement.

Callaghan said: 'Just a minute.'

The man stopped. Callaghan flashed his torch upwards.

The man's face was an olive colour. It was very thin, very bitter. The thin mouth looked like a slit.

Callaghan said: 'I saw your car parked across the corner, on the pavement, when we drove up. You were waiting for Miss Varette . . .?'

The man said: 'Yes.' The word sounded sibilant.

Callaghan got the idea that he was a Cuban. He went on:

'If you wanted to speak to her why didn't you take the opportunity then? When we were going in. Or did you think you might be interrupting us?'

The other smiled. There was something pitying in the smile. After a moment he said:

'Senor, please believe tha-at you cannot do yourself any advantage in thees matter. Not at all. The Senora Varette is so-och a stranger to the trut'. You know? She makes fools of peepul. Maybe she makes one of you, Senor?'

Callaghan said: 'Maybe . . . I hadn't thought of that.'

The Cuban laughed. It was an odd laugh. It started in the throat and trailed off. It sounded as if it came from a long way away.

'Eef you are a wise man you will theenk of tha-at *now*,' he said. 'You can take some good advice, hey, Senor?'

Callaghan felt in his pocket. He brought out a cigarette. He snapped on his lighter and lit the cigarette.

He said: 'Why do I have to take advice from you?'

The Cuban shrugged his shoulders. Then he put a thin hand into the inside pocket of his jacket and brought out a leather case. He opened the case and took out two bank-notes. Callaghan dropped the beam of light from his torch an inch or two. He could see that they were fifty-pound notes.

The man put the case back in his pocket and folded up the notes. He held them towards Callaghan.

'The Senora Varette,' he said softly, 'she is a one tha-at does not always know just wha-at she ees doing. Some-times she takes a leetle piece of drug, sabe, Senor? A peench of thees . . . a leetle drop of tha-at. She ees what you call not so reliable . . . hey, Senor?'

Callaghan said: 'Maybe. . . . I never thought of that either. . . .'

He took the two banknotes.

The Cuban stopped smiling. His eyes became very narrow. Callaghan could see them like pin points. When he spoke his voice was like a rasp. He said:

'So now you theenk . . . hey, Senor. You theenk it better tha-at you mind your own business?'

Callaghan nodded. He undid his overcoat and put the two banknotes into his waistcoat pocket. He was looking round the Cuban's shoulders, towards the car. He could not see it. It was too dark.

He said: 'Thanks for the information. Good-night.'

He took his electric torch in his left hand and held out his right.

The Cuban looked very surprised. He smiled a little cynically and shrugged his shoulders very slightly. Then he put out his hand.

Callaghan swung his right hand over the hand that came towards him. He brought up his elbow with all the force of his body behind it. He hit the Cuban under the point of the jaw with a thud that jerked his shoulder muscle. Simul-taneously he stepped forward on his left foot, put out his left arm and caught the man as he fell backwards.

Callaghan, moving quietly, dragged the limp figure a few yards down the street. He propped it up half a dozen yards from the Knightsbridge Post Office, against the wall.

He crossed the road and began to walk towards Piccadilly. He stopped in the shadow of the cabman's shelter and examined the two banknotes under the light of his torch. He was glad to observe that they were genuine.

The moon, arriving from a bank of clouds, threw a half light down Piccadilly and made shadows in St James's Park.

Callaghan put the notes away and continued on his walk. He stopped half-way down Piccadilly and fumbled in his fob-pocket for a couple of aspirin tablets.

His head felt a little better. He began to whistle very softly. He was whistling a tune called 'It Was Good While It Lasted.'

2

The Morning After

The jangling of the telephone awakened Callaghan. He realized, vaguely, that it was morning, that his head was aching. He opened his eyes and switched on the electric light. He closed his eyes again quickly. After a while he opened them again and found he could keep them so without flinching.

He lay looking at the ceiling thinking about Doria Varette. He began to wonder about her. He remembered other women who had come into his existence through the medium of a case, played their part and then taken their exit. He remembered that most of his worst best cases or best worst cases had begun through a woman. Sometimes it had been amusing . . . sometimes not so amusing.

Pictures of Cynthis Meraulton – from the old Chancery Lane days; Thorla Riverton – who had started off by being very tough and finished by being very kind – and Audrey Vendayne – followed each other in quick succession. Callaghan smiled at the recollection of Audrey Vendayne.

The telephone continued to jangle. He muttered something under his breath, threw aside the bedclothes, slid his feet out on to the floor. He was wearing the top half of a pair of violet silk pyjamas covered with small white *fleur-de-lys*. When he looked at the pattern he felt sick.

He got off the bed and walked to the telephone. It was Effie Thompson. She said brightly:

'Good morning, Mr Callaghan. I hope you're well this morning. It's eleven o'clock and Mr Nikolls has just come in. He asked me to see if you were awake. I thought I'd better ring through.' She paused for a moment, then: 'I

27

hope you had a happy birthday.' There was the sound of a decided sniff.

Callaghan said tersely: 'Ring down to the services and tell them to send me up some strong tea. Then put Nikolls on to this line. I want to talk to him.'

Nikolls came on.

'Hallo, Slim. How's it goin'?'

'Not so bad,' said Callaghan. 'Listen, Windy, I want you to do something. A young fellow by the name of Lionel Wilbery used to live at Roedean House. It's an apartment place just off Shepherd Market. Find out what you can about him.'

Nikolls said: 'O.K. Anything else?'

'Yes,' said Callaghan. 'I want to know who his people are. He's a poet or something. He doesn't pay his debts; he used to drink and gave it up when he took to drugs.'

'Sounds an interestin' guy, don't he?' said Nikolls.

'Maybe,' Callaghan said. 'That's all I've got to give you. Try and have something for me by this afternoon.'

Nikolls said: 'Right, Slim.'

He was hanging up when Callaghan continued: 'Just a minute. Here's a hint – it might mean something. Find out if a man who looks as if he might be a Cuban, a Brazilian or a Chilean – about five feet nine inches, with an olive skin and a thin face – a man who dresses rather too well and with very small feet – used to get around to Roedean House. Find out if there is any connection between him and Wilbery.'

He hung up the receiver. He stood in the middle of the sitting-room by the telephone table, looking reluctantly through the open doorway at his bed. Then he walked across to the windows, pulled the black-out curtains and looked out.

It was a cold grey February day. The corner of Berkeley Square that Callaghan could see was deserted. He yawned; then he walked across the bedroom into the bathroom and brushed his teeth. He came out, went to the sideboard and poured out a stiff four fingers of bourbon.

He drank it off at one gulp. He shuddered a little, lit a cigarette, began to dress.

At twelve o'clock he went downstairs. Effie Thompson, busily engaged in typing in the outer office, threw him a quick look. Callaghan told her to order some more tea. He went into his room and began to look through his morning mail.

A few minutes later the tea came up. Callaghan drank a cup, went over to the door. He said:

'Effie, get through to Mr Gringall at Scotland Yard. Tell him I'd like to see him. Ask if it would be convenient if I went down there at twelve-thirty.'

He went back to his office. Five minutes afterwards Effie came in. She said:

'I've been through to Mr Gringall. He said he'd be glad to see you. He hoped you had a nice birthday.'

'It was nice of him to remember,' said Callaghan.

He lit a cigarette, lay back in his arm-chair inhaling tobacco smoke, looking up at the ceiling. At a quarter-past twelve he got up, took a cab, went to Scotland Yard. A few minutes later he was shown into Gringall's room.

Gringall said: 'Hello, Slim. It's a long time since I've seen you.'

'Yes,' said Callaghan. 'It was very nice of you to think of me yesterday.'

Gringall lit his pipe.

'I keep your birthday down in my diary,' he said.

'Do you?' said Callaghan. 'Nikolls said that *he* told you it was my birthday.'

'I believe he did,' said Gringall. 'But I had it down all the same.'

Callaghan said: 'You don't say. Do you put everybody's birthday down in your diary?'

'No,' Gringall replied. 'But I thought it would be a good thing to remember *yours*. After all, I've got to admit you've been useful once or twice even if you've been a damned nuisance most of the time.'

There was a pause. Then Callaghan said:

'If you wanted to remember my birthday, why didn't you remember it till midnight? You know, a person's birthday is over at midnight.'

Gringall said: 'I know, but I wanted to have a word with that fellow Ferdinand about something. While I was having a drink there I thought it would be a good idea if you came over and had a drink with me for your birthday.'

Callaghan nodded.

He said: 'I see.'

He lit a cigarette, smoked silently for a few minutes.

Then: 'That woman Doria Varette is a hell of a woman, Gringall.'

Gringall raised his eyebrows.

'So you went over?' he said.

Callaghan grinned.

'Yes, I went over,' he said. 'When I got there I found you'd gone, but Ferdinand asked me to have a drink. So I stayed and listened to Varette sing.'

Gringall smiled.

'Well, then I did contribute something towards your birthday.'

Callaghan said: 'I wonder.'

Gringall began to draw a water-melon on his blotting pad. After a moment he looked up.

'What are you wondering about?' he asked.

Callaghan said: 'I thought I'd like to talk to Miss Varette, so I sent her a note round. She came back to my flat and had a drink. She asked me if I could find somebody for her – somebody she believes is missing.'

Gringall looked surprised.

'Did she now?' he said. 'Well, it looks as if you've got a case. Congratulations.'

Callaghan said: 'Yes. But it is an odd sort of case, isn't it, Gringall? That's why I came down here.'

Gringall, who had finished drawing the water-melon, began to draw a tomato.

He asked: 'Why is it an odd case?'

Callaghan went on: 'If you want to find somebody, the

right people to go to are the police. The police have much more chance of finding somebody than a private detective has.' He grinned at Gringall. 'You ought to know that,' he said.

Gringall said: 'Good God! You're not telling me we can do anything better than you can?'

'I didn't say *that*,' said Callaghan.

Gringall re-lit his pipe. He said:

'There might be something in what you say.'

Callaghan said: 'Why is it if this Wilbery fellow – that was the name, I think – has disappeared, his family aren't interested in it, that is if he has a family?'

'Quite,' said Gringall. 'Why was Doria Varette interested in Wilbery?'

'She's in love with him,' said Callaghan.

Gringall said: 'Well, let's see what we can find out. What did you say the name was?'

Callaghan gave him the name and address of Lionel Wilbery. Gringall rang the bell on his desk. After a minute a detective-constable came in. Gringall said:

'See if there's anything on the file about this name. See if it's been reported as a missing person and whether anybody's been in touch with us about it.'

Callaghan nodded.

'That's nice of you, Gringall.'

Gringall smiled.

'Not at all,' he said. 'Maybe you'll do something for me one day.'

Callaghan grinned amiably. He lit a cigarette, began to blow smokes rings.

Gringall got up from his desk and walked over to the window. He looked out. After a few minutes he turned.

He said: 'You're not losing your grip, are you, Slim?'

Callaghan said: 'You damned policemen are always so mysterious. What does that mean?'

Gringall smiled.

'Let me do a little deduction for you,' he said. 'Last night you go to a night club. You meet a good-looking lady. You take her back to your flat. She goes because' – Gringall looked a trifle quizzical – 'she probably likes the cut of your jib in the first place – they tell me you've got a way with women, although I could never see it personally – and, secondly, because she wants you to do something for her. She wants you to find this Wilbery. Is that all right?'

'That's all right,' said Callaghan.

'Well,' Gringall continued, 'then you come down here to find out if Wilbery has been reported to us as a missing person.'

'You don't say,' said Callaghan. 'And why do I do that?'

'You do that,' said Gringall, 'because if he hasn't been reported to us as a missing person you get in touch with the family. You tell them that you've been approached by Miss Varette to find Wilbery. You've already made up your mind that the Wilbery family wouldn't be too keen on an investigation being made at the instigation of some young woman they probably don't know. You think they'll probably commission you to find Wilbery. So you get paid both ways.'

'Just fancy that now,' said Callaghan. 'That's all right, but it only works if the family haven't already been in touch with Scotland Yard – you realize that?'

Gringall nodded.

'We'll know in a minute,' he said.

He went back to his desk and began to draw a pineapple. Callaghan blew more smoke rings. Two minutes afterwards the detective-constable returned.

'There's nothing on the file, sir,' he said to Gringall. 'There's been no inquiry about Wilbery.'

Gringall said: 'Thanks.'

The detective-constable went away. Gringall cocked an eye at Callaghan.

'So it looks as though it's come off, Slim,' he said.

Callaghan got up.

'It looks as if it has,' he answered.

He picked up his hat and went out.

Five minutes afterwards a very slim, elderly and rather distinguished looking gentleman walked into Gringall's room. He said:

'Do you think he fell for it?'

Gringall said: 'I'm certain he did, sir. Hook, line and sinker.'

Callaghan came into the office at five o'clock. He went into his room, sat down at the desk. He opened one of the drawers, took out a bottle of rye whisky and a medicine glass and drank a stiff three fingers. He felt better afterwards. He put his feet on the desk and smoked cigarettes.

At five-twenty Nikolls came in. Callaghan said:

'Well, Windy?'

Nikolls hung up his hat. He eased himself into the big leather arm-chair by the fire took out a packet of Lucky Strikes. He looked at the medicine glass. Callaghan passed the bottle.

Nikolls said: 'This guy Wilbery is a punk. He's been livin' around at Roedean Apartments for ten months. He's got a small allowance from his mother. She lives in a house called Deeplands at Norton Fitzwarren in Somerset. From what I can hear she's lousy with dough. His father's dead. His mother's cut his allowance two or three times because she's heard stories about his drinkin' an' goin' on.'

Callaghan said: 'I see. Did he do anything?'

'Not so you'd notice it,' said Nikolls. 'But he used to write poetry – I ask you! About four or five months ago he started gettin' around with an odd crowd. I think he started on the hop then. He's the sort of guy who goes for drugs. Sometimes he comes home an' sometimes he don't. He's been way for two three weeks or a month. He owes five months' rent, an' if it wasn't for his family the people at the apartments would pinch his furniture.'

'Nice work,' said Callaghan. 'What was the housemaid like?'

'It wasn't a housemaid. They got a housekeeper there.

She's all right too. That dame has nice hips an' ankles that strike right home.'

Callaghan said: 'Does she know any more?'

Nikolls grinned.

'I got a date with her sometime,' he said. 'She sorta likes me. Maybe I'll find something else out.'

Callaghan said: 'I shouldn't worry. You said it was the mother who lived down in Somerset?'

'Yeah,' said Nikolls.

He poured out his second shot of whisky.

Callaghan said: 'Get through on the telephone. See if you can get her. I want to talk to her.'

Nikolls said: 'Is this case a secret or do I know somethin' about it?'

Callaghan lit a fresh cigarette. He said:

'I saw Gringall this morning. I asked him what he wanted to see me about last night. He said he wanted to wish me a happy birthday. He said he had the date down in his diary.' Callaghan grinned cynically. 'He didn't *know* it was my birthday till you told him on the 'phone last night,' he said.

Nikolls said: 'Well, what's the answer?'

Callaghan said: 'Gringall wanted me to go to Ferdie's Place last night. When I got there I thought Ferdie was a little too affable. He'd been told I was coming over.'

'I get it,' said Nikolls. 'All that stuff about the lovely dame over there who was right up your street was just to make sure you did go over?'

Callaghan nodded.

'Gringall wanted me to meet the Varette woman last night,' he said. He drew the cigarette smoke down into his lungs. 'When I meet her I ask her to come round here and have a drink. It is rather a coincidence that when she gets here she wants me to find Wilbery. That's the reason I went to see Gringall at the Yard this morning.' Callaghan began to grin. 'Gringall suggested,' he went on, 'that the family might be annoyed at my being commissioned by a young woman they didn't know to look for Wilbery. He thought it might be a good thing for me if I got in touch with the family – that they might like to give me a job.'

Nikolls said: 'But if the family was worryin' about Wilbery, wouldn't they have been in touch with the Yard?'

'Right,' said Callaghan. 'But it's obvious that the family haven't been worrying about Wilbery, because Gringall went out of his way to let me know that they *haven't* been in touch with the Yard.'

Nikolls nodded.

'It's goddam mysterious, I reckon,' he said. 'It just proves somethin' or other, but I don't know what.'

Callaghan said: 'When you were making a play for that housekeeper round at the Roedean Apartments, she didn't say anything about the man I told you about – the man who looked like a Cuban?'

Nikolls shook his head.

'No,' he said. 'I talked to her about that. She didn't know a thing.' He sighed audibly. 'A dame with a shape like that don't *have* to know much.'

He went out.

Callaghan sat blowing smoke rings, looking at the ceiling, wondering about Gringall. Outside he could hear Nikolls trying to get through to Mrs Wilbery at Norton Fitzwarren, being told that there was a delay on the line.

He wondered what Gringall's game was. Gringall was no fool – Callaghan had been up against him too often since the days of the Meraulton case to have any delusions on that point – and it was certain that Gringall had some scheme in the back of his mind; something which concerned Callaghan or needed Callaghan unconsciously to bring that scheme to fruition.

And Gringall would have no scruples about using Callaghan. Why should he? Callaghan remembered, with a grin, the numerous occasions during the past two years when he had made good use of the police officer. And Gringall had a long memory.

Was it a sudden idea which had caused him to telephone through the night before? Obviously he had wanted to get

Callaghan over to Ferdie's Place. Obviously he had wanted Callaghan to meet Doria Varette. Why? It was just as obvious that he had not wanted to be present during the interview, otherwise he would have stayed at the bottle party on the off-chance of Callaghan turning up.

Callaghan began to think about the Cuban. He wondered why Doria Varette's late caller had been so generous with the two fifty pound notes. Fifty pound notes did not grow on apple trees and there was no consideration for the pay-off. Maybe, the private detective thought, the Cuban had taken him for someone else. Why not?

What the hell . . .? Callaghan, who seldom worried about looking at anything that happened beyond the end of his nose, who believed that Sherlock Holmes' methods of deduction looked wonderful in novels but flopped badly when it came down to cases, was concerned with the facts that *were*, at the moment, right under his nose. The facts were Gringall planting him, Callaghan, at Ferdie's Place at a crucial moment, the interview with Doria Varette, the encounter with the Cuban and the fact that nobody seemed to give a damn what had happened to Lionel Wilbery – *except* Doria Varette.

As facts they added up, at the moment, to sweet nothing at all. But they constituted a good kicking-off ground. Callaghan, whose motto Gringall had, in a caustic moment, once said was 'We Get There Somehow and Who The Hell Cares How,' thought that, as a kicking-off ground, the facts were all right.

Callaghan wondered if Lionel Wilbery *had* disappeared. He might easily be on a bout of drink or drugs or something. The Varette woman might be panicking about him because she was crazy about him or because she was trying to get away with something. . . You never knew with women.

He began to grin. That was about the truest thing that anybody had ever said. You never knew with women. At least you knew some things but nothing that ever added up to anything logical. Women were the true individualists.

They were so damned keen on being themselves that, very often, their simplicity of outlook made you think they were much more mysterious, much more dangerous, than they really were. The essential difference between men and women – especially when they got into some sort of trouble – was that a man did things by reason and a woman by what she thought was 'instinct', but which was, in reality, the quickest method of getting what she wanted – a point of view which was, in fact, much more logical than that of the male. A man always saw certain things sticking up in his way. He would try to evade them if he could. A woman saw nothing she did not wish to see – not even the inevitable.

He took his feet off the desk, stubbed out his cigarette end in the ash-tray, lit a fresh one. He opened the bottom drawer, took out the rye bottle and the medicine glass which Nikolls had replaced and poured himself a drink. The rye tasted acid and bitter. Callaghan thought that maybe he'd been drinking a little too much lately, then qualified the idea with the thought that you could not really drink too much anyhow.

Nikolls stuck his head round the doorway. He said:

'She's on the line. She's got a voice like the Queen of Sheba after she'd graduated from Vassar. She's so god-damned county it hurts. She's all yours.'

Callaghan picked up the telephone. He said:

'Is that Mrs Wilbery?'

The voice at the other end said yes.

Callaghan went on talking. He sounded quite imperso-nal and quite dispassionate. But he managed to imbue his words with a certain urgency intended to do something to the listener. He said:

'This is Mr Callaghan of Callaghan Investigations, Lon-don. I am calling you, Mrs Wilbery, because I understand from the Scotland Yard authorities that you have *not* reported the fact that your son, Mr Lionel Wilbery, is believed to be missing. . . .'

She said: 'But I don't understand. Why should I have

reported that fact? Is Lionel missing . . . and missing from *where*?'

'Exactly,' said Callaghan briskly. 'My whole point in calling you, Mrs Wilbery, is that this organization is not keen on undertaking an investigation in which the nearest relatives of the missing person are not particularly interested.'

There was a pause. Then the cool voice at the other end asked:

'Mr Callaghan. *Is* my son missing? *Who* believes him to be missing? Please explain.'

Callaghan said: 'Of course. Yesterday, Mrs Wilbery, a young lady by the name of Varette – Miss Doria Varette – assigned us to investigate the whereabouts of Lionel Wilbery. She suggested that he had not been seen for some weeks; that she was very worried about him. She also informed us that he was a person of not very good habits, that he had been in the habit of taking drugs, that he was in the habit of mixing with people who were not-so-good. She has offered to pay us a considerable sum to try and find him. Naturally we took up the matter with the Scotland Yard authorities. They tell us that you have not indicated that you considered him to be missing.'

She said coolly: 'But I am naturally very interested, Mr Callaghan. I want to know what has happened to Lionel, *if* anything has happened to him.'

Callaghan grinned into the receiver. He said:

'Well, Mrs Wilbery, you surely aren't *very* surprised. After all, you knew the sort of people he was getting around with . . . didn't you?'

'Really, Mr Callaghan . . .' The voice was caustic. 'And may I ask how you come to that conclusion?'

Callaghan said: 'Why did you cut his allowance?'

There was a pause. Then she said, as coolly as ever:

'I don't think we ought to talk about this on the telephone, Mr Callaghan. First of all if there are any grounds for believing that Lionel has disappeared I should naturally want him found. But I really don't see why a Miss Varette should concern herself. Who *is* Miss Varette?'

Callaghan said: 'Apparently Miss Varette is, or was, your son's fiancée. Didn't you know?'

'No,' she answered. 'I didn't know Miss Varette. But then there are many of my son's friends whom I haven't met.'

Callaghan said: 'Thanks, Mrs Wilbery. I'm sorry if I've troubled you. . . .'

'Just a moment, Mr Callaghan,' said Mrs Wilbery. 'I suppose if you are investigating this business for Miss Varette there is no reason why you should not also represent us?'

Callaghan looked up at Nikolls who was leaning against the office door. His wink was comprehensive. He said into the telephone:

'No reason at all, Mrs Wilbery.'

'Excellent,' she said. 'Well . . . I wonder if you could come and see me. You see I don't go to London very often. I would like to talk to you about this.'

'Of course,' said Callaghan. 'I'll try and see you tomorrow.'

'Perhaps,' she went on, 'you might see my daughter first. She's in London. Perhaps she may know something of Lionel. I'm afraid he's an extraordinary boy. Will you go and see her and let me know if she has any ideas when you come down?'

Callaghan said he would. He took a note of Miss Leonore Wilbery's address – 15 Claremont House, Welbeck Street, murmured a few words of farewell and hung up the receiver.

Nikolls said: 'Nice work . . . hookin' two clients on one job.'

Callaghan did not reply. He was wondering if Leonore Wilbery was going to look as good as her mother sounded.

Callaghan and Nikolls sat on high stools in the upstairs bar at the Premier in Dover Street. They were drinking double rye whiskies.

Nikolls said: 'It looks goddam screwy to me. You don't

know anythin' about this Varette baby an' she's slipped up already, ain't she?'

Callaghan said: 'Has she? How?'

'What about the two hundred she was goin' to send you today?'

Callaghan wondered if he would be too drunk if he had another double rye. He thought the matter over for some seconds – then ordered it. He said:

'True, Windy. I'd forgotten about that. But we're still a hundred ahead of the market.'

Nikolls asked how. Callaghan told him about the Cuban, about the two fifty-pound notes. Nikolls grunted.

'Ain't life a scream?' he said. 'Guys walkin' about London givin' away fifty-pound notes an' all they get for it is a bust on the nose.'

Nikolls finished his drink and rapped on the counter for another.

'Maybe he thought you were somebody else,' he concluded.

Callaghan shook his head.

'I don't think so now,' he said. 'I think that hundred pounds was the pay-off.'

'What for?' Nikolls asked. 'Have you got a theory?'

Callaghan nodded.

'There's only one theory that fits,' he said. 'This fellow was following Varette and myself after we left Ferdie's Place. He saw her come into the flat with me. He could have looked at the indicator on the ground floor and discovered who I was.'

Nikolls grunted.

'I get it,' he said. 'So he concludes that the Varette is comin' to see you about somethin', an' he thinks he'll talk to her about it. Maybe he don't like it. So he gets into his car an' drives round to her place an' waits for her. How's that?'

'Right,' said Callaghan.

'When you get there,' Nikolls continued, 'he sees the cab arrive an' he knows it's her cab because it stops outside the alley-way that leads to her place, but he don't know you're with her. He can't see – it's too dark, hey?'

Callaghan said: 'You're doing very well, Windy.'

'Swell,' said Nikolls. 'He can't see because he's got his car parked on the other side of the road, but he can see when the cab goes. So he walks for a bit an' he goes over to see the Varette. He wants to ask her what the hell she's been doin' talkin' to Callaghan Investigations; an' Varette knows him. Not only does she know him, but she don't like him. So she smacks the door in his face. So he gives up.'

Callaghan wondered whether he could stand *another* double rye. After debating the matter for some moments he ordered two more. He said:

'When he's about to leave the alleyway he finds me there, so he's in a spot. He knows I'm Callaghan. He thinks Varette's been talking to me about something and he's got to make up his mind quickly. He tells me to mind my own business and gives me one hundred pounds to clinch the bargain.'

Nikolls said: 'What a mug that guy is.'

Callaghan said: 'I wouldn't be too sure of that.'

Nikolls swallowed his drink ponderously.

'All right,' he said. 'So we've got a sweet set-up. We got the Varette who is a swell baby with a swell voice an' what it takes. We got her – she owes you two hundred anyway. Then we got this Cuban or Chilean or Brazilian guy – he's just sorta floatin' around. He don't owe you anythin' except a bust in the puss. We're doin' swell.'

Callaghan said: 'We've got more than that. We've got Mrs Wilbery.'

Nikolls said: 'I forgot her. All right. We'll count her in. We've got her too, and another thing, we might even have the Leonore dame. We'll have a baseball team in a minute.'

Callaghan said: 'Which reminds me, what time did you say she'd be in?'

Nikolls looked at his watch.

'They said she'd be in at half-past seven an' it's eight o'clock now. As detectives I don't think we're so hot. We're lettin' somebody slip through our fingers.'

Nikolls hiccupped gravely.

'You never know,' he said. 'She might give us a hundred pounds too.'

Callaghan said: 'Windy, I believe you're drunk. Go and telephone Leonore.'

Nikolls got off the stool and wandered downstairs. Callaghan came to the conclusion that he was drinking too much whisky. He ordered a large Bacardi. He wondered whether drink helped a private detective to think – then came to the conclusion that private detectives didn't think anyway. This thought comforted him.

Five minutes afterwards Nikolls appeared. He said:

'Miss Wilbery's gone out. She's gone to a party. She says if the business is very urgent you might like to go along.'

Callaghan said: 'Do I like going to parties?'

'I wouldn't know,' said Nikolls. 'When I go to a party I like to have some guarantee as to what it's goin' to be like. I don't think parties are so hot – there's too much talkin' an' not enough liquor. I can only remember one good party I went to – that was in Chicago. I met some dame there . . .'

'I know,' said Callaghan. 'This is that strawberry blonde story again.'

Nikolls said: 'For cryin' out loud. Nobody ever lets me finish a story.'

Callaghan drank the Bacardi. He said:

'Where's the party?'

Nikolls said: 'It's at an apartment block called the Collier Arms at Hampstead – No. 76.'

Callaghan got off the stool. He said:

'I think I'm going to the party.'

Nikolls said: 'What about me? Can't I go somewhere an' get a hundred pounds, an' then bust somebody on the nose?'

Callaghan said: 'You go home, Windy. If I need you tonight, I'll give you a ring.'

'Please do,' said Nikolls gushingly. 'It would be so nice if we discovered some more guys in this case. I'll be seein' you.'

He went away.

3

Prelude to a Party

Callaghan walked down Dover Street, turned down Hay Hill, across Berkeley Square. An 'alert' was sounding. When the sirens had ceased there was an eerie stillness.

Arrived at his flat, he threw his hat and coat on the settee in the sitting-room, went into the bedroom, undressed, ran a bath full of fairly hot water, tried it with his toe, hiccupped a little, got into the bath. Safely there, he turned on the cold water tap, lay back and relaxed.

He was thinking. Mainly he was thinking about Gringall. He was rather uncertain about Gringall. During the years that Callaghan had known the police officer he had learned that Gringall was no fool. Police officers seldom are. But he knew also that, during the same period, the Chief Detective-Inspector had had ample opportunity to realize that he – Callaghan – was no fool either. That being so, the present situation did not add up.

Callaghan wondered whether it would be better to have a showdown with Gringall. After a moment's consideration he thought not. If Gringall had wanted to talk straight, he would have talked straight at the beginning. It seemed to Callaghan, groping rather vaguely for the bits and pieces of the kaleidoscope that was beginning to shape in his mind, that whichever way you looked at the job Gringall expected some specific line of conduct from him. Callaghan grinned at the ceiling, remembering that on previous occasions the specific line of conduct had been somewhat different from that which Gringall had anticipated. It was possible that history might repeat itself.

After a while he got out of the bath and dried himself.

He sat for a few minutes in front of the mirror rubbing eau-de-cologne into his hair. He went into the bedroom and began to dress. He was feeling better. His mind was working and the birthday hangover was rapidly becoming a memory.

As he tied his black tie and got into his double-breasted dinner jacket, he put in a little time thinking about Mrs Wilbery and her daughter Leonore. He liked Mrs Wilbery's voice. It was decided, incisive. It possessed a peculiar quality of directness. Mrs Wilbery was no fool.

Callaghan walked into the sitting-room. He went to the side-board and poured himself one for the road. While he drank the bourbon he was trying to conjure up a mental picture of Mrs Wilbery – a process to which he was addicted – but which, on this occasion, was quite unsuccessful.

He lit a cigarette, began to walk up and down the sitting-room. Now he was thinking about the Cuban – because Callaghan had decided that he was a Cuban and in any event that was an easy description. Callaghan, whose experience of men was nearly as varied as his ideas about women, came to the conclusion that the Cuban might easily be very bad medicine. He was that type – effeminate, dandified, soft-voiced and cruel – a nasty type. He wondered what the Cuban was doing wandering about at large at a time like this in England; stopped wondering when he realized that all sorts of odd people were wandering about at large in England.

At ten o'clock he put on his overcoat and hat, went downstairs, walked into Piccadilly, got a taxi and drove to No. 76 Collier Arms at Hampstead. He relaxed easily in the corner of the cab, his black hat tilted over his eyes, his head still aching slightly.

The butler who opened the door looked as if he had stepped off the conventional St James's stage of fifty years ago. He had grey side-whiskers and an urbanity quite unique. He was benign. Callaghan thought he liked benign butlers. He said:

'My name's Callaghan. Miss Wilbery said she'd be here.'

The butler said; 'Oh, yes. Will you come in, sir?'

Callaghan stepped into the thickly carpeted hall. The butler helped him off with his coat and hat. The place was large, expensively furnished. There were three doors leading off the hallway – two of them were open. Sounds of talking, laughter and the clinking of glasses struck Callaghan's ears.

A woman came out of the centre door. Her hair was the colour of new carrots. She had on a pink gown. Callaghan thought she looked like hell. In a vague way she was beautiful. He noticed that the first and second fingers of her left hand were stained almost dark brown with nicotine from cigarettes. She said:

'Are you Mr Callaghan – the detective?'

Callaghan said he was.

She said: 'I think that's wizard. I've never had a detective at a party before. Tell me, is it interesting?'

Callaghan said he wouldn't know but that he once went to a party where there were two performing seals.

She said: 'Now you're pulling my leg! Tell me, Mr Callaghan, do you like my frock? Everybody thinks it's terrible.'

Callaghan said that he disagreed; he thought it was a very good frock. He said he had never seen one like it before.

The woman said: 'I'm glad. Come in.'

Callaghan followed her through the open door. He expected to find a lot of people in the room, but he was wrong. It was a small and almost deserted ante-room. There were folding doors on the other side wide open. On the other side of the doors were a pack of people, most of them glass in hand.

The woman said: 'My name's Mrs Martindale, and I feel rather bilious. I'm interested in art when I get around to it. Would you get me a brandy and soda? The drinks are in the corner over there.' She pointed vaguely in the direction of the folding doors.

Callaghan said he would. He went into the other room. In the corner two men in white jackets were serving drinks. In front of them were an immense array of bottles. Callaghan thought it might be an expensive party.

He asked for a large brandy and soda and threaded his way carefully through the throng back into the ante-room. Mrs Martindale had passed out in the corner of the settee. Her mouth was half-open and Callaghan noted that her teeth were false. He drank the brandy and soda, went back into the other room. He stood just inside the doorway, the glass in his hand, looking about him.

There were about thirty people in the room – all sorts and conditions of people. A few of them were men in khaki. The rest of the men were nondescript. If anything they were inclined to run to stomach and jowl. The women he thought were of much better class. They were slim, well-dressed, effective. Callaghan found himself thinking that taken by and large any given bunch of women looked better than any given bunch of men. A plump and entirely bald man of about forty jostled past him.

Callaghan said: 'Excuse me, but do you know Miss Leonore Wilbery?'

The bald man said yes. He pointed over to the far corner of the room.

Callaghan looked. Reclining on a large antique couch was a young woman. He imagined she was about twenty-seven years of age. She was quite lovely. She was a brunette and he could see that her figure was superb, that her ankles were wonderful, and that not only did she possess a peculiarly striking type of beauty, but she might even be intelligent. He used the word 'might' in his mind because at the moment she was staring straight across the room towards him with eyes which appeared to be glazed. One slender hand, drooped gracefully over the head of the couch, held a cocktail glass at an angle; the liquor inside the glass was spilling over the edge, dropping on to the beige carpet, forming a dark patch.

Callaghan walked across the room. He said:

'Miss Wilbery, my name's Callaghan. I wanted to talk to you and I thought it was urgent enough to come here. I hope I'm not disturbing you.'

She opened her mouth but she did not say anything. It was apparent to Callaghan that she was trying to say something. After a second attempt she succeeded. She said:

'That's marvellous. I'm fearfully glad to meet you, Mr Callaghan. There's only one thing . . .'

Callaghan raised his eyebrows.

'Yes?' he queried. He was thinking that the peculiar low pitch of her voice was unique and attractive.

She said: 'The fact of the matter is I'm cockeyed. I'm one of those women who've never realized that if you have one more you're going to be cockeyed. I think I've had one more.'

Callaghan said: 'Are you certain? It seemed to me that the carpet was getting the last one.'

She looked up at him. He saw that her eyes were the colour of amethysts. Then he thought that possibly they tinged towards violet.

She said: 'I think you're quite delicious. Won't you sit down? I think I like you. I'm never quite certain whether I like men or not. I think I have a complex against men.'

Callaghan sat down. He said:

'I know. I knew another woman like that once.'

Her eyes were wide.

'What – only one?' she said. 'Surely you must have known more women than that who didn't like men.'

'This one was a very special one. She disliked them intensely,' said Callaghan.

The fingers which held the glass opened involuntarily. The glass, which was a thin one, fell on to the carpet and smashed.

She said: 'Wasn't that silly? Would you get me a drink?'

Callaghan said he would. He went to the serving table in the corner. He was feeling rather bored. He got a double brandy and soda for himself and a mild cocktail for her. He went back, gave her the cocktail, sat down.

She got the edge of the cocktail glass to her lips with a certain amount of difficulty. Callaghan, apparently gazing at the crowd in front of him but with the corner of his eyes on her, watched as she held the glass against her lip, tilted it with an effort and swallowed the cocktail.

He noted the superb curving of her mouth, wondered why it was that women who were lovely and presumably intelligent should want to get drunk.

Her glass was empty. She held it by the stem in much the same way as she had held the first one, her hand hanging over the end of the settee. Callaghan waited for the glass to drop. It dropped.

She said, enunciating with a certain amount of difficulty: 'I s'pose you think women ought not to drink, Mr Callaghan. Isn't that what you're thinking?'

Callaghan said: 'I wouldn't say that. I think women ought not to drink too much. You're drinking too much. You're cockeyed. I don't think I like women who get cockeyed.'

She looked at him with an expression that was intended to be antagonistic. She pursed up her beautiful mouth and waggled her head. She said:

'Now you're merely being antagonistic. I don't like antagonistic men.'

Callaghan said: 'What am I supposed to do – jump off the end of the pier?'

She said: 'No, I don't want you to do that. I like you.' She considered this gravely for a moment. 'Yes, I definitely conclude I like you.'

She looked round the room dazedly, trying to remember what she was talking about. Then she went on:

'Of course you're the detective, aren't you? You wanted to see me about something. Mother telephoned me about you, although I must say she was rather vague.'

A man near Callaghan, with a green satin tie on a pink shirt, leaned up against the wall. He said to a woman who was wearing a brocade bodice made like a painter's blouse: 'When I love a woman I love her. I never do things by half measures. . . .' He ended the sentence with a staccato belch.

Callaghan looked at the man. Leonore Wilbery said: 'He *is* awful, isn't he? But then all men are awful. Love's a terrible thing.'

Callaghan said to her: 'So your mother telephoned, did she? So you know all about it?'

Leonore said: 'I'm not certain. I'm not certain that I know anything now.'

She leaned back against the side the settee. Callaghan took out his cigarette case and lit a cigarette. He was looking at her. He was beginning to get ideas about Leonore Wilbery.

He went on: 'Do you think you're sober enough to understand what I'm talking about, because I think it's rather important?'

She said: 'I wouldn't know. But if it was fearfully important it might impress itself on me, mightn't it?'

Callaghan said brusquely: 'Look at me.'

She looked at him. She began to smile, even if the smile was something like a drunken smile. He liked the way her lips parted over her white teeth. He was still undecided whether her eyes were amethyst or violet.

'Well, I hope this will impress itself on you,' he went on. 'The position is this: Last night I met a young woman by the name of Varette. Have you ever heard of her?'

She asked: 'What's her first name or hasn't she got one?'

He said: 'Of course she has a first name. Her first name is Doria – Doria Varette. Does that mean anything to you?'

'Nothing could mean less,' she said. 'And incidentally, I take a very poor view of a woman with a name like that. I've never heard of her and I shouldn't like to meet her.'

Callaghan said: 'That doesn't matter. The point is that *I* met her last night and *I* thought she was rather nice. That, however, isn't important. The important thing is this. It seems that Miss Varette is in love with your brother Lionel. She has a definite idea in her head that Lionel is missing. She commissioned me to try and find him. Do you understand that?'

'Perfectly,' she said. 'But I'm not frightfully interested. Tell me, do you undertake divorce cases?'

Callaghan said: 'No, I don't like divorce cases – unless the case has a redeeming feature.'

She laughed. She laughed for such a long time that people turned round and looked at her. She said:

'O-oh, my God! Fancy employing a detective to look for a redeeming feature in a divorce case.'

Callaghan lit a fresh cigarette. He was thinking that he would like to smack her. She stopped laughing suddenly. She said:

'Yes, I understand all that. So this Doria Varette, whom you think is rather nice, thinks Lionel is missing.'

She leaned forward. Solemnly she put her hand on Callaghan's knee. She said dramatically:

'Tell me, Mr Callaghan, do you love her?'

Callaghan began to grin. He said:

'Not at the moment. To tell you the truth I haven't had a chance. But let's get back to Lionel. You're not particularly worried about him?'

She nodded gravely.

'O-oh, yes,' she said, 'fearfully worried. I've always been worried about Lionel.'

Callaghan asked why.

'Lionel is a strange person – a very strange young man. If you're sister to a strange young man, you *must* worry about him. But go on, Mr Callaghan.'

'I went to Scotland Yard to find out if anybody had reported Lionel Wilbery as a missing person,' Callaghan went on. 'Nobody had. Naturally I was rather curious as to why Miss Varette should believe he was missing and yet the family weren't worrying. So I telephoned through to your mother. She's asked me to go and see her.'

She nodded.

'When are you going?' she asked.

'Tomorrow maybe,' Callaghan replied. 'She suggested I might see you first. She thought you might have something to tell me – that you might know something about Lionel.'

She said mysteriously: 'I think there's a lot I could tell you about Lionel – all sorts of strange, odd things that you ought to know. But not here.'

'No?' said Callaghan. 'Why?'

She went on: 'I don't like this party. I don't like the people. I don't even like myself particularly. But I think I like you. Let's go to another party. I know a much better party than this one.'

Callaghan said: 'I see. But will that be any good? Will that help?'

She said: 'Definitely! There'll be some people there and I *think* they'll be able to tell you something about Lionel. In fact, I'm sure they will.'

Callaghan said: 'All right. Let's go to the other party.'

She said: 'First of all I want to go home. I want to change my frock. I think you'd better take me home. Then you'd better come back for me. Then you can come on with me to the other party. It will be *much* better than this one.'

Callaghan said: 'All right.'

She got up and walked with a little difficulty across the room. He followed her. When she got into the ante-room she stopped before the settee on which the recumbent figure of Mrs Martindale still lay. Callaghan stood looking at Mrs Martindale.

Leonore said: 'I know exactly what you're thinking. You're thinking that hair that colour ought never to be seen against a violet settee. I agree.' She said to Mrs Martindale: 'Dearest, can you hear me?'

Mrs Martindale opened one eye with difficulty. Leonore went on:

'My dear, we've decided either you've got to have your hair dyed or change the cover of that settee. It just doesn't match. Goodnight, my dear.'

Mrs Martindale said nothing. She was already asleep.

The taxi-cab ambled through the black-out in the direction of Welbeck Street at about fifteen miles an hour. In one corner Leonore Wilbery sat up perfectly straight, looking out of the window. Her eyes were wide.

She said suddenly: 'Did you ever hear the story of the man that criticized a girl's figure?'

He said he had not. She gurgled. She said:

'It couldn't matter less. She just didn't hold it against him.'

Callaghan sighed. After a minute he asked:

'Tell me, do you ever suffer from hangovers?'

She turned her head towards him. She said:

'No, I've heard of them. I've never met one. You were thinking about me?'

Callaghan said: 'Yes, I was.'

'What were you thinking?' she asked.

Callaghan said: 'I'm not certain.'

She said: 'You were wondering whether I'm nice or not, weren't you? Wasn't that it?'

There was a pause.

Callaghan said: 'Possibly.'

She leaned towards him with a sudden movement.

'Mr Callaghan,' she said in an odd voice, 'let me tell you something —'

Callaghan realized that her face was close to his in the darkness. There came to his nostrils a vague and rather attractive perfume – not the heavy oriental perfume which one met so often, but something rather light and subtle. He put out his hands and took her by the shoulders. He turned her round towards him and kissed her fully on the mouth.

She said: 'I suppose I ought to shriek for help or something, oughtn't I?'

Callaghan grinned.

He said: 'Why? Didn't you like it?'

She looked out of the window. She said:

'I don't know.'

Callaghan relaxed back in his corner, took out his case, lit a cigarette. He said:

'Would you like to go on talking about Lionel?'

'I don't think so,' she said. 'We'll leave that till later. I want to think.'

Callaghan said: 'That's all right with me.'

He tipped his hat over his eyes. He began to blow smoke rings in the darkness. She sat bolt upright – almost rigid – staring out of the window.

Callaghan paid off the cab in Welbeck Street. Leonore Wilbery stood on the pavement in front of the house with one hand resting on the door-knob. She seemed to appreciate its support.

Callaghan, by the tiny light behind the taxi-meter glanced at his wrist-watch, saw that it was nearly eleven o'clock. His birthday hangover was quite gone. He was wondering whether he was tired or merely bored.

The cab drove off. Callaghan said:

'Where do we go from here?'

She said: 'It's a nice night, isn't it. Dark but otherwise rather good. I'm feeling rather better. I'm not half so cockeyed now. I'll probably be quite intelligent by the time you come for me.'

He asked what time that would be.

'Come back about oneish,' she said. 'I'll be waiting for you here. I'd ask you to come in for a drink but a girl has to be so careful of her reputation these days . . . don't you think?'

He did not bother to ask her why. He watched her as, with a certain amount of trouble, she eventually unlocked the door and went in. He said:

'I'll come back for you at one o'clock.'

From somewhere in the dark hall she said all right.

Callaghan began to walk in the direction of Berkeley Square. An air-raid alert was on and heavy gunfire was sounding on the other side of the river. High above him the intermittent drone of enemy bombers formed a background for the noise of the guns.

He went into a doorway and lit a cigarette. He was thinking about Leonore, wondering whether it was true that she had never met Doria Varette.

Only one aspect interested him at the moment and that was an aspect which he proposed to leave severely alone – at least for the time being. In any event it was something tangible – something he could deal with when the time came . . . if it ever got as far as that.

It was just after eleven when he went into his flat in Berkeley Square. He threw his hat on the settee, helped himself to three fingers of rye, lit a cigarette and began to pace up and down the sitting-room. Somewhere, he concluded, there must be an indication of who was doing what and why.

After a bit he stopped pacing and went to the telephone. He dialled a Mayfair number. Nikolls answered.

Callaghan said: 'What are you doing, Windy?'

'Nothin' much,' said Nikolls. 'I'm in bed readin' a detective story. This story is about a detective who has got such a helluva instinct that every time he looks at a dame the dame knows the detective knows just what she is thinkin'.'

'That must be inconvenient sometimes,' said Callaghan.

'Yeah,' said Nikolls. 'That's what I thought. I was just wonderin' about my instinct when you called through. I gotta theory . . .'

Callaghan grinned into the transmitter.

'You don't say?' he said.

'I do say,' said Nikolls. 'I been working it out. Look. Supposin' you are talkin' to a dame an' she tells you somethin'. O.K. Well, she's either tellin' you the truth or she ain't, ain't she?'

Callaghan said: 'I'll grant that.'

'Well,' said Nikolls. 'If she's tellin' you the truth, that's O.K. an' you don't haveta worry. But supposin' she ain't tellin' you the truth – that's the snag. My theory is this – that the number of times a dame tells you the truth is so goddam small that it don't amount to anythin'. You got that?'

Callaghan said he had got it.

'O.K.,' Nikolls continued. 'Well then, all you got to do is to reckon that every time a dame tells you somethin' it's just a goddam lie an' in about eighty per cent of cases you're gonna be right.'

'All right,' said Callaghan. 'But what about the other twenty per cent.'

'The percentage is too small to matter,' said Nikolls wisely. 'It just don't matter a damn.

'In other words the idea is that everything that any woman tells you is a lie?' asked Callaghan.

'Yeah,' said Nikolls. 'That's my theory.'

Callaghan sighed.

'You're going to get brain fever one day, Windy,' he said. 'Just get dressed and come round to the flat – and don't do any more thinking today. Something might break.'

'O.K.,' said Nikolls. 'But I reckon a detective ought to be sorta logical an' I'm tryin' to get that way. I remember some dame I met up with in Kansas City. This dame was the belle of the dump. She had everything an' she went for me like hell. Well . . .'

Callaghan laid the receiver down on the table, very quietly. He had heard the one about the Kansas City dame before. He lit a fresh cigarette. After a while the drone of Nikolls' voice from the transmitter ceased. Callaghan put it back on the hook. Then he dragged the armchair in front of the fire, put his feet on the mantelpiece and relaxed.

During the fifteen minutes that elapsed before the arrival of Nikolls, Callaghan gave himself up to a consideration of women and drink. He was trying to find the answer to a question that, at first, seemed easy. The question concerned the exact difference between the mental attitude of a woman who was sober and that of one who was not. Callaghan considered that, from the point of view of a man, a woman who was cockeyed would in all probability, be easier to deal with, to take advantage of, to delude and possibly to cross-examine.

But it was the point of view of a woman on the same point that intrigued him. What would be the reactions of a not-so-sober woman to a man *from the point of view of a woman?*

He pondered the point but got nowhere. After a while he heard the lift ascending, then the sound of Nikolls – who had a key – opening the front door of the flat.

Callaghan screwed his head round as his assistant appeared in the doorway. Nikolls was carrying under his arm the book he had been reading when Callaghan had telephoned.

He said: 'I brought it along. It's a helluva book. It tells you all the things you've been wonderin' about all your life – about dames I mean. I reckon the guy who wrote this book knew his groceries all right.'

Callaghan said: 'That's fine. Help yourself to a drink, Windy.'

Nikolls said thanks. He put his hat on the table, went to the sideboard and poured a stiff one. He produced a small fat cigar from his pocket and lit it. Then he came over to the fireplace and stood leaning against one end of it, the whisky-glass in his hand, looking at Callaghan. After a while he said:

'That dame Leonore is a swell dame. . . . I'm tellin' *you*. That dame has got looks an' personality. Yes, sir.'

Callaghan said: 'How do you know?'

Nikolls grinned. 'It's my trainin' as a detective,' he said. 'An' my over developed instinct for the feminine sex. Like it says in this book. Believe it or not,' he continued, 'I got myself trained to such a pass already that I reckon I could tell you a helluva lot about Leonore Wilbery just through instinct.'

Callaghan raised an eyebrow.

'Go on,' he said. 'Tell me.'

Nikolls drew on his cigar and inhaled deeply. Then he screwed up his eyes and looked at the ceiling. His expression was intended to denote concentration of the deepest and most urgent type. After a minute:

'I reckon she ain't a blonde an' she's sorta tall and willowy. Yeah . . . she's got a helluva good figure. She's the sort that you just gotta watch when she's walkin'. You know, the type with the swell hip-line. I reckon she's a brunette. I can't tell you about her eyes exactly, but I'll take a shot that they're either violet or sorta grey-blue. An' she's got sorta sweepin' eyelashes. Maybe her voice is pretty good too. Sorta low an' soothin'. In fact,' concluded Nikolls, 'I would go so far as to say that this Leonore baby is just what the doctor ordered.'

Callaghan smiled at the fire. He said:

'It's not at all a bad description. How did you know what she looked like, Windy? What's your system?'

Nikolls grinned.

'I ain't got a system. I just made that up,' he said. 'But I took a shot at what the dame was like by tryin' to remember the sort of dame you go for. So I figured up a sorta composite picture.'

'Yes,' said Callaghan. 'That's interesting. And how did you know I went for her?'

Nikolls said mysteriously: 'I got a reason.'

'Well, what is the reason?' demanded Callaghan. 'Come on, Windy, get it off your chest.'

Nikolls removed the cigar from his mouth and flicked off the ash.

'First of all,' he said. 'You didn't stay at that party long. So I reckon you got out early an' I also reckon she went with you. If that's O.K. then you two got somethin' in common – either connected with this Wilbery case or sorta personal. So I reckon you went off with her an' went a cab-ride some place. O.K.?'

'That's all right,' said Callaghan. 'But what do you mean by saying that we had something in common either connected with this case or "sorta personal"? What do you mean by "sorta personal"?'

Nikolls said ponderously: 'My years of trainin' as a detective tells me that you been kissin' Leonore in a taxi-cab. O.K.?'

Callaghan sat up.

'How the hell did you know?' he asked.

'You got lipstick all over your pan,' said Nikolls, with a happy grin. 'An' it looks terrible. I think that calls for another little drink.'

He went to the sideboard and got it. Callaghan, after looking in the mirror above the mantelpiece, went into the bathroom and cleaned his face. When he came back he said:

'Maybe your years of training can tell you something else?'

'Why not?' asked Nikolls. 'Such as . . .?'

Callaghan lit a cigarette. He said:

'When I got to the party tonight Leonore was putting on an act. She pretended to be stewed. She went out of her way to tell me that she was cockeyed; that she'd been drinking all the evening. . . .'

'I got it,' said Nikolls. 'That was why you necked the dame in the cab. You wanted to see if she had liquor on her breath.'

'Right,' said Callaghan. 'And she hadn't. I don't believe she'd had more than one drink.'

Nikolls exuded a mouthful of cigar smoke.

'I reckon she was scared,' he said. 'Maybe she's heard about you an' that you are a pretty cute guy when it comes to talkin' to people. Maybe she reckoned you was goin' to do a little quiet third degree on her. So she thinks that if she puts up a front that she's cockeyed you ain't goin' to take very much notice of what *she* says, an' you ain't goin' to be so careful about what you say. That way she scores a point.'

'Right,' said Callaghan. 'And who would it be that told her she'd got to be careful?'

Nikolls considered for a moment. Then he said:

'There's only one person an' that would be the one who sent you along to see her an' telephoned her that you was goin' to see her. I reckon that would be mama Wilbery.'

He wandered over to the sideboard and took another shot

of rye, holding up the bottle to see what was left in it. 'I wonder what these dames are playin' at,' he concluded. He took the rye at a gulp.

Callaghan said: 'I'm not a mind reader. But somebody's going to try and suck me in in a minute. Leonore's taking me on to another party. She tells me that there'll be some people there who can tell me about Lionel. I'm meeting her at one o'clock. That gives her plenty of time to do what she wants to do.'

'And what does she want to do?' said Nikolls.

'Telephone through to the people I'm going to meet and tell them what to tell me.'

'I got it,' said Nikolls. 'This is goin' to be a nice case, I reckon. Everybody is double-crossin' everybody else before we even get started.'

Callaghan said: 'Listen, Windy. And no slip-ups.' He looked at his watch. 'It's nearly eleven-thirty. Doria Varette does her turn at Ferdie's Place at twelve o'clock. She'll do two songs and probably an encore. That's going to take over ten minutes. Then she goes to her dressing-room and does her face and changes. That'll take another twenty at least. That's eighty minutes from now. Then she's got to get a cab and get from Ferdie's Place to her house off Wilton Place. That's going to take another ten minutes at least. That gives you ninety minutes.'

Nikolls nodded.

'What do I do . . . case the Varette dump? Inside or out . . . or are you still lookin' for that Cuban?'

Callaghan said: 'Get inside. You ought to be there in fifteen minutes and inside in half an hour. Take a cab and get out of Knightsbridge. Don't use a torch. Turn round into Wilton Place and keep along the wall past the Post Office. Twenty yards or so along Wilton Place you'll find a little *cul-de-sac*. The bottom of the alley is the front door of Varette's house. The front door will probably be open. It was last night. Inside is a little flight of stairs curving round to the left. At the top is the real front door. It's probably got a good lock on it. You may have to spend ten minutes on that.'

Nikolls said: 'O.K. What am I lookin' for?'

'I don't know,' said Callaghan. 'Get a general impression of the place and look round as much as you can. Don't waste time being clever with desk and drawer locks – just use a small jemmy and be as quick as you can. The great thing to do is to read any correspondence you find. Look for papers, letters, bills, anything that will give us a lead on Varette.'

'All right,' said Nikolls. He knocked the ash from his cigar. 'I'll telephone through from a call-box first an' see if there's anybody there.'

'Right,' said Callaghan. 'If there is any one there, say you're speaking from Ferdie's Place and Miss Varette wants whoever you're speaking to to go to the Club at once. Get 'em out somehow. Have you got that, Windy?'

Nikolls said: 'I got it.'

'You'll find a spider and two or three other tools in the bottom drawer in my desk downstairs. Get a ripple on, Windy. And you'd better have a story ready in case she gets home early.'

Nikolls grinned.

'Sure,' he said. 'I'll tell her I'm a fire-watcher who's lost his way in the black-out. That oughta please the dame. Well, what do I do afterwards?'

'Go to bed,' said Callaghan, 'and talk to me in the morning. Unless, of course, you find something that looks like something. If you do, telephone Effie. She'll be able to tell you where I am. I'm going to a party.'

'O.K.,' said Nikolls. He went to the door. He said: 'Say, wouldn't it be goddam funny if I found that Cuban guy under the bed? Maybe he'd give *me* a hundred pounds too. . . . Well, so-long, Slim. I'll be seein' you.'

He went out.

The Chinese clock on the mantelpiece struck the half-hour. Callaghan went over to the sideboard and poured out four fingers of rye. The whisky tasted good. He lit a cigarette. He went into the bedroom and took off his coat, collar, tie and shoes. He switched on the electric fire, turned off the light, lay down on the settee at the foot of the big bed.

He began to blow smoke rings and watched them in the light from the fire. He was wondering about Leonore Wilbery, Lionel Wilbery, Mrs Wilbery.

He got up and went over to the house telephone. He spoke to the night porter downstairs.

'I'm going to sleep, Wilkie,' he said. 'Call me on this line at half-past twelve and send me up a cup of strong tea at a quarter to one. Have you got that?'

Wilkie said he had got it.

Callaghan went back to the settee and lay down. He went to sleep at once.

4

Meet Sabine – Meet Milta

Wilkie brought up the tea at twelve forty-five. Callaghan was in the bathroom. He came out, put on a fresh shirt and collar, drank a little rye and then the tea. He felt very good.

He was putting on his overcoat when the telephone in the sitting-room rang. It was Leonore. She said:

'Mr Callaghan? This is Leonore Wilbery. Have you got a car?'

Callaghan said he had.

'Could you bring it round?' she asked. 'I want to go to a place called The Dene, in Forest Row, Ashdown Forest. Is that all right?'

'Certainly,' he replied. 'How are you feeling now?'

'Quite all right,' she said. 'I've had a rest and changed my frock. I've just had a double martini and I feel wonderful.'

'I'll get the car and call for you in ten minutes,' said Callaghan.

He hung up. He waited a moment or two, then dialled a Kensington number. He heard the telephone at the other end ringing for some time before Effie Thompson came on the line.

He asked: 'Were you asleep, Effie?'

'Yes,' she replied. 'Sound asleep.' Her voice was mildly sarcastic. 'You don't want to do any dictation or anything – do you?' she asked. 'Because this time is as good as any other.'

'That's nice of you, Effie,' said Callaghan. He grinned into the transmitter. 'Would you be surprised if I asked you to keep awake for a bit?'

'That depends,' she answered. 'Since I've been working for you I've lost the ability to be surprised at anything. But I'd like to help.' She yawned.

'Excellent,' said Callaghan. 'Nikolls may be calling you tonight. He *may* be. I don't suppose he will. If he does you might tell him I've gone to a place called The Dene, Forest Row, Ashdown Forest. It's somewhere near East Grinstead, I believe. Have you got that?'

'I've got it,' said Effie 'I hope I'll be awake when Mr Nikolls rings through.'

'You'd better be,' said Callaghan. 'If you aren't he'll probably come round in person.'

'I'll keep awake then,' said Effie. 'Any time Mr Nikolls calls in the small hours I'm going to wear chain mail and talk through the letter box. Goodnight.' She hung up.

Callaghan put on a thick overcoat, picked up his hat, walked round to the garage in Charles Street. He drove quietly round to the Cavendish Street end of Welbeck Street. The moon was up and the empty streets looked delightful.

Leonore Wilbery was waiting on her doorstep. She was wearing a three-quarter mink coat. Callaghan eyed it appreciatively. He thought it had cost a lot of money.

He got out of the car. He said:

'One of the advantages of being a private detective is that you get opportunities of meeting women as lovely as you are, as well turned out as you are, on doorsteps in Welbeck Street after midnight.'

She smiled. Callaghan watched her lips curved back over white teeth. He thought she had a delightful mouth.

She said: 'A very charming speech. I suppose another of the advantages of being a private detective is that you can kiss women in taxi-cabs any time you feel like it. Right, Mr Callaghan?'

'Wrong,' said Callaghan. 'I consider it unprofessional to kiss women in cabs unless it's in the interests of my client.'

He walked round the car and held the door open for her. She got in.

'I see,' she murmured. 'So I was kissed in the interests of your client. So that's that. I hope the process was successful – from a *professional* point of view I mean.'

'It was all right,' he replied. 'But from the personal angle it wasn't so good.'

He walked round the back of the car and slipped into the driving seat. As he started the Jaguar she said:

'You're rather a difficult person, aren't you. You *won't* do what one expects you to do. You take odd lines and fly off at tangents. So one doesn't know if one can trust you particularly or not.'

'That's all right,' said Callaghan. He put his foot down on the accelerator as the car curved into Wigmore Street. The Jaguar shot forward.

'If I did what people expected me to do I should be in a hell of a jam most of the time,' he went on. 'The majority of the people I come in contact with – when I'm working I mean – expect me to do something that they'd *like* me to do. If I did that I'd get nowhere. I've usually got to do something drastic to get the effect I want. Incidentally, the question of whether you trust me or not doesn't particularly interest me.'

'Delightful,' she said. 'You can be fearfully rude when you want to, can't you, Mr Callaghan? Did you get the effect you wanted by kissing me?'

'Pretty well,' said Callaghan. 'I didn't want to kiss you particularly. Why should I?' He grinned at her sideways. His eyes were mischievous. 'I wanted to find out what sort of condition you were in. I found out that you weren't drunk. So you'd been lying when you put that act on. . . .'

'I see. . . .' Her voice was very soft. Callaghan thought it sounded a little dangerous. 'So I was lying. Why?'

'Because you've got some scheme, of which the party we're going to forms an important part,' said Callaghan. 'If you'd professed to be sober when I first met you there would have been no reason for your taking me on to this party. You could have talked to me there and then. If you'd appeared sober I might have been surprised at being asked to go off somewhere in the country at this hour of night. But from a woman who was cockeyed the request might appear fairly normal.'

She sighed.

'You're not such a bad detective,' she said. She was smiling.

Callaghan grinned at the windscreen. He said:

'We'll see about that.'

It was a long time before she spoke. Then:

'I'll tell you the truth. I'll tell you the truth about why I pretended to be a little drunk and why I suggested we went on to this party.'

Callaghan said: 'When a woman tells me something and prefixes her remarks with the statement that she's going to tell me the truth I get very suspicious.'

She stiffened.

'That was unnecessarily rude,' she said. 'Don't you want to know anything about what you're going to try to find out. Even the cleverest people like some information to work on.'

'I'm not the cleverest people,' said Callaghan. 'Any information I want in this case I'm going to get in my own particular way. Then I'll know it's good information.'

'I see,' she said. Her voice was icy. 'Then I'll say nothing about it. I won't talk at all.'

'Yes you will,' said Callaghan amiably. 'You'll talk just as soon as I want you to – whether you like it or not. At the moment I don't need any informaton.'

She gave a little exclamation of disgust. She said coldly:

'You think you're damned clever, don't you, Mr Callaghan?'

Callaghan looked at her. He was smiling beatifically. Her eyes were bright with anger. He thought she looked quite superb.

'I wouldn't know about that,' he said. 'I'm content with the fact that you think I am.'

There was a long silence. Callaghan, driving with one hand, produced his cigarette case from an overcoat pocket, handed it to her. She took out two cigarettes, gave one to him, lit both from the electric lighter on the dashboard, slipped the case back into his pocket.

The car was doing a steady fifty. By now they were outside Croydon.

She said: 'You're a pretty cool customer, aren't you?'

'Am I?' asked Callaghan. 'Why?'

'You've sufficient nerve to be rude to the daughter of a client who will probably over-pay you,' she said. 'I believe detectives are always over-paid, aren't they?'

'Sometimes,' said Callaghan. 'Usually when they run a little blackmail on the side. But in any event you're still wrong.'

He drew the tobacco smoke down into his lungs, held it there for a moment or two, then exhaled. The cigarette tasted good. He was beginning to enjoy himself.

'Why am I still wrong?' she asked.

'I'm not working for your mother yet, so she hasn't got the chance of over-paying me,' said Callaghan. 'She *may* have the chance. We'll see. . . .'

'Really!' Her voice held a note of surprise. 'Is one permitted to ask then for whom you *are* working?'

'Certainly,' said Callaghan. 'I'm working for Miss Doria Varette. She's my only client at the moment. Possibly, tomorrow, I may decide to work for Mrs Wilbery, and then again I may not.'

'It must be nice to be so fearfully independent,' she said. 'I suppose Miss Varette will pay you a great deal of money – or hasn't she got any money?'

Callaghan grinned. He lied glibly.

'She had enough money to pay me five hundred pounds as a retainer,' he said coolly. He looked sideways at her. 'That's about the price of the coat you're wearing.'

She said: 'I don't see what the price of my coat has to do with it, do you?'

Callaghan nodded.

'It hasn't,' he agreed. 'It has just as much to do with it as the price that Miss Varette is paying for my services.'

She sighed. She said sarcastically:

'I asked for that snub and I got it. Tell me something. Are you ever *nice* to women?'

Callaghan looked at the road ahead.

'You'd be surprised,' he said.

She nodded.

'Yes . . .' she said. 'I probably should be.'

There was another silence.

They ran into Purley. Callaghan took the left fork to Godstone. The moonlight illuminated the road. He accelerated to sixty, let in the supercharger, raced the Jaguar up to eighty for a three-mile stretch and settled down to a steady seventy. She leaned back into her seat and drew her coat close about her. Callaghan slowed down a little, dropped the window on his side a few inches. The night air was cold and refreshing. He felt almost contented.

He began to think about Doria Varette, wondered how Nikolls had got on, whether he had found something – no matter what – or whether the hunch had been merely a hunch.

He accelerated a little. The Jaguar at a sweet seventy-five ran past the last house in Blindley Heath and settled down for the final stretch. He began to think of Leonore Wilbery. Out of the corner of his eye he could see her profile, admire the carefully planned simplicity of her hair-dressing. Her dark brown hair, naturally wavy, was parted at the side, caught up in a small bow of dull black silk ribbon, and curled delightfully round the nape of her neck. He wondered what she would try next.

She said: 'I like being driven fast. Especially when I have confidence in the driver. May I have another cigarette?'

Callaghan nodded. She slipped her hand into the side pocket of his coat, found the cigarette case.

'Would you like one too?' she asked.

When Callaghan nodded, she took two cigarettes from the case, put them in her mouth, lit them, put one into his mouth. There was something delightfully intimate in the process. She sat looking at the open case, holding it under the fading light of the electric cigarette lighter on the dashboard.

She read the inscription inside the case: 'To Slim Callaghan from Audrey Vendayne.'* She shut the case with a snap. She said:

'The woman who gave you this cigarette case – was she nice? And was she a client?'

Callaghan said: 'Both.'

'I suppose she paid you lots of money?' she went on.

Callaghan did not answer.

There was a long pause. She said suddenly:

'We'll be there in a minute or two. I think you and I ought to talk sensibly.'

Callaghan said: 'Nobody's stopping you.'

She said: 'I know. I'm the one who's been idiotic. I ought to have been quite frank with you from the start. I ought to have told you what I know about Lionel and what I think about it all.'

Callaghan slowed down as they ran past Hartfield.

She said: 'You take the little turning about a mile up the road, on the right. Go right on and through the lodge gates – they'll be open.'

He said: 'All right.'

He slowed down to forty, turned on to the dirt road.

She said: 'Will you stop for a minute?'

Callaghan put on the brake and drew in to the left. The narrow road was bounded by thick trees. He sat looking at her in the darkness.

She said: 'I want to tell you about Lionel.'

Callaghan interrupted. He said:

'Did you know that Lionel was in love with Doria Varette? Was it true that you'd never met her?'

She nodded.

'I've never met her,' she said. 'And I didn't know that she and Lionel were in love with each other.'

*You Can't Keep the Change

'All right,' said Callaghan. 'Then what's the good of you trying to tell me about Lionel? You don't know anything about Lionel. You only think you know something, and what you do know probably isn't true. If you didn't know about Varette how can you know anything about him that really matters? I imagine that all you know of him is what he has told you. Is that right?'

She bit her lip.

'That's true enough,' she said. 'But I can't understand your attitude. I . . .'

'Of course you can't,' said Callaghan. His voice was mildly sarcastic. 'Why should you. However, I'll make it quite plain. Shall I?'

She stubbed out her cigarette in the dashboard ash-tray. She said:

'Please do. It would be most interesting.'

'It probably will be,' said Callaghan. 'But, as I believe I told you before, I like dealing in facts and not fiction. That's why I'm not inclined to waste any more time listening to you.'

'So you think it would be a waste of time,' she said. 'That's awfully interesting. Perhaps you'll tell me why.'

'Certainly,' said Callaghan. 'I'll tell you. I've got certain facts to work on and I'm going ahead from there. I never allow myself to be deflected by fairy stories – even when they are told me by a woman as beautiful, as attractive, as completely charming as you are.'

She said coldly: 'Thank you for nothing. But you haven't any facts. You can't have any facts. When you saw me tonight at Mrs Martindale's party, you didn't know anything.'

'I knew a lot,' said Callaghan. 'I'd spoken to your mother. Your mother wasn't very interested in Lionel's disappearance until she heard that Miss Varette had commissioned me to try and find him. Then she was interested. Is that a fact, or is it? Then she asks me to see you first before I go to see her. She suggests that you may have some information for me. I meet you and you put on that silly act of being cockeyed. You say you've never heard of Miss Varette. That's a damned lie. And that's fact number two . . .'

She interrupted quickly. She said angrily:

'I detest your attitude. How can you know that was a lie?'

Callaghan grinned at her. She was losing her temper. He liked women to lose their tempers – especially when they were beautiful women. Then they told the truth – sometimes. He said pleasantly:

'Your mother had telephoned you and told you I was going to see you. Obviously she told you about Doria Varette. You considered seeing me a matter of sufficient importance to leave a message for me that would get me along to the Martindale party, where you could put on an act of being cockeyed, tell me that you knew nothing of Varette, so that you might eventually pump me and find out what *I* knew of her, knowing that as a young woman in a half-cut state you could evade answering any question you didn't want to answer. And that's fact number three.'

She looked at him.

'Aren't you *too* wonderful?' she said. Her low voice was intense to the point of bitterness.

'Not too bad,' said Callaghan cheerfully. 'You then arrange to get me to come along to *this* party, where I am going to meet somebody or other who *can* tell me about Lionel. If you know what this person or persons know about Lionel, why the devil couldn't you tell me yourself? The reason must be that the person or persons I'm going to meet are better able to put over the story that you want me to believe than you yourself are. That's fact number four.'

She said: 'You're stupid. I wanted to tell you the truth. . . .'

'Rubbish,' said Callaghan smilingly. 'You didn't, otherwise you'd have done it. Now you've lost the chance.'

He fished out his cigarette case and extracted a cigarette.

'You were asking about Audrey Vandayne,' he went on,

'the woman who gave me this cigarette case. She wouldn't mind my telling you that when I started to work for *her* she tried to lead me up the garden path too. It was only when someone pretty close to her was as near as damn it to swinging on the end of a six foot rope that she decided to talk sense.' He lit the cigarette. 'But I don't suppose the example will be of use to you.'

She did not reply. Callaghan started the car.

'The trouble with women who are as pretty as you are,' he said amiably, 'is that you think you can get away with anything. You even think you can take *me* for a walk up the garden path any time you want to. And that's a dangerous process. Because I might take you for a walk up the garden, and if ever I do you'll walk and like it.' He blew a smoke ring and watched it dissolve against the windscreen. 'Let's go to the party,' he said. 'I need a drink.'

She said coldly: 'I'm sorry you've been so bored.'

He grinned at her.

'I accept the apology,' he said. 'But I probably shan't do it again.'

She made a little hissing noise like a snake. She was furious. She said:

'Very well. Let's go to the party, Mr Callaghan, and be damned to you!'

Callaghan eased the Jaguar to a standstill at the end of a long row of cars that were parked outside The Dene. He looked round him appreciatively. The Dene was a big country house surrounded by lawns and shrubberies, adequately concealed by a ring of thick forest. He thought it was a good place for doing anything not intended to be seen by those not concerned.

He followed her across the gravel courtyard, through the big doorway guarded by two stone pillars, into the hall. The place was expensively furnished, the lighting and decorations perfect.

A butler, who was on duty in the hall with two menservants, came forward to meet them. Callaghan said:

'This is funny. Do any of these people know there's a war on?'

She said: 'Why ask me? There's a room over there where you can leave your things. I'm going upstairs. Come up when you're ready. I'll introduce you to the people I told you of.' She smiled cynically. 'And then,' she added, 'my responsibility so far as you're concerned ends.'

Callaghan smiled.

'I wonder . . .?' he said.

She looked at him for a moment, started to say something, checked herself, went up the wide thickly carpeted staircase.

He crossed the hall, went into the room she had indicated. It was a cloakroom. On the other side was a door leading to a similar room which Callaghan could see was being used as a cocktail bar. Half a dozen men, most of them in lounge suits, were there drinking.

Callaghan went in, asked for a brandy and soda. He drank it slowly. He was looking at the men about him. He thought they were an odd-looking crowd. You could not put them into any particular class or type except that they were all well dressed.

He finished his drink, went out into the hall, up the curving staircase, through the double doors of the room at the top. There were a lot of people there. A heavy buzz of conversation, an airy badinage, created an almost pre-war atmosphere.

Leonore Wilbery was deep in conversation with a woman on the other side of the room. She saw Callaghan and smiled. He went over.

As he crossed the room he took a long look at Leonore. He thought she was definitely breath-taking. She had taken off her fur coat and the clothes she was wearing enhanced the beauty of an almost perfect figure and carriage.

She wore a black watered silk coat and skirt of exquisite cut. The coat was tailored rather on the severe lines of a man's lounge jacket with a single diamond link button at the waist. Beneath, Callaghan caught a glimpse of a soft pale pink angora wool blouse, high in the neck, caught with a diamond link to catch the coat button. She wore the sheerest black silk stockings so cobwebby that it seemed at first glance that she wore none. The plain black glacé court shoes set off a foot that would have made clogs appear graceful.

A hell of a woman, thought Callaghan. A woman who could start a packet of trouble any time she felt like it – and finish it too.

As she approached she said: 'This is my friend Mr Callaghan, Sabine. You will like him. Mr Callaghan is a very famous private detective. His methods – and you will agree, my dear, if you ever get close enough to them – are unique if not interesting. Mother is proposing that Mr Callaghan should look for Lionel because somebody or other thinks he's disappeared. Mr Callaghan, this is Miss Sabine Haragos. . . .'

Callaghan said how do you do. Miss Haragos put out a very small hand, the fingers of which were almost entirely covered with jewels. When she spoke the words came out of her mouth so softly that you were surprised that you heard so distinctly. Her accent was delightful. All the vowels were long and spoken with an odd drawl. It was like listening to someone reciting the words of a song.

She said: 'Meester Cala-aghan. I am so-o-o pliz to meet with you. . . .'

Callaghan took a quick look at her. Her beauty was peculiar and devastating. She looked like a resuscitated mummy of an Egyptian princess. Her face was very white, peculiarly flat. Her cheek bones stood out. Her nose was wide at the base, but with nostrils sensitively cut. She had black eyes, blue-black hair with curls piled high on her head. A broad wine-coloured velvet ribbon was threaded through the curls. She reminded Callaghan of a picture of the Medusa.

She was wearing wide wine-coloured velvet trousers that looked like a skirt when she stood still, a silk shirt of a rare duck-egg blue colour under a wine-coloured velvet jacket. She wore no stockings. On her feet were flat-heeled sandals of wine-coloured kid, and her toe-nails were painted scarlet.

Callaghan said: 'I'm glad to meet *you*, Miss Haragos.'

She looked away from him. From the other side of the wide room a man was approaching. She said to Callaghan:

'My na-ame is Sa-abine. So pliz ca-all me Sa-abine. . . .'

Callaghan grinned. He said:

'All right. I'll call you Sabine.'

The man joined them. He was immense. He was six feet three or four inches in height, with a great breadth of shoulder. His hair was black and he had a large handlebar moustache. Beneath it, when he smiled, his big white teeth shone.

Leonore Wilbery said: 'Mr Callaghan, this is Milta Haragos – Sabine's brother. I think they'll amuse you. *Au revoir*, Mr Callaghan.' She threw him an enigmatic look and disappeared into the crowd.

Milta Haragos looked at Callaghan. He looked him over carefully, as one looks at a horse. He said to Sabine:

'Dees one is strong. Plenty muscle. Nice an' strong.'

He put out a hand as big as a plate. Callaghan took it. Milta Haragos began to squeeze Callaghan's hand in his, exerting more and more pressure. Callaghan began to wonder when his finger bones would break.

Haragos said: 'Me . . . I am verry strrong too. . . You soo . . . ?'

He smiled amiably at the detective and went on squeezing.

Callaghan put his left hand gently on Haragos's wrist. He slipped his fingers round it, pulled and, as the other tried to draw his hand away, put on a Japanese wrist lock.

Haragos's face contracted in agony. His right hand opened. Callaghan kept on with the wrist lock. He said:

'Don't be funny, Haragos. I know some better holds than this one. *Judo* will always beat beef, you know.'

He took off the lock, dropped his hand. Haragos began to rub his wrist.

Sabine said: 'Lo-ovely. . . . I liked tha-at. . . . Beautiful. . . . Milta, you a-are alwa-ays so godda-am clever.' She looked at Callaghan with eyes that were like glistening slits. She said: 'Co-ome with me. I wa-ant to ta-alk wiz you. . . . Come. . . .'

Callaghan said to Milta Haragos: 'I expect I'll be seeing you later.' He went after Sabine.

She led the way through the groups of laughing, drinking people, opened a french window at the right hand end of the room and stepped out. Following her, Callaghan could see that they were on a wide balcony that, at the height of the first floor, ran right round the house. She moved along the balcony with a peculiar, gliding walk that gave her the appearance of floating rather than walking. Almost at the end of the house she stopped, pushed open another french window and stepped into the room beyond.

He followed her, shutting the blacked-out window behind him. The room was a small square room, panelled in oak and sombrely furnished. It was lit by an electric standard lamp which gave a bad light. He thought it a very depressing room.

Sabine Haragos said: 'Pliz to sit do-own, my friend, and give me a ciga-arette. . . .'

Callaghan gave her a cigarette, sat down in a leather arm-chair. She sat down, quite suddenly, and with a single movement, on the floor, drew up her legs under her and regarded him gravely. There was something feline about her graceful and quick movements.

He lit his own cigarette and sat looking at her. Her eyes were quite amazing. She had some trick with her eyelids that almost entirely covered them. She said:

'Wha-at a-are you theenking? I kno-ow. . . . You are theenking that Milta is joost a beeg godda-am fool. . . . Me also. . . . Alwa-ays he moos' try to show off about hees strengt'. Because he is so-o stro-ong he does not realize that he is almo-ost entirely brainless.' She laughed in her throat.

Callaghan said: 'I wasn't thinking about Milta. Milta doesn't interest me. Even if he's not brainless I still don't care.'

'A-all right,' she went on. 'Pliz leesten. . . . Leonore says you wa-ant to kno-ow about Lionel. . . . She says that you theenk that Lionel ha-as disappeared somewhere. Pliz don't worry about Lionel. He will re-a-appear almos' like a ba-ad penny.'

She laughed again. It was quite a pleasant laugh, even if it did rasp a little.

Callaghan asked: 'Is he in the habit of disappearing?'

She inhaled deeply. Then she began to blow the tobacco smoke out of her nostrils. She took quite a time over this process. Eventually:

'Ye-es, Lionel is ver' seely. He is a moos' seely young man. He smokes too mooch . . . he drink too mooch . . . then he take some drugs also too mooch. . . . He is a-alwa-ays that ver' weak young man tryeeng to make-out that he's so-o stro-ong. He 'as disappearaed befo-ore . . . but he alwa-ays co-omes ba-ack.'

'I see,' said Callaghan. 'And so you think he'll come back this time?'

She nodded. Her eyes were still fixed steadily on his.

He said: 'Did you ever meet a woman called Doria Varette?'

She nodded again.

'Ye-es,' she said. 'Mees Varctte is a fren' of Lionel. They were clo-ose fren's . . . I theenk. Lionel spo-oke to me of her. I theenk he thought he was in lo-ove with her. I do not theenk that Mees Varette is ver' nice. I do not theenk tha-at she was ver' good for Lionel.'

'Why not?' Callaghan asked.

She shrugged her shoulders.

'Mees Varette is one of tho-ose mysterious people,' she said softly. 'No one kno-ows how she lives or what she does. Lionel tol' me tha-at she uses some drugs . . . tha-at she likes drugs. I theenk tha-at maybe she gave so-ome to Lionel.' She smiled at Callaghan. 'Lionel was a godda-am fool,' she concluded.

Callaghan got up.

'Thanks,' he said. 'You've been very useful.'

She did not move.

'*Au revoir*, Meester Callaghan,' she said, smiling at him. 'Maybe Milta ca-an tell you so-ome more. Milta ees ra-ather a great lo-over of women. Lionel ha-ad an inclination to be the sa-ame. I should speak wiz Milta.'

'Thanks,' said Callaghan. 'I probably will.'

He moved towards the french windows, opened one side, stepped out on to the balcony. He walked back and entered the room where he had met Sabine Haragos.

The crowd had thinned out, but there was still quite a number of people exchanging badinage. Callaghan wondered what went on at The Dene. He looked about him, but could see no sign of either Milta Haragos or Leonore. He went down the stairs into the hall and crossed into the cloakroom, walked through it into the bar. He asked for Canadian rye.

There was no one else in the bar. Callaghan took a long look at the man behind the limed oak counter. He was young, thin, dark-haired and wore long side-whiskers. He looked like any one of the *commis* waiters one sees in a West End restaurant.

Callaghan said: 'What do I do when I get tired of drinking?'

The man said: 'If that's possible you can always take a chance in the card-room. They play everything. Most of the crowd are in there. You can stake to suit yourself and the game's so straight it almost hurts.' He grinned cheerfully.

Callaghan said thanks, finished his whisky, walked back into the hall. On each side of the wide staircase was a passage-way, thickly carpeted, lit with dim lights. Callaghan took the right hand passage. At the end was a door. He pushed it open a little and looked in.

There were many more people in the room. They were all playing something or other. The room was big, well lit, cheerfully decorated. There were about twenty tables going. Callaghan saw that *Chemie, baccarat, roulette*, a dice-cage, poker – practically every sort of game of chance, including a Chinese dragon game – was being played. At each table was a *croupier* with all the hall-marks of the professional.

Callaghan looked round to his right. He looked at the floor. He saw a very small pair of patent shoes with wide trouser ends draping over them too beautifully. The man had his back to him and was busily engaged in using his *croupier's* rake on a *roulette* table.

It was the Cuban. Callaghan gave a little sigh.

He shut the door and wandered back to the bar off the hallway. It was still empty except for the bartender. Callaghan ordered more rye whisky. He lit a cigarette, smoked silently for a few minutes. Then he asked:

'Who runs the game here – the house?'

The bartender looked at him for quite a while. Then:

'You wouldn't be a dick, would you?' he asked.

Callaghan grinned.

'Do I look like a dick?'

'No,' said the bartender. 'But you never know these days. Coppers get everywhere. They look the part too. But *you* don't look like a dick. Who'd you come with?'

'I came with Miss Wilbery,' said Callaghan. 'I'm an old friend of hers.'

The bartender smiled.

'That's different,' he said. 'I like her, an' so does everybody. She's cute.' He began to polish the bar counter. 'Santos runs the games here,' he said. 'He's a nice boy . . . very generous. He's got a big connection. And he's very straight. He's got the dough too.'

Callaghan nodded. He passed his glass over. The bartender poured more rye.

'Theres' no gambling in London these days,' said Callaghan. 'At least not what *I* call gambling. I used to play at Garoldi's place. Did you ever hear of Garoldi?'

The bartender grinned.

'My brother used to work for him. He was night-waiter,' he said. 'That was a helluva game, wasn't it?'

Callaghan nodded.

'Does this Santos run any games in town?' he asked. 'You know – a quiet nice game with the money on the table, no nonsense and the house taking a straight *cagnotte* and no funny business?'

'You bet he does,' said the bartender. 'You have a word with him. He'll put you right.'

Callaghan drank the rye. He said thanks and went out into the hall. He stood there leaning up against the wall, smoking. After a few minutes he walked across the hall, took the latch off the main door, went out, closed the door behind him.

The open space in front of him was still bright in the moonlight and there were still many cars drawn up. He walked past them and along a pathway that led across the lawn. On the other side of the lawn the pathway ran through a copse. At the other end of the copse, deep in the shadows formed by the thickening trees, stood a little summer-house. It was open on the side farthest from the house, and on the small veranda were a couple of garden chairs.

Callaghan went back to the hallway. He stood there, leaning against the wall, watching the main staircase. Several people came down and turned into one or other of the passages leading to the card-rooms.

After a while a fat man came down the stairs. He was holding on to the banister rails. His face was very flushed, and the dull silk lapels of his dinner coat were white with cigar ash. Half-way down the stairs he paused, hiccupped solemnly, then continued on his careful way.

Callaghan went over to meet him. He said:

'I wonder if you'd do me a favour?'

The fat man laughed.

'Anything in reason, dear boy,' he said. 'Except I won't

lend anybody any money. Beyond that you can have anything I've got – even my wife – that's if you want her.' He laughed for a long time. 'I don't,' he added seriously.

Callaghan smiled at him.

'It's just a little thing,' he said. 'Of course you know Santos. . . .'

'You bet,' said the fat man. 'I've lost a lot of money to him, and won a little from him.' He became ponderous. 'I s'pose I've known Santos D'Ianazzi as long as any other gambler who plays three or four times a week.'

'Excellent,' said Callaghan. 'Well . . . here's the favour. Would you ask him if he could come outside and meet me for a moment in the summer-house on the other side of the lawn. I've a little gaming proposition I'd like to talk over. But I want it kept quiet . . . you know. . . .' Callaghan looked mysterious.

'Surely,' said the fat man. 'I'll tell him. Happy landings.'

He lurched down the passage.

Callaghan stubbed out his cigarette in a wall ash-tray. He crossed the hall, went out of the main door, across the lawn and round behind the summer-house. He stood, on the corner of the veranda, in the shadow, watching the path.

Two or three minutes afterwards he saw the Cuban coming down the path. He was walking quickly and easily. As the moonlight fell on his face Callaghan saw that he was half smiling.

Callaghan took out his cigarette case, lit a cigarette. He put his hands in his trouser pockets. As the Cuban reached the end of the path and turned the corner on the far side of the summerhouse Callaghan stepped out of the shadows.

He said: 'Hallo, Santos.'

The Cuban stopped. His face froze. He stiffened. Then, as suddenly, his shoulders relaxed, his thin lips opened and his white teeth showed in a smile that was intended to be amiable. He said:

'Senor Callaghan. . . . I did not expect the pleasure of meeting you here. . . .'

Callaghan said: 'I know. It's just one of those pleasant surprises, isn't it?'

The Cuban said nothing. There was a silence. Then he said: 'Well?'

Callaghan said: 'I want to ask you a few questions. Maybe you'll answer them, maybe you'll want to be funny about answering 'em, but before we go any further let me tell you this:

'I can make things pretty hot for you – one way or another, I mean. I'm not suggesting that I've anything on you, that I know anything about you, except that you run a pretty big game somewhere around the West End. If you use your imagination you will realize it would be fairly easy for me to be a trouble.'

The Cuban was still smiling. He said:

'Pliz go on. . . .'

'Why were you waiting for Doria Varette – what was it that you had to see her about last night – that was of sufficient importance for you to hang about till she came home? And why doesn't she like you? You remember she slammed the door in your face. Those questions will do for a start.'

The Cuban shrugged his shoulders. Then he spread his hands in a gesture of vague bewilderment. Then, quite suddenly, he kicked Callaghan in the stomach. Callaghan doubled up, his knees sagged under him. He fell forward on to the gravel path. The Cuban stood quite still watching him. Callaghan was retching violently. After a minute he got up on to his knees and began to crawl towards the two wooden steps that led up to the summer-house veranda. The Cuban, his lips drawn back over his teeth, watched this process with mild approval.

Callaghan reached the steps. He put up his hand, caught hold of the verandah rail, pulled himself up to his feet. Then he collapsed again on to his knees. He began to be sick. He felt a little better. The sharp tearing pain in his abdomen was turning into an ache, his head was clearing. He put up his hand and caught hold of the verandah rail again.

The Cuban took two little mincing steps forward. He looked at Callaghan and began to laugh softly in his throat. Then he looked at the pointed toe of his patent leather shoe. He drew back his leg for the second kick almost slowly.

Nikolls came round the other side of the summer-house. He was wearing a chauffeur's uniform that was quite three sizes too small for him. A peak cap with a Rolls Royce badge on the front was perched precariously on one side of his head. He drew back his arm, turning back his fist like a sledge-hammer and hit the Cuban in the face with such force that the impact sounded as a dull thud. The Cuban described an arc. He landed in a thick rhododendron bush almost on his head. Nikolls watched him with interest. The Cuban's face was covered with blood; a thin stream was running down his chin over his collar on to his immaculate shirt front.

Nikolls spat artistically. He fumbled in the side pocket of his uniform jacket and produced a packet of Lucky Strikes. He selected one, lit it with a wax vesta which he struck on the underneath part of his thigh, flicked the used match away and walked over to the Cuban. He reached down and put his left hand inside the stiff collar and shirt front. He pulled the Cuban to his feet.

D'Ianazzi stood swaying backwards and forwards like a pendulum. Nikolls took a short pace backwards, measured him, hit him again in the face. The Cuban, right out, disappeared in the rhododendron bush.

Callaghan was sitting on the bottom step of the veranda. After a moment he got up, held the veranda rail with his hands, began to stretch himself. After a minute he stood up straight, began to massage his stomach muscles.

Nikolls said: 'It don't feel so good, does it? I remember a dame kicked me in the guts up in Wichita. She was a tough momma all right. She had ridin' boots on. While I was lyin' on the ground she tried a few back kicks with the spur in the belly. I still got the marks. I oughta tell you that this dame . . .'

Callaghan said: 'I've heard that one.'

'O.K. . . . O.K.,' said Nikolls.

Callaghan sat down on the veranda steps. He said:

'What have you got those funny clothes on for?'

Nikolls said: 'I reckoned I oughta see you, an' I didn't know what the set-up was down here. I rang through to Effie. She told me where you were. So I went round to the garage and borrowed this stuff. I hired their Rolls Royce an' drove it down. I thought it'd look better. I told the butler at the house I was your chauffeur.'

Callaghan nodded.

'Go over that,' he said, jerking his head towards the Cuban. 'You might find something.'

Nikolls pulled the recumbent figure out of the rhododendron bush. He searched it. He found a pocket-book, went through it carefully. In the pocket-book were some visiting cards and a passport. He handed them to Callaghan, who put them in his pocket. Nikolls went on searching. After a minute he said:

'There's nothin' else. I was hopin' the bastard might have a hundred pounds on him for me. This ain't my lucky day.'

Callaghan got up. He said:

'We'll get back to the house.'

Nikolls said: 'What're you goin' to do about the boy-friend?' He jerked his head in the direction of D'Ianazzi, who was lying on his back breathing stertorously.

'He'll do where he is,' said Callaghan. He lit a cigarette. He said:

'What did you come down for, Windy?'

Nikolls said: 'Oh, I forgot, I thought it was important. I thought I'd better let you know.'

Callaghan cocked one eyebrow. He grinned.

'It must be damned important for you to get into a

make-up like the one you've got on. You look like a music-hall turn. Well, what is it?'

Nikolls inhaled. He opened his mouth and allowed a large volume of tobacco smoke to escape. He said:

'It's about that Varette dame. I thought I oughta tell you. Somebody's bumped her.'

5

Reconstruction Piece

Callaghan sat down on the running-board of a Cadillac car that was parked in the shadows at the north end of The Dene. His guts were aching dully. He wanted a drink. He said:

'Stay here, Windy, I shan't be long.'

As he got up he felt in his jacket pocket and produced the passport and the few visiting cards, held together by a rubber band, that Nikolls had taken off the Cuban.

'You're sure there wasn't anything else on him?' he asked.

Nikolls shook his head.

'Not a goddam thing besides,' he said. 'Not even any dough. That seems damn' funny to me.'

Callaghan said: 'It doesn't make sense. D'Ianazzi is not the sort of bird to be running a big game like this without money on him. I bet he's wearing a belt next his skin. Go back and have a look. Then wait for me here.'

'O.K.,' said Nikolls. 'That suits me. I just love undressin' guys in rhododendron bushes by moonlight. I'll be seein' you.'

He went off.

Callaghan got up and went into the house. He walked through the cloakroom, through the little passage on the left of the bar into the lavatory. He locked the door and examined the things that Nikolls had taken from the Cuban.

He looked at the passport. Santos D'Ianazzi was a Cuban citizen. By the look of the *visas* he had travelled a great deal during the last year or so. The last *visa* bore the stamp of his country's Consular Office in Naples. And there was no mistaking the passport photograph.

Callaghan looked at the top card of the little packet of visiting cards. Printed on it were the words in copperplate: *'Mr Santos D'Ianazzi – Representing the Santiago Cigar & Tobacco Company – Rochelle Court, St John's Wood, N.W.8. Maida Vale 67543.'*

He put the passport and the visiting cards back into his pocket, went out of the lavatory, along the passage into the bar. He asked the bartender for a double brandy and soda.

He drank it slowly, felt better afterwards.

He waited a little, lit a cigarette, drank another brandy and soda. He was thinking about Doria Varette. After a few minutes he left the bar, slipped quietly out of the front door, walked along the forecourt. Nikolls was waiting by the Cadillac.

He said: 'Ain't you the brain guy? He *was* wearin' a body belt. There was two thousand in it in banknotes – tens and fifties. Just fancy me missin' that.' He held out the notes.

Callaghan put out his hand and took them. He put them in the inside breast pocket of his jacket. He said:

'What happened to the Varette?'

'Search me,' said Nikolls. 'I wasn't takin' any chances of leaving prints or anything about the place. I just took a look at her an' scrammed. She was as dead as a herrin'.'

Callaghan asked: 'What was she dead of?'

Nikolls shrugged.

'I wouldn't know,' he said. 'She was lyin' on the bed upstairs. She didn't look disturbed except her eyes were pretty scared. There was a little blood had run out of her mouth. Not much – just a bit.'

Callaghan nodded.

'You didn't see anybody else about the place? When you were going there, I mean.'

'No,' said Nikolls. 'I called through there about a quarter to twelve. I heard the telephone ringin' at the other end. There wasn't any reply, so I went straight along there. I didn't see anybody at all. I got the door open with the No. 3 spider. I took a look around the ground floor, an' when I decided that I'd got the place to myself I went upstairs. When I'm casin' a joint I always like to work from the top downwards. When I got up to the first floor I could see a door open along the passage an' some light comin' out. So I eased along and took a gander quietly. I could see her lyin' on the bed from around the door, but I couldn't see her face. I thought maybe she was cockeyed and had passed out. So I went inside an' had a real look, after which I decided to beat it. So I got out. I phoned through to Effie to find out where you'd gone to, went around to the garage, got this outfit an' the car an' came down here.'

Callaghan nodded.

'Give me the No. 3 spider,' he said.

Nikolls took the small bunch of skeleton keys from his pocket, took one off, handed it to Callaghan.

'You're gonna have a look?' he asked.

Callaghan nodded again.

'Where's your car?' he asked.

Nikolls indicated the end of the car line with his head.

'Get in the driving seat,' said Callaghan. 'I'm going to wish Leonore Wilbery on to you. You're a hire-service chauffeur. I've telephoned for you to come down to take her back. See?'

'I got it,' said Nikolls. 'What do I do when I've delivered her?'

'Go to bed,' said Callaghan. 'Come in at ten o'clock tomorrow. I want some action on this case. It's getting boring.'

Nikolls cocked an eyebrow.

'Ain't you the little glutton?' he said. 'You got a swell corpse on your hands, you get yourself kicked in the guts by some dago baby with pointed shoes, an' you're bored. Maybe if some Jerry dropped a five hundred pound bomb on your dome you'd get a little excited.'

He pulled his too-tight uniform jacket down.

'This lousy coat is stranglin me,' he said. 'An' it's a

goddam shame about Varette. Here's one of your clients getting' herself bumped off before we'd even got a chance to send in an expense account. It ain't ethical. I reckon we gotta make 'em pay in advance in future before some guys fog 'em.'

Callaghan said: 'Good-night, Windy.'

He went back to the house. In the hallway the butler was stifling a polite yawn. Callaghan went up to him.

He said: 'Will you find Miss Wilbery, give her Mr Callaghan's compliments and tell her that he's had to leave quickly.'

The butler said he would do that at once.

Callaghan gave him a pound note.

'You might also tell her that I've arranged for a hired car to take her back. I know the driver well. She'll be quite safe – even if he does drive a little fast.'

'Very well, sir,' said the butler. He went away.

Callaghan got his coat and hat from the cloakroom. He went outside, started the Jaguar and looked at his watch. It was three o'clock. He drove the car quietly down the drive. Outside, on the dirt road, he warmed up the Jaguar, took her down the road at forty, swung on to the main road and put his foot down hard.

The needle shot up to fifty, sixty, sixty-five. At that speed he let in the supercharger. Most of the way back he was doing eighty.

Callaghan stood in the dark hallway of Doria Varette's house listening. In the distance an out-of-town 'All Clear' faded into nothingness. Everything was very quiet.

He snapped on his lighter, found the electric light switch. He put his handkerchief over his fingers, turned it on for a few minutes until he had the lay-out of the staircase in his head, then switched it off, snapped on his lighter and began to walk up the stairs. A minute later he had switched on the light in Varette's bedroom; stood, looking down at her as she lay on the bed.

Her eyes were wide open. They looked straight above

them at the ceiling. They were scared. Callaghan thought that Varette had had a moment or two to get frightened before the end.

Very gently he turned the body over. He saw what he was looking for. Under the right shoulder-blade was a tiny stain of blood on the silk blouse; in the middle of the stain was the small puncture wound.

Callaghan took out his cigarette case and lit a cigarette. He put on his gloves. He wiped the electric light switch with his handkerchief. Then he walked across the bedroom, through the doorway leading to the room beyond. He found the switch, flicked it on.

The room was small, charming, well lighted. In the corner was a desk with a typewriter standing on it. Callaghan took off his hat and coat, folded his coat carefully, placed it in the middle of the floor with his hat, looked at his watch, saw it was nearly a quarter to four, began to search. He worked systematically through all the rooms in the small house.

He finished at four-thirty. He found nothing.

He squeezed out his cigarette, put the stub in his jacket pocket, lit another. He went back to the bedroom, stood looking at the lifeless figure lying on its face on the bed. As he bent over it to turn it gently into its original position he heard the soft crackle of the Cuban's banknotes in his breast pocket.

He went over and stood in front of the fireplace in which the embers were cold. His face relaxed, he began to grin. He went quickly across the bedroom, into the sitting-room. With his gloved hands he extracted an envelope from the stationery rack, slipped it into the typewriter. He took the Cuban's visiting card from his pocket, studied it for a moment, began to type. He addressed the envelope to 'Senor Santos D'Ianazzi, Rochelle Court, St John's Wood, N.W.8. He laid the envelope by the side of the typewriter.

He took a sheet of notepaper bearing the Wilton Place address from the rack, inserted it in the typewriter, tapped out a letter. It said:

'*Dear Santos*

It isn't any good you trying to see me. I don't want to see you. Also I don't want to talk to you on the telephone. Your threats only bore me and you don't frighten me either. So you'd better call it off.

Why should I return the money to you? I won it fairly. I'm not going to return it. Besides, surely you're making enough to stand a loss of nineteen hundred pounds. That shouldn't mean a lot to you. I won this money and I'm going to keep it.

I think it's time you and I had a showdown. I tell you, quite frankly, that I don't want to see you, or speak to you again, that I'm not going to return the money or any part of it, and if you threaten any more on the telephone or anyhow else I'm going to the police.

Incidentally I thi—'

Callaghan stopped typing in the middle of the word 'think.' He picked up the typewriter, carried it into the bedroom. He put the typewriter on the floor, moved a chair to the side of the bed, put the machine on it, cleaned the keys with his handkerchief, then pressed the finger-tips of the first and second fingers of Doria Varette's left and right hands on the keys on the left and right sides of the keyboard respectively. The process was not particu-larly nice or particularly easy.

When it was done he carried the typewriter into the other room, put it on the desk, went back to the bedroom, put the chair back in its place, squeezed out his cigarette end, put it in his pocket and lit another. Then he went into the sitting-room. He sat down at the desk in front of the typewriter and rehearsed a scene in his mind.

He imagined he was Doria Varette typing the letter to Santos D'Ianazzi. He imagined that just as she had begun to type the unfinished word the front door bell had rung. This, he thought, would have startled her. She would be scared because she would think that the caller would be D'Ianazzi. She would make up her mind to tell him that she had paid the money mentioned in the letter into a bank. She would make up her mind not to let him know that it was in the house, and she would tell him that unless he stopped pestering her she would go to the police.

Then she would hear the bell ring again. She would step back, she would knock the chair over. . . .

Callaghan got up, took a small step backwards and knocked the chair over.

Then he walked quickly to the door, snapped off the light, closed the door behind him.

This is what Varette would have done, thought Callaghan, *if* she had been typing that letter *if* she had heard the bell ring and suspected D'Ianazzi was there.

He stood in the middle of the bedroom looking at what remained of Doria Varette. He took the cigarette out of his mouth and carefully dropped the ash into the side pocket of his jacket.

He took the packet of D'Ianazzi's banknotes out of his pocket. The notes were folded once. Callaghan removed the two top notes. He removed them because they were both fifty-pound notes and their removal left the sum mentioned in the letter – nineteen hundred pounds, because the top folded note bore both his and Nikolls' fingerprints, and because Doria Varette owed Callaghan Investigations a hundred pounds.

He thought for a moment, moved over to the chest of drawers, opened two or three drawers, eventually found a flimsy nightgown with a pink ribbon threaded through it. He drew out the ribbon carefully, folded the packet of banknotes into a small oblong shape, tied the ribbon round the package.

He went over to the bed. Very gently he raised the skirt on the still figure and slipped the packet into the silk stocking-top. He replaced the skirt.

He pinched out his cigarette, put the stub in his pocket, switched off the light, left the door as he and Nikolls had found it. He went back into the sitting-room, put on his hat and coat, closed the door as he went out. He stood at the top of the stairs in the darkness.

He was thinking about Doria Varette. He came to the conclusion that it was tough being the sort of person that she had been, having to do the things she had to do, to meet the odd sort of people she had to meet. He remembered her singing at Ferdie's Place, and the name of the song: 'I could Learn . . .' Well, she'd learned something all right.

He wondered how well she knew the Cuban. An odd thought struck him. It would be damned funny if she hadn't known the Cuban at all. If, when he had called at the house the night before, when she had slammed the door in his face, it had been their first meeting. But that would have meant that she had heard something about him, that she was scared of him anyway and did not want to talk to him.

He stood at the top of the stairs listening. Then he shrugged his shoulders and descended. He closed the front door quietly behind him, stood for a minute in the cul-de-sac listening, then walked quietly into the street, across it into Knightsbridge.

He began to walk towards Berkeley Square. He took off his gloves, undid his overcoat and jacket and fumbled in the fob pocket of his evening trousers for a couple of aspirins. He swallowed them and continued on his way. He was whistling softly to himself. It was the same tune: 'It Was Good While It Lasted.'

After a while he stopped whistling and began to think about Leonore Wilbery. He wondered just what sort of a person she really was . . . what made her 'tick over' . . . what her motives were for doing whatever she was doing, or trying to do. He wondered just how much her attitude about Lionel was truth and just how much was 'theatre.' It was certain that before their first meeting at Mrs Martindale's party, Mrs Wilbery had telephoned her and told her all there was to be told. He wondered why, as a result of that conversation, Leonore had decided to pretend she was cockeyed in order to see how the land lay as regards himself. Why should she want to do that?'

You never knew with women. Women were damned odd. They flew off at tangents. The trouble with women was that they were quite definite about what they wanted – for the *moment*. They went all out for it even if they discovered a few minutes later that they didn't want it and wanted something quite different.

He wondered what Leonore was like when you got to know her. When the superficial attitude which she had adopted on the occasions when he had spoken to her was shed, and she was her ordinary normal self.

He switched his mind on to the Haragos pair. He wondered if they were brother and sister or husband and wife. Vaguely they reminded him of a continental music-hall turn. He did not know why. Sabine was a character. A very definite character and they could both be very tough. And Sabine had seemed to know Lionel Wilbery fairly well, had volunteered information about him.

He turned down Clarges Street. An air-raid 'alert' sounded. By the time he was half-way down Piccadilly there was a glow in the sky from the east. Two auxiliary fire-engines, speeding as fast as they could make it, passed down Piccadilly.

Callaghan lit a cigarette. He thought that being firemen in these times must call for a lot of nerve. The 'raiders passed' signal was sounding as he entered his apartment block. He took the electric lift, stopped it at the office floor, opened the outer door, switched on the light. He turned on the dictaphone on Effie Thompson's desk. He spoke into. He said:

'Effie, Nikolls is coming in at ten o'clock. Directly he comes in give me a ring and have some tea sent up. See that I wake up.'

He turned off the dictaphone.

He switched off the light, locked the door, took the lift to his flat on the floor above, undressed, turned on a warm bath and got into it. He lay there looking at the ceiling, relaxed.

The kaleidoscope was beginning to take shape.

The morning sun brightened the office as Nikolls came in. He grinned at Effie Thompson, went into Callaghan's room, opened the bottom right-hand drawer of the desk, extracted the rye bottle and medicine glass, swallowed a neat two ounces.

He sighed pleasurably, fumbled for his pack of Lucky Strikes, lit one, wandered back into the outer office.

Effie Thompson was calling Callaghan. Nikolls could hear the crackle of Callaghan's voice as it came through the transmitter. When it stopped, Effie said:

'Yes, Mr Callaghan, I've ordered your tea. I'll call Miss Wilbery at once. Mr Nikolls has just come in. . . . Very good. . . .'

She hung up.

'He wants you,' she said. 'I suppose you don't know the telephone number of a Miss Leonore Wilbery?'

Nikolls shook his head.

'I wouldn't know,' he said. He made a gloomy face. 'I never get the telephone numbers of dames like that,' he continued.

She smiled cynically.

'You don't do so badly, I dare say,' she said.

She dialled 'Directory' and asked for the number of Miss Leonore Wilbery of Welbeck Street. She hung up. She said, almost casually:

'I suppose she's another of the usual Callaghan clients. One of these days we're going to get a case with an ugly woman in it. It would be a nice change. I suppose she's very beautiful and very smart?'

'Yeah,' said Nikolls. 'Slim finds 'em all right. This one is the works. The ultimate berries. That dame's got so much atmosphere that any time she tried to vamp a clergyman he'd haveta wear stained-glass spectacles.'

'Really,' said Effie. 'So she's like that?' She sniffed. 'I suppose she's one of these women with too much money and too little to do. Desirable but decadent.'

Nikolls grinned at her.

'What's the matter?' he asked. 'Gettin' jealous?' He opened his mouth and let a cloud of cigarette smoke emerge. 'You're wrong about this baby,' he said with a grin. 'She's the picture of health and she's got the swell frame that goes with it.'

The telephone rang. It was the Welbeck number. Effie dialled it. She said:

'One of these days one of these marvellous women is going to take this firm for a ride.'

'That sounds to me like the wish was father to the thought,' said Nikolls. He grinned broadly, showing his big white teeth. 'I s'pose when that happens the boss realizes that all the while that this marvellous woman has been takin' the firm for a ride he'd got a beautiful red-haired secretary who was ready an' willin' to give her all at any moment . . . ?'

She looked at him. Her eyes were furious.

'You low-minded colonial,' she said. 'Don't you ever think about *anything* else but sex? Isn't there *anything* else in life that interests that thing you call a mind?'

'Not much,' said Nikolls cheerfully. 'You find me some-thin' better an' I'll go for it.' He inhaled tobacco smoke, opened his large mouth and watched it float out. 'Did I ever tell you the story about that dame I met up with in Mariana, New Mexico? This baby was a streamlined model with sex appeal that was so supercharged that it nearly hurt. Some guy I knew tried to marry her. He was a mean guy. That guy was so goddam mean that he was always wishin' he was under sixteen so's he could travel half-fare. Anyway, he proposes to this dame an' she tur-ned him down for about fifteen reasons.'

Effie raised her eyebrows. 'Fifteen?' she queried.

'Well,' said Nikolls, 'the first one was that he was a mean guy so the other fourteen didn't matter. Well, right then I blew into this baby's life just at the right moment – for *her*, I mean. I was packin' a wad so big that it was nearly killin' me. I'd been playin' the Chicago stock market an' it had run for me. I was lousy with jack. In six months she took me for every red cent an' I hadta do some very heavy thinkin' to get it back. . . .'

The two telephones on Effie's desk began to jangle. She picked up a receiver in each hand. She said into the house telephone:

'Yes, Mr Callaghan, Mr Nikolls is on his way up.' She said into the other receiver: 'Is that Miss Leonore Wilbery? Hold on, please, this is Mr Callaghan of Callaghan Investigations calling you; I'll connect you.'

Nikolls went to the door. As he opened it, she said:

'And how did you get it back?'

Nikolls said over his shoulder: 'I taught her to play poker. I *won* it back. She was so dumb that she usta bet on a pair of deuces. But she had a shape that put a crick in guys' necks looking back – somethin' like yours, you know – everything in the right place an' under proper control. . . .'

He closed the door quickly.

Callaghan took off the receiver. He was wearing the top half of a pair of pillar-box red pyjamas, a pair of eau-de-nil silk shorts and one black sock.

He said: 'Is that Miss Wilbery? Good-morning. I'm sorry I had to run out on you last night.'

Her low voice sounded charming. She said:

'It couldn't matter less. Your hire-chauffeur drove me home quite adequately. I rather liked him. He told me a marvellous story about some woman he once knew in Iceland. I *do* hope I meet him again.'

Callaghan grinned.

'I expect you will,' he said.

There was a little pause.

'Can I do something for you?' she asked.

'You might,' said Callaghan. 'I thought we might dine together one evening soon. I'd like to talk to you.'

'Really?' she said. 'That is indeed a compliment coming from Mr Callaghan. So you've decided to like me a little?'

'Not particularly,' said Callaghan. 'I wanted to talk to you about Lionel.'

'I see,' her voice altered. 'I'm not particularly interested in Lionel at the moment. He's becoming a little boring.'

'Is he?' said Callaghan. 'That's too bad.'

There was another pause. Then she asked:

'Are you going to Norton Fitzwarren to see mother?'

Callaghan looked at the ceiling. After a moment he said:

'I think not – that is unless she's absolutely certain she wants me to go on with the investigation. You see I've got one client already?'

'You mean Miss Varette?' she asked.

'Yes,' said Callaghan. 'I mean Miss Varette.'

'I'm awfully curious about her,' said Leonore Wilbery. 'Is it permitted to ask what she's like?'

Callaghan smiled. He looked at the ceiling for inspiration. He said:

'She's rather wonderful. She has a charming and attractive figure, a delightful voice, an almost perfect carriage and quite beautiful eyes. Her taste in dress is exquisite.'

'Dear me,' she murmured. 'She's quite wonderful, isn't she? It must be marvellous to look like that so much that a man remembers everything so well. Your description makes me feel quite a frump.'

'I'm sorry about that,' said Callaghan, 'but there isn't anything you can do very much about it, is there?'

'No,' she said. Her voice had an acid tinge. 'So I take it that while you represent Miss Varette you're not very inclined to investigate Lionel for mother?'

Callaghan said amiably: 'I don't like working for two people whose interests might clash. That's all.'

'I see.' Her voice was sarcastic. 'But if mother offered you more than the five hundred pounds which you said Miss Varette had paid you, I expect you'd do it, wouldn't you?'

'I might,' said Callaghan. He grinned into the receiver. 'It depends on *how* much more. . . .'

'Quite,' she said. 'Well, goodbye, Mr Callaghan.'

His grin broadened.

'*Au revoir*, Miss Wilbery,' he said. His voice was almost insolent.

She said sharply: 'Why "*au revoir*." Are you so certain that we shall meet again?'

'I'm never certain of anything where a woman's concerned,' said Callaghan brightly. 'The "*au revoir*" was more of a habit than anything else. *Au revoir*.'

'Goodbye, Mr Callaghan,' she said. He heard the sharp click as she hung up.

Callaghan replaced the receiver. Nikolls, who had been leaning up against the wall by the door, said:

'She's a swell dish, ain't she? When they was servin' out alure that baby got right up in front.'

Callaghan sat on the edge of his bed. He said:

'Somebody knifed Varette.'

Nikolls nodded. He fumbled for a cigarette.

'So that's how it was. I wonder who it was didn't like her.'

Callaghan said: 'I planted a little evidence. Enough to get D'Ianazzi pulled in. That'll help a bit for the moment.'

Nikolls looked out of the window. After a minute he said:

'Maybe I'm sorta dense but I can't get the hang of the way you're playin' this. I suppose you wouldn't know anything I don't know?'

Callaghan said: 'You know as much as I do. Or you ought to. Work it out for yourself. Gringall throws Varette at us. Why? There's only one answer to that one. He throws her at us because he knows she wants Lionel Wilbery's disappearance investigated.'

Nikolls asked: 'Why does he throw her at us. Why don't he investigate it himself. He's got the whole goddam police force to do it, ain't he?'

'Right,' said Callaghan. 'But he's got no official reason to investigate Wilbery's disappearance. Nobody's complained that Wilbery has disappeared. The family don't think he's disappeared. They probably think he's on one of his jags and that in due course he'll come back. But Gringall wants to *force* the family to investigate Wilbery's disappearance. So he throws Varette at us. He knows that I shall go down to the Yard to find out if the family have asked for an official investigation. He knows that when I discover they haven't I'll try an' make 'em put me on the job. He actually suggests that to me. He knows they'll have to agree when they find out that some young woman they don't like is employing me to do it. They'll have to because it'll look odd if they don't.'

Nikolls said: 'All right. I'll give you that. Now tell me why Gringall wants you employed by the family to find Wilbery, an' why he goes to such a helluva lot of trouble to get you on the job by a roundabout route. Why don't he do it himself?'

Callaghan walked to the wardrobe, took out a purple silk dressing-gown, put it on, went into the sitting-room. Nikolls followed him. Callaghan lit a cigarette and indulged in his usual morning cough.

'If I could answer that one I'd know who killed Varette,' he said.

Nikolls asked: 'What's the idea in planting evidence on that Cuban mug? Why're you tryin' to hang it on to him?'

'Why not?' asked Callaghan. 'It's logical, isn't it? The Cuban was waiting for Varette when she and I went back to Wilton Place the night before last. He wanted to talk to her. She wasn't playing. She slammed the door in his face. Probably he knew she'd been to see me. Maybe he'd followed us from Ferdie's Place as you suggested. Possibly he thinks she's been talking to me about something that he doesn't want talked about.'

'That's O.K.,' said Nikolls. 'Well . . . he tried to graft you to keep out. He gives you a hundred pounds an' you bust him on the nose. That's O.K. But why does he have to wanta bump Varette? What's his motive?'

'I don't know,' said Callaghan. 'But work it out for yourself. Somehow the Cuban and Varette are mixed up.

And Varette is mixed up with young Wilbery. There's a triangle for you. The Cuban turns up the first time I meet Varette. He turns up again last night. He happens to be running a game at a place to which I'm taken by Leonore, who is Wilbery's sister. If he didn't kill Varette he'll have an alibi, won't he? If he did and there's no other evidence, there's the stuff I planted.'

'Yeah,' said Nikolls. 'How did you do it?'

Callaghan blew a smoke ring.

'I typed a letter from her to him,' he said, 'an unfinished letter. It suggested she'd won nineteen hundred from him, that he wanted it back and she wasn't having any, that he'd threatened her, and that she intended going to the police unless he laid off. I left nineteen of the two thousand you took off him on Varette. I kept the odd hundred because the notes had our prints on them and because Varette owed us a hundred anyway.'

Nikolls grinned.

'That's *two* hundred you've had offa that Cuban,' he said. 'That guy is a charitable institution.'

'They'll check on the notes,' Callaghan went on. 'They'll find the notes were notes that D'Ianazzi had probably drawn from some bank or other. They'll pull him in. Maybe he'll get scared and talk.'

'What good will that do *you*?' said Nikolls. 'Is Gringall gonna tell *you* what the Cuban says if he talks?'

'Why shouldn't he?' asked Callaghan.

'Why should he?' asked Nikolls.

Callaghan grinned.

'For the same reason that he threw the Varette business at us from the start,' he said. 'Gringall's making use of me. He thinks I don't know it.'

Nikolls grinned.

'That guy always thinks you don't know something or other,' he said. 'One of these days he's gonna get a surprise.'

'I doubt it,' said Callaghan. 'I've never known a police officer to be surprised at anything yet.'

He went over to the sideboard. He took out a bottle of bourbon and a bottle of rum. He looked at the two bottles and decided on the bourbon. He poured out three fingers, drank it, shuddered a little.

Nikolls said: 'The way you drink spirits on an empty stomach gives me the willies. One of these fine days you're gonna take the linin' offa your tank.'

'Don't you ever drink spirits in the morning?' asked Callaghan.

Nikolls shook his head.

'Then it must be Santa Claus who's practically drunk the bottle of rye that's in my desk,' said Callaghan. 'Him or Effie . . . and she doesn't drink.'

Nikolls looked hurt.

'I may have taken a swig,' he said. 'But only when I got asthma.'

Callaghan grinned.

'You ought to see a specialist,' he said. 'You've got chronic asthma.'

He lit a fresh cigarette.

'Go round to the garage and hire yourself a car,' he said. 'Go down to Norton Fitzwarren and do a little snooping. Find out when Lionel Wilbery was last down there. Find out what you can about the family. Find out especially anything that's going about Leonore. Get the local tradesmen's reactions to Mrs Wilbery. And you'd better take a suitcase. You may be down there for a bit.'

'O.K.,' said Nikolls. 'Are you goin' down there?'

Callaghan nodded.

'I've just been talking to Leonore,' he said. 'She doesn't like me a lot at the moment. I told her that I wasn't keen on handling the case for Mrs Wilbery because I'd got another client, the Varette, and that their interests might clash. She suggested that I'd do the job for Mrs Wilbery if I was paid more than Varette is supposed to be paying.'

'What's the idea in that?' asked Nikolls.

'She'll get through to her mother and tell her,' said Callaghan. 'Then, if Ma Wilbery is really interested in finding out *why* Varette commissioned us to find Lionel, *why* she thinks he's disappeared and *who* and what Varette is, she'll come through and raise the price. Then I'll know that there's really something to this disappearance. I'll know that in effect Ma Wilbery is worried about Lionel. Then I'll really begin to believe that he *has* disappeared.'

Nikolls pondered for a moment.

'They'll know Varette is bumped in a minute,' he said. 'Today's papers will have the whole goddam story.'

'They won't,' said Callaghan. 'Gringall won't let that story go yet. He'll keep it dark. He won't release it to the press, but he'll telephone through and tell me that Varette is dead. He'll want to talk to me about the killing.'

Nikolls asked: 'Why the hell should he do that? Why should he hold up the story and talk to *you* about it? I don't get it.'

'No?' said Callaghan. 'You will – eventually.'

The house telephone rang. Nikolls went over and answered it. After a moment he looked at Callaghan. He was surprised.

'Ain't you the little marvel?' he said. 'Effie says that Gringall's on the line. He wants to know if you could go down to the Yard an' have a word with him. He says he don't want to talk on the telephone.'

Callaghan smiled.

'Tell Effie to tell him I'm coming right down. You get off to Somerset, Windy. Do what you can and play it carefully.'

'O.K.,' said Nikolls. 'I hadda date with that housekeeper at Lionel's place. But I suppose it can keep. I thought I might find something. . . .'

'It'll keep,' said Callaghan. 'You can make a pass at the housekeeper some other time. On your way, Windy.'

Nikolls went over to the door. He said:

'I've always been a misunderstood guy. An' I ain't really interested in that housekeeper. I just think she's got a nice hip-line, that's all.'

'The hip-line will keep,' said Callaghan. 'There'll be another time – or, alternatively, there'll be another hip-line.'

Nikolls grinned.

'I *hope* . . .' he said as he closed the door.

6

Week End

It was eleven-thirty when Callaghan was shown into Gringall's room at Scotland Yard. He said:

'Hallo, Gringall. It's nice seeing you again so soon.'

Gringall smiled.

'Yes,' he agreed. 'You and I go for years and don't see each other, and then we meet a lot. Life's strange, isn't it?'

Callaghan nodded.

'It is,' he said. 'And all because you remembered my birthday. I hope you'll remember it next year. Did you want anything?'

He put his hat on the corner of Gringall's desk, lit a cigarette. Gringall got up from his chair. He said:

'That's a nice suit you're wearing – but then you always wear good clothes. And a silk shirt, too – you private detectives must make a lot of money.'

'That's because we're so clever,' Callaghan said. 'We find things out – sometimes.'

The Chief Detective Inspector walked over to the window and stood looking out. He produced a short briar pipe from his pocket and began to fill it. He turned round and said to Callaghan, who was busy blowing smoke rings:

'Doria Varette's been murdered.'

Callaghan raised his eyebrows.

'You don't say?' he said. His expression was one of complete astonishment.

Gringall lit his pipe. He went back to his desk, sat down and began to draw a Jerusalem artichoke on the blotter. He said:

'Early this morning, just before five, there was an air-raid alert. They dropped a couple of incendiaries somewhere near Wilton Place. One of the air-raid wardens, who knew that Miss

Varette was living by herself (her maid went off at nights) in the house there, tried to get in to see if she was all right. There was no reply to his ringing and knocking, so he had a word with the constable on duty. The constable had seen Varette go in soon after eleven. They thought it looked a little odd so they got through a window at the back.

'She was killed with a thin dagger of some sort – probably of the stiletto type. She must have died very quickly.'

Callaghan said: 'That's too bad. There's quite enough trouble going on in the world these days without people getting themselves killed. Have you got any ideas about it?'

Gringall finished the Jerusalem artichoke and began work on a pineapple. Callaghan thought that Gringall must draw a lot of pineapples in the course of the year; that it must be his favourite fruit.

'I've got too many ideas,' said Gringall. 'But they don't match up.' He went on drawing.

'Don't think I'm curious,' said Callaghan, 'but exactly what has all this got to do with me?'

Gringall looked up.

'She was your client, wasn't she?' he asked.

Callaghan nodded.

'Definitely,' he said. 'She was our client – just as you intended she should be. The way you threw that woman at me made a creaking noise – it was so obvious.'

Gringall said: 'Rubbish. I don't know what you're talking about.'

'Don't worry,' said Callaghan. 'It couldn't matter less.'

Gringall cocked an eyebrow.

'That's a new one,' he said. 'I never heard that one before . . . *"It Couldn't Matter Less"* . . . But then you know all the catchphrases.'

'It's a new one on *me*,' said Callaghan. 'I learned it from a young woman I've been getting around with. I think it's very apt.'

Gringall went on: 'I thought I'd like to ask you just what Doria Varette had asked you to do and just what you'd done. I thought it might give us something to go on.'

Callaghan said: 'Rubbish. You knew what Doria Varette was going to ask us to do. What we've done up to the moment is our business.'

Gringall grinned.

'Now don't get annoyed,' he said. 'You always get so touchy.'

'I've never been less touchy in my life,' said Callaghan. 'I'd do anything for you, Gringall.'

They sat smiling at each other.

Callaghan stubbed out his cigarette in the ash-tray, lit a fresh one. He said:

'I always like to help. Varette told me she was worried about Lionel Wilbery. She wanted us to find him. I came down here to see if anybody else had thought he was missing. You knew I'd come down here. You told me that the family had not asked for an investigation. On the strength of that I did what you knew I'd do. I got through to Mrs Wilbery. She didn't seem particularly interested at first, but when I told her that we'd been commissioned by the Varette to find Lionel she got interested. I'm probably going down to see her.'

Gringall said: 'Probably?'

'That's how it is,' said Callaghan. 'If she likes to pay more money than she thinks Varette was paying me I'll work for her.'

'What was Varette supposed to be paying you?' asked Gringall.

Callaghan smiled.

'We never got a penny from Varette,' he said. 'She promised to send us a hundred pounds. She never sent it. I told Leonore Wilbery she'd paid us a retainer of five hundred pounds – that ought to push the ante up for Mrs Wilbery. She'll have to pay the same at least.'

Gringall sighed.

'You ought to be in the Ministry of Economic Warfare. I don't wonder you can afford Savile Row clothes.'

Callaghan said: 'All men get what they deserve.'

'Don't you believe it,' said Gringall. 'If you got what you deserve you'd be wearing a grey suit with broad arrows on it.'

Callaghan murmured: 'You're *always* so charming.'

Gringall began to draw a banana. He asked:

'You think she'll pay that?'

Callaghan nodded.

'I think she'll try to get in touch with me some time today,' he said. 'I told her daughter Leonore on the telephone this morning that I wasn't keen on working for two clients at once, that their interests might clash. She suggested that I'd work for her mother if Mrs Wilbery paid enough. I said I'd see what her offer was first of all. I think she'll want me to work for her *now*.'

Gringall said: 'Why *now*?'

Callaghan said: 'You wouldn't know, would you? One of these fine days somebody is going to start a course for Scotland Yard officers – a course to teach 'em how to tell lies and look as if they're telling the truth.'

'It's a good idea,' said Gringall. 'If the Chief Commissioner agrees we'll get you to come down here and run it.'

Callaghan said: 'It wouldn't be any good. You can't teach people anything unless they've got intelligence to start with.' He blew a smoke ring. 'The reason why Mrs Wilbery will want me to go on with this job *now*, and why she'll raise the ante to five hundred, is because Varette is dead.'

Gringall said: 'But she doesn't know that.'

'She will,' said Callaghan. 'I'm going to tell her.'

'Why?' asked Gringall. He laid the pencil down.

Callaghan said: 'Look, I went to a little party last night. I met some people there – who they are, what they are, doesn't matter to you. One of 'em evidently knew something about Wilbery. This person suggested that Varette took drugs; that *she* was the person who introduced Wilbery to dope. This person suggested that Doria Varette was the nigger in the woodpile.'

Gringall nodded.

'I see,' he said. 'But I still don't get the idea.'

Callaghan looked at the ceiling. The expression on his face was bland and innocent. He said:

'People who take drugs do funny things, don't they?'

Gringall said: 'I've heard so.'

'All right,' said Callaghan. 'If I were to suggest to Mrs Wilbery that possibly Doria Varette was the woman who started Lionel taking drugs for some reason best known to herself; that he used to get his supplies through her and that she'd suddenly stopped his supplies, it might not be unreasonable to suppose that little Lionel might have lost his head and killed her.'

Gringall opened his eyes.

'I see . . .' he said. 'And what then?'

'Well,' said Callaghan, 'Mrs Wilbery wouldn't believe a thing like that. She'd begin to take a real interest in finding and producing Lionel so that he could refute such a lousy story, wouldn't she?'

Gringall said: 'I've met some tough propositions in my time, but you take the cake.'

Callaghan said: 'Wasn't it you who said the motto of Callaghan Investigations was: "We get there somehow and who the hell cares how"?'

Gringall sighed.

'I didn't know how true it was,' he said. 'You can play it that way if you like though – that's your business.' He began to draw a bunch of grapes. 'I thought I'd got the murderer this morning,' he said. 'As a matter of fact he's in a cell at Cannon Row Police Station now.'

'No?' said Callaghan. 'That's interesting. Who was it?'

'A foreigner by the name of D'Ianazzi,' said Gringall. 'When I went down to Varette's house with the doctor and the rest of the boys I found an unfinished letter in her typewriter. Apparently she was typing that letter when D'Ianazzi arrived. She went out of the sitting-room where the typewriter was, turned the light off and shut the door. Apparently she talked to D'Ianazzi in her bedroom. Apparently he killed her in there and got out quickly.'

Callaghan said: 'What did the letter say?'

'It was to D'Ianazzi,' said Gringall. 'Apparently Varette had won some money off D'Ianazzi, and he wanted it back. She wasn't having any. She told him in the letter that if he pestered her she was going to the police. We found the money on her,' Gringall concluded.

Callaghan said: 'Well, there's one case that's in the bag.'

'I'm afraid it isn't,' said Gringall. He began to do a little shading work on the bunch of grapes. 'Needless to say,' he went on, looking at Callaghan, 'we tested the typewriter for fingerprints. Doria Varette's fingerprints were on the keys all right. Apparently she'd typed the letter, as most people do, using the first and second fingers of her left and right hand. That's the snag.'

'It is?' said Callaghan. 'Why is it a snag?'

'Varette was a touch typist,' said Gringall. 'You know what that means – she used all the fingers of both hands to type with.'

Callaghan said: 'That just shows you, doesn't it?'

'It does,' said Gringall. 'So it looks to me as if that letter was a plant. It looks to me as if somebody was trying to hang this murder on to D'Ianazzi.' He put down his pencil and folded his hands. 'I wonder who could want to do a thing like that?' he said.

Callaghan blew a smoke ring.

'People do the strangest things, don't they?' he said. He knocked the ash from his cigarette into the ash-tray on Gringall's desk. 'What is this D'Ianazzi?' he asked.

'He says he's a Cuban,' said Gringall. 'But he's got no passport and no identity card.'

Callaghan said: 'Really! That's not too good at a time like this, is it?'

'No,' said the police officer. 'D'Ianazzi says he had a quarrel with some fellow, that they got to fisticuffs, that the other man knocked him out and, when he came to, his passport and papers and two thousand pounds that he had in a body-belt were gone.'

Callaghan nodded.

'That sounds phoney to me,' he said.

Gringall said: 'I wonder. We checked with the bank. We found that D'Ianazzi drew that money from his own banking account. We also discovered that the notes that were found on Doria Varette were the identical notes that were issued by the bank to D'Ianazzi, less one hundred pounds.

Callaghan said: 'Isn't that strange? So somebody had a hundred pounds.'

'Yes,' said Gringall. 'Somebody who was clever enough to know that the note on the outside of the packet would have their fingerprints on it. Or' – he smiled quizzically – 'it might have been somebody who thought they were owed a hundred pounds,' he said.

Callaghan stubbed out his cigarette.

'You don't say?' he said.

Gringall re-lit his pipe.

'I thought you might have had some additional information – something that would have helped me,' he said. 'But if you've told me all you know, that's that.'

Callaghan got up.

'I'm sorry I can't be of more use to you, Gringall,' he said. 'You know I'd like to be.'

Gringall got up. They stood smiling at each other.

Gringall said: 'What are you going to do now, that is supposing Mrs Wilbery asks you to find Lionel? Have you got a plan of campaign?'

Callaghan grinned.

'That's my business,' he said. 'I never discuss my client's affairs with police officers.'

Gringall said: 'You're a hard case, Slim.' He held out his hand. 'Come in and see me sometime.'

'I'm looking forward to it,' said Callaghan.

He went to the door and opened it; then he turned with his hand on the doorknob.

'By the way,' he said, 'you wouldn't have change for a hundred pound note, would you?'

'Thanks for the compliment,' said Gringall, 'but they don't pay us enough.'

Callaghan nodded.

'Too bad,' he said. 'I suppose you're going to hang on to that Cuban?'

Gringall said: 'Well, I suppose I'll have to until I find

whether he's got a passport or not. Strangely enough, the Cuban Legation say they don't know anything about him.'

Callaghan said: 'They're like the rest of us. None of us knows anything about anything. So long, Gringall.'

He closed the door quietly behind him.

Callaghan sat on a high stool at the Premier Lounge in Dover Street. He ordered a sandwich and a double Canadian rye. He was thinking about Gringall.

He drank the rye, ordered another. He came to the conclusion that the Wilbery case needed a little action and that he was not inclined to be too particular as to what form that action took. The thought pleased him.

Callaghan was not prone to theorizing – even to himself – about the technique of the business of being a private detective. He left such things as 'clues' (invariably described in the press reports as 'important'), experiments with test tubes, psychological cross-examinations, deductions which – in the majority of cases – were based on an entirely false premise, and all the rest of the paraphernalia of fictional detectives, to those people who believed in them. His own method – which incidentally and, whether they admit it or not, constitutes the main stock-in-trade of all those individuals whose business it is to inquire into the underneath side of life – was to draw a broad canvas incorporating all the people who came into the picture of a case, or were in some way concerned in it, examine it carefully, and then to create such circumstances as would make people talk. Then all you had to do was to listen.

You could also do a little talking yourself. And this is where you scored over the professional policeman who had to be careful what he said, when he said it and to whom he spoke. You could secure all sorts of results by being rude to the right – or wrong – people, by flattering, by sympathizing or by being tough. If it was necessary, and the case merited it, you could be very tough. Providing you were tough with the *right* people nothing much ever went *wrong* with the system. If it did, who cared?

It was four o'clock when he got back to the office. He

went into his room and sat down. He smoked and thought about Leonore Wilbery.

Effie Thompson came in. She said:

'Nikolls has been through. He's staying at an inn called The Grasscutter – it's about three miles out of Taunton on the Norton Fitzwarren side. It is a mile and a half from the Wilbery house.'

Callaghan nodded. He put his feet on the desk and blew smoke rings. The telephone in the outer office rang. Effie Thompson hurried out, took the call, then came back.

'It's Mrs Wilbery,' she said. 'She wants to talk to you. She says it's urgent.'

Callaghan took off the receiver. He said:

'Good-afternoon, Mrs Wilbery.'

The very quiet and cool voice at the other end said good-afternoon. Then:

'Mr Callaghan, my daughter has been talking to me on the telephone. She says that you seem undecided as to whether you could undertake the business of trying to find Lionel for me. She says that you have some idea in your head that my interests might clash with those of your other client – Miss Varette. I thought I'd like to know what you mean by "my interests". After all, we all want Lionel to be found.'

'Do you?' asked Callaghan pleasantly.

'Of course,' said Mrs Wilbery. There was a note of surprise in her voice. 'Why ever shouldn't we?'

'I had the idea in my head that you didn't *really* believe that Lionel was missing,' said Callaghan amiably. 'I had the idea that you thought that Miss Varette was panicking a little – unnecessarily I mean. Incidentally, my idea about your interests clashing with those of Miss Varette doesn't matter *now*.'

'I'm glad,' said Mrs Wilbery. 'And why doesn't it matter *now*?' She sounded mildly amused.

Callaghan said: 'Miss Varette's dead. Somebody murdered her.'

There was a long pause. Then she said:

'How terrible. . . . I suppose the police have an idea who did it?'

'*Why* should the police have an idea who did it?' asked Callaghan quickly.

'I don't know . . .' said Mrs Wilbery. 'Except that Miss Varette seems to have been a rather extraordinary sort of young woman. And she used to sing at a night club, didn't she? And she did odd things too, I believe. . . .'

'Such as taking drugs?' asked Callaghan.

'Well . . . yes . . .' said Mrs Wilbery slowly.

'Quite,' said Callaghan.

He lit a fresh cigarette with his free hand. There was another pause.

'Of course,' said Mrs Wilbery, 'I know that this business of trying to find someone like Lionel is rather like looking for a needle in a haystack. He's inclined to be a little irresponsible and foolish sometimes. I realize that you would probably be put to a great deal of expense. I've talked to my lawyer about it and he thinks that it would be proper – at this stage – for me to pay you say five hundred pounds as a retainer and to cover expenses for the time being. Would that be all right?'

Callaghan said: 'Mrs Wilbery, about this business of Lionel being a little irresponsible and foolish sometimes. I'm rather interested in that angle. You mean by that, that he's inclined to be headstrong and do silly things; that he's one of those weak people who sometimes like to give a bad imitation of being strong. Is that it?'

'Well . . . yes . . . I suppose so,' said Mrs Wilbery.

Callaghan said: 'Lionel was in love or thought he was in love with Miss Varette. For some reason or other he disappeared without telling her where he was going. We know she didn't know where he was because she'd employed us to find out. It occurred to me – and I regret I haven't been able to ask Miss Varette this question – that he may have disappeared in a fit of temper because he had some sort of disagreement with her.'

'Quite,' said Mrs Wilbery. 'That's quite possible.'

Callaghan grinned at the telephone transmitter. Mrs Wilbery was walking straight into the trap. He went on:

'Very well then. If Lionel went off without a word to

114

Doria Varette because he'd quarrelled with her, do you think it possible that he might suddenly decide to see her and have another quarrel . . . that he might suddenly decide to come to London – that is if he was somewhere else – and that they might have quarrelled again?'

There was an exclamation at the other end of the line. Then Mrs Wilbery said quickly:

'I don't see why, having gone off, Lionel should suddenly decide that he would see her. Why should he? The very fact that he'd gone off shows that he *didn't* want to see her.'

Callaghan interrupted.

'He might have wanted to see her in spite of himself,' he said. 'There's quite a good reason, you know.'

'Is there?' asked Mrs Wilbery. 'What is it?'

'You suggested it to me yourself,' said Callaghan. 'You suggested that Miss Varette was not quite all that she should be, that possibly she took drugs. You have also suggested that Lionel was irresponsible and foolish. And he and Miss Varette were in love it occurred to me that she might have got him to do a little drug-taking too. The process isn't unusual between two people who are supposed to be in love and of whom one takes drugs. That being so, it would be obvious that Lionel would get any drugs he used from Miss Varette; that being so, when he went off, his supply would be cut off, and that being so he might suddenly decide *in spite of himself* that he would come back and see Miss Varette. She, however, might not have been too amenable to reason. She might have refused. All sorts of things might have happened.'

There was a little pause. Then she said, very coolly:

'I don't think we ought to talk about this on the telephone, Mr Callaghan. Are you coming down here? I'd like to see you. We could talk freely then.'

'Quite,' said Callaghan. 'Candidly, I'm rather intrigued with the idea of finding Lionel. I'd like a retainer of a thousand pounds. As you said, it might be an expensive business.'

'So it seems,' said Mrs Wilbery wryly. 'My daughter suggested . . .' she stopped suddenly.

Callaghan completed the sentence for her.

'Your daughter suggested that I'd told her that private detectives sometimes do a little blackmail on the side,' he said amiably. 'You probably think I'm trying the process. I'm not. I charge more than a thousand when I blackmail clients.'

'I'm sure you do,' said Mrs Wilbery. 'Anyhow Leonore thinks that you're rather clever, so I'll pay the thousand pounds. I'll have a cheque sent to you today.'

Callaghan said: 'Thanks. I'll come down this afternoon. I'll try to get down by nine tonight. You're about a hundred and fifty miles from town, aren't you?'

'Yes,' said Mrs Wilbery. 'So you *did* intend to come down. You'd looked it up.'

Callaghan grinned.

'Yes,' he said. 'I intended to come down and I'd looked it up.'

'Well . . .' said Mrs Wilbery. She began to laugh. It was an extremely attractive laugh. 'You're rather a unique investigator, aren't you, Mr Callaghan?'

Callaghan said: 'I wouldn't know. Perhaps we can discuss that angle too. I hope to be with you about nine o'clock tonight.'

She said: 'Will you try to be here by nine. We shall dine at that time. Leonore's coming down about then.'

'I shall be with you at nine,' said Callaghan. 'Goodbye, Mrs Wilbery.'

He hung up, rang the bell for Effie Thompson. When she came in he said:

'You remember that fellow who did some snooping for me in the Riverton case. I've forgotten his name.'

'I remember,' said Effie. 'It was a Mr Maninway.'

'All right,' said Callaghan. 'Just get your book and make a note of this.'

He waited while she got her notebook. Then he went on:

'I want Maninway to get next to two people called Sabine and Milta Haragos. I want to know who and what they are. I've got an idea they've an interest in running gambling games round town and possibly elsewhere. Ask him to find out. Ask him to get anything he can. He's to put anything he gets through here. You can let me have it over the telephone at Norton Fitzwarren. When you call through to me there be careful. If I'm on a direct line and no one can listen in I'll call you Effie. But if I call you Miss Thompson you'll know I'm speaking on an extension line and you'll have to watch your step.'

'Very well,' said Effie. 'I suppose you don't know when you'll be back.'

'No,' said Callaghan. 'Just keep an eye on things. If you want any help, get Wintor or Blane to come to the office and stand by.'

'Very well,' said Effie. 'And I'll ring through to the valet downstairs to pack your things.'

'Thanks,' said Callaghan.

He lit another cigarette, put his feet back on the desk.

Somewhere in the house a clock chimed ten. Callaghan knocked the ash off his cigarette, stood looking over the wide expanse of lawn that ran down to the woodland at the back of Deeplands.

A nice place to live in, he thought, lots of space and air and not too many people.

He walked along the wide veranda that ran the entire width of the back of the house, let himself into the smoking-room, through the french window, crossed the room, walked down the long oak wainscoted passage into the library.

Mrs Wilbery was pouring out coffee. She was alone. Callaghan looked at her appreciatively. She wore a long bottle-green velvet housecoat. Under the hem a beige silk-clad ankle showed itself over a gold sandal.

He went and stood by the fireplace, watching her as she poured and held out his cup of black coffee. A very good-looking forty-four or five, he thought. Leonore had to be about twenty-six or seven, so that Mrs Wilbery must be at least forty-five or so. Callaghan thought she looked a good ten years younger.

Her figure was good, her movements quick and graceful. Her complexion would have been good for a girl, and the auburn hair that set off her oval-shaped face showed no trace of grey.

He took the cup. She said:

'Now we can talk. I did not like to talk to you on the telephone. I think it is so much better to see people face to face. First of all I want to know what you think about Lionel?'

Callaghan smiled at her. He said:

'I want to hear what *you* think. Then, when I've digested that I'll give you any ideas I've got.'

'I don't think anything at all – very much,' she said. 'I think Lionel is stupid. But then all young men are stupid, aren't they? At some time or other they have to do silly things. If they don't, one feels they're not normal.'

'So you think Lionel was normal?' asked Callaghan.

'I'm not quite sure about that,' she said. 'He was odd, of course, but then he was a poet. Poets are always a little eccentric, don't you think, Mr Callaghan?'

'I think most people are eccentric in some way or another,' said Callaghan. 'Lionel has disappeared before, hasn't he?'

'Well . . . yes,' she replied. 'That is to say he's gone off and never told anyone where he was going. He's always turned up though, usually when he's broke. I shouldn't have worried this time except for this unfortunate Miss Varette.'

Callaghan said: 'When we talked on the telephone you seemed to know quite a bit about her. Where did you get your information?'

She shrugged her shoulders.

'Leonore is my only source,' she said. 'And I think that she has been talking to Milta and Sabine. You've met them, I suppose?'

'Yes,' said Callaghan. 'Just how do they come into the picture?'

'Lionel introduced them to Leonore, some time ago,'

said Mrs Wilbery. 'They seem to have been the one steadying influence in his life. They're nice people. Leonore likes them. They're amusing, she says. They're White Russians who managed to get out of the country just after the Revolution. They've lived in England ever since. They have money and they're interested in things and people. They drink a little but not too much, and gamble a little but not too much. Sabine was interested in Lionel's work. She tried to get him to give up all sorts of odd people that he'd got to know, and settle down to serious writing. Milta – who knows publishers and people like that – had practically arranged to get the book on which Lionel was working published. In fact we all thought that possibly Lionel had turned over a new leaf. Then, apparently, Miss Varette turned up.'

'And she wasn't very good for Lionel?' queried Callaghan.

She looked into the fire.

'That's what they tell Leonore,' she said. 'Milta is certain that Miss Varette took drugs – which isn't very nice. Also he says that she seemed to have some sort of hold over Lionel. Milta, apparently, is an expert on women –' She smiled at Callaghan. 'Most Russians consider themselves experts on women, don't they?' she said. 'But Milta definitely did not like Miss Varette. He'd met her with Lionel half a dozen times and thought that she was just another of the rather odd women that Lionel met and thought he admired from time to time.'

'What made Milta think that she wasn't so good, that she drugged?' asked Callaghan.

'Lionel did,' she said. 'Apparently Lionel talked to Milta some time ago about her. His attitude was a little strange. He seemed afraid of her. Milta got the idea that Lionel was definitely under Miss Varette's thumb. And now this terrible thing has happened to the girl. It rather makes one think that Milta was right, doesn't it?'

She took a cigarette from the silver box on the table. Callaghan lit it for her. She smiled her thanks.

'I wonder why Miss Wilbery didn't tell me all this before?' he asked.

She laughed.

'I think she thought you were a little breath-taking . . . a little forceful. She's a girl with a will of her own. I don't think she likes you a lot.'

Callaghan grinned.

'I don't think she does either,' he said.

'Women are inclined to make up their minds very quickly on such matters,' she said. 'Sometimes too quickly. I like you very much. I think you're quite delightful.'

Callaghan said: 'I hope you won't alter your opinion.'

She loked at him.

'Why should I?' she asked. She settled back in her chair. 'Now tell me,' she said, 'what do you propose to do about finding Lionel? May one know how you are going to set about it?'

Callaghan said: 'I'd tell you if I knew. I don't know yet. I've got one or two ideas, but nothing very definite.'

She looked into the fire.

'I want him found quickly,' she said. Her voice was decided. 'I want him found quickly because of what you suggested on the telephone. I didn't like it!'

'Why not?' asked Callaghan. 'If you thought it was untrue.'

'Whether I thought it might be untrue or not doesn't come into it,' she said quickly. 'Milta says that he is certain that Miss Varette introduced Lionel to the nasty habit of taking drugs. That matched up with your suggestion. It matched up with the suggestion that they might have quarrelled, and that Lionel, having gone away, might return because he wanted more drugs, and then . . .' She shrugged her shoulders. 'It's not a particularly nice thought,' she said.

'Murder's not a particularly nice thing,' said Callaghan. 'Not that I'm suggesting for a moment that Lionel had anything to do with Miss Varette being killed. I had to bring up that angle because it's certain that the police will begin to consider him as a suspect unless they find somebody else. After all, if a girl gets killed it's rather natural for them to look for a lover who's disappeared, isn't it?'

'I suppose it is,' said Mrs Wilbery. 'That's where you come in, Mr Callaghan.' She smiled at him prettily. 'You've got to find Lionel first. So that we can know exactly what he's been doing and exactly where he's been. So that we can refute any silly talk about his being responsible – in any way – for this unhappy young woman's death.'

She got up.

'I'm tired,' she said. 'I think I shall go to bed. Ring for anything you want and please consider the house your own. Good-night.'

Callaghan walked to the door, held it open for her. As she went out, she said:

'It's an odd thing to say, but I feel much more confident about Lionel now that you're looking after things.'

'Do you?' said Callaghan. He grinned at her. 'Maybe that's only because you like me,' he said mischievously.'

'Possibly,' she said. 'But that isn't a bad reason, is it?' She threw him a quick smile over her shoulder.

Callaghan closed the door. He went back to the fire. He thought that the Wilbery women were no fools – either of them.

He lit a cigarette, sat down and blew smoke rings. After a while he got up, went through the passage into the smoking-room, out of the french windows, down the verandah steps. He began to walk across the lawn.

It was a fine night. At the bottom of the first lawn was a terrace. Callaghan turned and looked at the big rambling house behind him. He wondered why it was that a young man with such a background had to play around with the very odd people that the half-world of London can produce.

He walked along the terrace, round the side of the

house to the garage. He pulled one of the sliding doors open, went in, started up the Jaguar, put on a tweed cap which he produced from the cubby hole in the dashboard, backed the car out of the garage and turned it.

He drove slowly down the drive.

He thought that he liked Mrs Wilbery. He thought that was what she had intended.

He stopped the car outside the big wrought-iron gates, fumbled in his dinner coat for a cigarette, lit it, settled down behind the wheel.

He was still thinking about Mrs Wilbery. Wondering if she had quite decided that Lionel had killed Doria Varette.

Nikolls filled a good half of the cocktail shaker with Bacardi rum. He added lemon juice, a spot of gin and some ice. He said:

'This is a helluva drink. It sorta gets the brain workin'.'

He shook the cocktail shaker expertly, poured out the mixture into whisky glasses, passed one to Callaghan and sat down on the opposite side of the fire, the cocktail shaker by his side.

Callaghan drained the glass and passed it back to Nikolls, who refilled it, handed it back.

Callaghan said: 'So you can get gin at the Grasscutter? This seems a good inn.'

'I brought it with me,' said Nikolls. 'I always like to have some liquor around. I remember one time – in the old Prohibition days – when I was stuck in some dry State that was really dry. It was terrible.'

'What did you do?' asked Callaghan.

'I got along,' replied Nikolls. 'I was workin' for the Transatlantic Detective Agency then. I was on a case tryin' to find some honeybelle who'd taken a runout on her husband because he was broke. Two days after she left him the guy came into a fortune – three-quarters of a million dollars – an' commissioned the Transatlantic to find. I won the job.'

Callaghan asked: 'Did you find her?'

'Yeah,' said Nikolls. 'I found her all right. We usta make gin in the bath-tub. She hadda recipe that was swell. One day she gotta bit high an' put the wrong stuff in. She took a drink while I was shavin' an' damn near passed right out. I heard a sorta gurgle an' found her in the bath. She'd fell in. That dame was a marvel. She had a sorta iron constitution. She must have, because the stuff she made took the enamel offa the bath. She was a nice dame. Just a little vague sometimes. . . .'

Callaghan finished his second glass of Bacardi mixture. He said:

'I suppose you haven't had time to get anything on Lionel?'

'I've got plenty,' said Nikolls. 'There's a helluva barmaid in the saloon bar here. A very nice line in dames. I been talkin' to her. I think she likes me a little.'

Callaghan nodded.

'I know . . .'

'This guy Lionel was a pup for the dames,' continued Nikolls. 'Any time he saw a pretty jane he usta rush around with his tongue hangin' out. He fell with a bump for this baby in the bar. He usta come an' read poetry to her – his own stuff – in the evenin' before the bar filled up. She said he was a good poet an' she'da liked it a lot if she'd known what it was all about. He gave her a picture. I've seen it. He's not a bad-lookin' guy either. A bit on the weak side but sorta spiritual – you know. He looks as if he'd been smacked in the pan with a blunt instrument an' never got over it. Side-whiskers too, an' wavy hair.'

Callaghan said: 'When did she see him last?'

'That's the thing,' said Nikolls. 'She says he's been around here plenty. She says he ain't been in here, but she's seen him around. She says she saw him around on the Deeplands road last night. Goin' towards the house.'

'Did she?' said Callaghan. 'That's interesting. Very interesting. Anything else?'

'That's the lot up to the moment,' said Nikolls. 'Maybe I'll do some real snoopin' tomorrow. You had any luck?'

Callaghan grinned.

'I'm not certain,' he said. 'Mrs Wilbery is a peach. She's come to the conclusion that she likes me. She's paying a retainer of a thousand for Callaghan Investigations to find Lionel.'

Nikolls whistled.

'She must be nuts,' he said. 'Callaghan Investigations would find the north pole for half that. What's the idea?'

'She's scared,' said Callaghan. 'She thinks it quite likely that Lionel killed the Varette. Some friends of his – people I met out at The Dene – named Haragos, believe that Varette got him on to drugs. She believes that there may have been a little trouble between him and Varette and that he might have lost his head and killed her. That's what she thinks. She didn't tell *me* so.'

'I got it,' said Nikolls. 'She likes you an' she's payin' a thousand so that if you do find Lionel you arrange it so that he couldn't have killed Varette. Maybe she thinks you can fix an alibi or somethin' for the poet?'

'It looks like that,' said Callaghan. 'And it looks like that still more if Lionel's been seen round here. If the barmaid here saw him last night it was certain that he was going up to the house.'

Nikolls nodded.

'Maybe he went to see mamma an' talked.'

Callaghan said: 'Who knows?'

He got up, lit a cigarette.

'Find out what you can tomorrow,' he said. 'Find out if your barmaid friend had ever heard of the Haragos couple – Milta and Sabine.'

Nikolls asked: 'Could they be Russians? An' would the Sabine proposition be a dame with a very white flat pan, but sorta attractive. Thin like a snake an' with a funny accent?'

'That's the pair,' said Callaghan.

Nikolls said: 'Well, they live around here. They got a house about five miles on the other side of Deeplands – a place called Vale Cottage – only it ain't a cottage. Lionel usta be very thick with 'em an' then they tried to reform him or somethin' so he gave 'em the air. One time he usta stay up there a lot. He told the barmaid downstairs that the atmosphere at their dump was O.K. for poetry.'

Callaghan said: 'All right. Carry on with the good work. I'll be seeing you, Windy.'

It was twelve-thirty when Callaghan drove the Jaguar into the garage at Deeplands. He parked the car neatly, closed the self-locking garage door behind him, began to walk towards the side door.

Away to the right, over the breast-high wall that bounded the side of the drive, Callaghan could see the thick woods, distinct in the moonlight. He crossed the drive and stood in the shadow of a tree, his elbows resting on the wall.

Behind him he heard the side door open. Callaghan turned quietly and stood, his hands in his pockets, looking towards the porch. Leonore came out. She wore a short fur coat over the attractive black frock she had worn at dinner, and driving gauntlets. He watched her as she walked to the garage, unlocked it and disappeared within. Two minutes later he heard the sound of a car being started, then a small blue touring Fiat which had been parked alongside Mrs Wilbery's Rolls, backed out.

Leonore swung the car expertly, switched on the parking lights, drove slowly down the drive towards the main country road.

Callaghan stood for a moment looking after the disappearing tail-light. Then he lit a cigarette, walked over to the side door, entered the house.

He hung his things on the stand in the passage, crossed the hall, went up the stairs to his room on the first floor.

He undressed, bathed, got into pyjamas and a dressing-gown, lit a cigarette.

Then he switched off the light, opened the bedroom window and the door and lay down on the bed.

He began to blow smoke rings in the darkness.

7

Bedroom Scene

It was nearly three o'clock when Callaghan heard the sound of the car coming up the drive towards the garage.

He swung himself off the bed, switched on the light, closed the bedroom door. He went to the wardrobe and took out a pair of blue sports trousers and a blue polo sweater. He put the trousers on over his pyjamas, pulled the sweater over his head, put on a pair of leather slippers.

He switched off the light, opened the door half-way, stood waiting, leaning up against the doorpost.

Two or three minutes later the passage light went on. He drew back into the shelter of the doorway, peered down the corridor.

Leonore turned into the corridor at the far end. She walked quickly, a little unsteadily. She dropped her handbag, bent down, picked it up, dropped it again, eventually retrieved it. She walked to the door of the bedroom third from the corridor end and went in. Callaghan saw the gleam of light between the time she snapped the electric light switch and the closing of the door. He walked quickly down the corridor, tapped on the door of Leonore's room.

She called out: 'Who is that? Who is it?' Her voice was shrill.

He said: 'Callaghan!'

'Oh, dear . . .' She sounded petulant. 'Has something happened?' Then sarcastically: 'Have you found a clue or something?'

He grinned in the darkness of the corridor.

'Yes,' he said. 'I found a nice clue wandering about looking for a home. I thought we might examine it.'

She opened the door. She stood, framed in the lighted doorway, looking at him oddly. Her eyes were antagonistic. They were very bright and the pupils were too small, he thought. She ran her tongue over her lips. She seemed excited about something.

She said: 'I'm fearfully tired. Is it important? What is it, please?'

Callaghan said: 'I want to talk to you. *I* consider it important, you may not. If you knew what was in my mind you'd probably want to discuss it. But I don't care whether I talk or not. I'd just as soon go to bed.'

'You're the most extraordinary person,' said Leonore. 'You do the strangest things at the most impossible times. You . . .'

Callaghan interrupted.

'I'm not doing anything strange,' he said, 'at the moment. And I didn't come here to hear about the sort of person I am. So please don't talk rubbish. It's much too late.'

He took out his cigarette case, extracted a cigarette. He radiated impertinence.

She said: 'I think you will agree that a bedroom isn't a very good place in which to discuss things. There's a time and place for everything.'

Callaghan sighed.

'How trite,' he said patiently. 'But I don't agree with you. *I* think a bedroom is a very good place to discuss anything. But if you don't like it let's go somewhere else.'

She began to laugh. Callaghan thought that there was a touch of hysteria in the laugh. She said:

'Aren't you amazing? You've had ample time to talk to me. I was here from dinner-time onwards. But you have to select three o'clock in the morning.'

'I didn't select the time,' said Callaghan. 'I had to wait till you came back, hadn't I? There wouldn't have been much to talk about before, would there?'

She raised her eyebrows. She leaned a shoulder against the edge of the door.

'I don't even know what you mean by that,' she said. 'Possibly I'm very stupid, but perhaps you'll explain why you couldn't talk to me before.'

'Certainly,' said Callaghan. 'And I don't think you're a bit stupid. On the contrary –' He lit his cigarette, taking quite a time over the process. 'It wouldn't have been very much use my talking to you before,' he went on. 'Before I talked to you it was necessary that you should have ample opportunity to talk to your mother and then further opportunity to decide what you were going to do about it.'

'I see,' she said. 'Go on . . .'

'After your mother went to her room tonight you went to see her,' said Callaghan. 'She told you of the conversation I'd had with her. As a direct result of what she told you, you decided that it was necessary for you to go and see Milta or Sabine Haragos – or both of them. And it was so necessary that you should see one or either of them that the lateness of the hour didn't matter. Isn't that right?'

She did not reply immediately. She looked at him along the edge of her eyelids. He thought she looked rather dangerous. He thought Leonore could be damned dangerous if she wanted to be. He thought she looked extremely attractive when she was like that, dismissed the idea immediately because it was interfering with his train of thought.

'You know everything,' she said bitterly. 'You're just too wonderful, aren't you, Mr Callaghan. I suppose this is another of your inspired guesses.'

He smiled cheerfully.

'That's not a bad description,' he said. 'I like "inspired guesses." It's good. But you haven't answered my question.'

'I don't think I'm going to answer your question,' she said casually. She was still looking at him through half-closed eyelids. 'You told me once – when we were driving down to The Dene – that when you wanted me to talk I'd talk and like it. Well . . . now you want me to talk and I don't like it. So I'm not going to talk.'

Callaghan blew smoke out of his nostrils. He said cheerfully:

'You are going to talk and you are going to like it. Just so that we shan't misunderstand one another I'll tell you just what I'm going to do . . . shall I?'

'Please do,' she said. 'It might be interesting. It might even be amusing.'

'It will be,' said Callaghan. 'It's going to amuse *me* a lot. Good-night.'

She took her hand away from the door and stood up straight. Callaghan had already begun to move when she spoke.

'I thought you were going to tell me what you were going to do,' she said. 'I thought I was going to be made to talk.'

Callaghan grinned at her.

'*When* I want you to,' he said. 'And that will be some time tomorrow morning. I'm not going to waste any more time tonight talking to you. You're beginning to bore me a little. You'd better go to bed and get some sleep. You'll need to have a clear brain tomorrow morning. You'll have a certain amount of explaining to do to your mother.'

She stiffened.

'Exactly what do you mean by that?'

Callaghan said: 'Quite obviously your mother has a definite idea in her head about Lionel. She thinks it extremely probable that he killed Doria Varette. Before, she was uncertain about it, but only because she couldn't find a definite motive for him doing such a thing. Now she's found the motive she's scared.'

'What nonsense,' said Leonore. She spoke a little too glibly. 'Anyhow, what is this motive? Why should Lionel want to have killed this unfortunate Varette person?'

'People who dope do all sorts of silly things,' said Callaghan, 'and when they're weak, fatuous people like Lionel they do anything – if and when they feel like it. I've no doubt that if Varette was supplying Lionel with drugs and she stopped his supplies he'd feel like killing her. Just for the moment, I mean. Probably – a moment or two afterwards – he'd be fearfully surprised at what he'd done. He'd give anything not to have done it. He would wonder why he had done it. But wondering wouldn't do him any good. The Varette killing would be a *fait accompli*, and there wouldn't be anything to do about it except to disappear again.'

'So that's what you think,' she said. She laughed.

'That's what I think,' Callaghan went on. 'Incidentally, Lionel would be doing the clever thing to play it that way. He's disappeared before, gone off to odd places where, apparently, he's never met people who knew him, and he can say he'd done the same thing again. Of course – if and when we find him – your mother will expect me to fake some sort of alibi for him.'

'Really! So mother expects you to fake *alibis* too. You can't realize how ridiculous you sound.'

'That never worries me,' said Callaghan cheerfully. 'So long as I don't think ridiculously. For instance, I should *be* ridiculous if I thought that your mother was paying me a thousand pounds just to hang about on the off-chance of finding Lionel. She could have had Lionel found for nothing. She could have gone to the police. Well . . . why didn't she go to them when she'd made up her mind that Lionel had disappeared? The reason is obvious. She knew I'd been to the Yard and seen them after Varette told me that he'd gone. She knew that she'd got to do something about it. But she didn't want to employ the police. She didn't want to do that because she didn't want the police to find out – in the course of their investigations – something or other connected with Lionel that she either knew about or guessed at.'

'But she's prepared to employ *you*,' said Leonore. 'I think you're much more dangerous. The police couldn't be half as dangerous – whatever they found out or didn't find out – as you could be if you felt like it.'

'Quite,' said Callaghan. 'At the same time that's amusing coming from you and having regard to the fact that it was really through you that I'm working for your mother.'

She raised her eyebrows.

'How amazing,' she said. 'Please tell me about that too. I just love hearing what I've done and what I haven't done – from you.'

'After I'd spoken to your mother the first time and told her about Lionel,' said Callaghan amiably, 'she put me on to you. She suggested that I should see you before coming down here. The reason she gave me was that you might know something about Lionel. Really she wanted you to have a look at me, to make up your mind as to what sort of person I was and report to her before she went any further in the business. She told you about Varette then.

'When I picked you up at Mrs Martindale's party, you put on that drunk act so as not to give anything away about knowing Varette; so that you need not answer questions until you'd seen how the land lay.'

'Marvellous,' she said sarcastically. 'Wonderful. You're almost a thought reader. Tell me . . . what did I do then?'

'You put me on to the Haragos couple,' Callaghan went on, 'because you knew they'd give Varette a bad break. You knew they didn't like Varette, that Sabine, anyhow, believed that it was Varette who started Lionel off on drugs. I suppose the idea was then to make me lose confidence in my original client. . . .'

'And then?' asked Leonore seriously.

'Then you telephoned your mother and advised her to clinch the deal with me. You told her that Varette was paying me five hundred pounds and she ought to offer the same. You told her I'd probably want more and that if I did it was because I was beginning to guess things; that it would be better to have me working on your side and not worrying about what Varette wanted or didn't want. So Mrs Wilbery agreed to pay a thousand – especially when she heard that somebody had killed Varette. Especially when she was half-inclined to think that it might be Lionel.'

He stood looking at her, smiling pleasantly.

In spite of the fact that her head was aching, that she

felt, somehow, on the verge of hysteria, she found herself looking at him for the first time objectively. She noted the square strength of the broad shoulders outlined by the dark blue sweater, the lithe thinness of the hips, the relaxation of his long arms as they hung down by his side, the easy flexibility of his long fingers. Something in her brain was saying over and over again . . . 'This man is dangerous . . . this man is dangerous.' She felt a little drunk and did not know why.

She looked at his face. He was still smiling. Everything about him, thought Leonore, indicated a sureness, a confidence that was a little overpowering. She wondered why he was here. Why had they been such fools as to employ a man like this, a man who could, very easily, make a great deal of trouble if occasion arose. A man who would make the occasion arise if he wanted it.

Callaghan did not move. He was still looking at her. She thought that she disliked him intensely; that she had never, in the whole of her life, disliked any man so much.

'You're quite wrong,' she said. Her voice was hoarse. It sounded strange to her, as if someone else was speaking. 'Absolutely wrong.'

Callaghan moved another step down the corridor. Then he stopped and took his cigarette case out of his hip pocket. He took out a fresh cigarette, lit it and inhaled with pleasure.

'So I'm absolutely wrong,' he said. 'All right. Well, if that's so it makes things a great deal easier for everybody, doesn't it? I can go ahead with the business of finding Lionel with a clear conscience. Knowing that the family really *want* him found and with no strings attached to the process. Knowing that when he is found they *don't* want any fake alibis, that they don't want any covering-up done for Lionel in case he did kill the Varette, that's right, isn't it?'

He stood waiting for her reply. She did not answer. She was leaning against the door-post, her face very white, very strained.

'And it makes things a great deal easier for you,' Callaghan went on. 'You – *personally*, I mean – don't have to be afraid of anything. You'll be able to take part in our little interview tomorrow morning without a qualm, knowing that you're able to speak the truth, the whole truth and nothing but the truth. . . .'

She ran her tongue over her lips. She wondered why they were so dry.

There was a silence. Then she said:

'What interview?'

'I think I'll have a talk with your mother in the morning,' said Callaghan. 'You'll be there. You'll be there *and you'll talk*. Because there's been a certain amount of collusion so far as I've been concerned between your mother and yourself, I'm going to take damned good care that there aren't any secrets between *you* and her. After all, she's paying me a thousand, and when a client pays me a thousand the client is entitled to a square deal.'

She said: 'What do you mean, I'll talk. . . . What do you mean by that?' Her voice trailed away faintly.

Callaghan grinned at her. He showed all his white teeth in a comprehensive smile, a smile that was so frank, so open, that it would have indicated to her – if she had known Callaghan – that he was gathering his forces for the big guess, the 'inspired guess,' the guess he had been playing for all along.

'You'll explain,' he said easily, 'to your mother why you've been making a fool of me and a fool of her. You'll explain why, when all this business about finding Lionel has been set afoot, you haven't worried to tell either her or me that you've been meeting him here, recently, somewhere near Deeplands.'

He drew a long breath of tobacco smoke and exhaled slowly through his nostrils. He turned away. He said over his shoulder:

'Good-night, Leonore . . . pleasant dreams.'

He went down the corridor. She heard his door shut softly after him.

She stood leaning against the door-post. She began to cry. The process was involuntary. She stood there wondering why the tears were running down her cheeks and why she seemed powerless to stop crying. She told herself that this was unlike her, that she must pull herself together.

She went into her bedroom, forgot to close the door, came back closed it. She threw herself on the bed, clutching at the edges of the frilled pillows with her fingernails.

Somewhere in the house a clock struck four. Callaghan stretched out his hand and extracted another cigarette from the box on the bedside table. He lit it, relaxed on his pillow and lay, gazing at the ceiling.

He was thinking about Leonore Wilbery. When he had finished with her, he thought about Mrs Wilbery and Chief Detective-Inspector Gringall and Santos D'Ianazzi and Milta and Sabine Haragos. When he had thought about all of them he began to think about Lionel Wilbery.

Looking for Lionel Wilbery was going to be much more difficult than looking for a needle in a haystack. If you looked for a needle in a haystack you knew, at least, what you were looking for. You knew also that the needle *was* in the haystack. It was merely a matter of time.

But a person like Lionel could fly off at any angle. Might do anything. Go anywhere. Poets were damned difficult in their most normal moments. When they became abnormal they might easily be impossible, do impossible things. Go to impossible places.

The only thing about this poet was that, apparently, he had, for reasons best known to himself, decided to come back to the district, at any rate, in which his home was situated. Not that this helped. It might mean a lot and it might mean nothing at all.

It might mean nothing at all. . . . Yet at first thought it seemed odd that Lionel – if he had nothing to fear, no one to avoid – should not have gone directly to his home, in which case Callaghan's occupation, like that of Othello, would be gone.

And it might mean a lot. Taken in conjunction with the fact that Leonore *knew* that Lionel was in the neighbourhood, knowing that she had suggested to her mother that a more than ample retainer should he paid to Callaghan to find him, many things might be surmised. One of these things was that Leonore, knowing that Lionel was about, would, at the opportune moment, produce him to Callaghan who, in the process of appearing to 'find' him, might arrange (after all a thousand pounds was a thousand pounds) that his background during the time he had 'disappeared,' and especially during the operative time of the murder of Doria Varette, was positively stiff with *alibis*.

Callaghan, looking at the ceiling with unblinking eyes, brought his mind to bear on Santos D'Ianazzi. The Cuban would have been moved by this time, he thought, to Brixton. He would be sitting on his slim backside regarding his pointed patent shoes and cursing the unjust fate that had managed to get him pulled in as a suspect in a murder case.

And while Gringall could not hold him for long on the murder suspicion, he could, and would, hold him because he had no passport and because the Cuban Legation had said they knew nothing about him.

This point intrigued Callaghan, but not a great deal. Many Cuban nationals were, no doubt, mixed up in all sorts of funny businesses in these days, and when one of them got himself locked up in connection with a murder case, it would be no idea of the representatives of Cuba to press for a release or to concern themselves too greatly over the matter if the background of the individual in question was as shady as that of Santos D'Ianazzi might well be.

In the meantime – even if only as a red-herring – the Cuban would suit as a possible suspect. After all, if you were holding a man on a charge of murder on evidence which was not quite perfect, you were much more inclined to endeavour to perfect the evidence than to look for an entirely new suspect.

Callaghan smiled as he realized his error in not thinking that Doria Varette might be a skilled touch-typist, who used *all* her fingers in the process of typewriting.

And the error had not been so gross. After all, one does not think that a lovely lady, a star singer of night clubs, an almost ravishing beauty, would add to her other accomplishments by being a touch-typist!

An idea struck him. So forcibly that he sat up in bed in order to analyse it.

There was a knock on the door. Callaghan slipped quietly out of bed, turned on the bedside light, put on his dressing-gown, opened the door.

Leonore Wilbery stood outside. She was standing in the middle of the corridor. Her eyes were red, her face white and drawn in spite of the fact that she had attempted a quick renovation.

Callaghan stood in the doorway looking at her. She was wearing eau-de-nil pyjamas cut high in the neck – Russian fashion – caught with a silver cord. Her dressing-gown, made like a man's, was of black satin with an eau-de-nil belt. Callaghan saw that her hands were trembling.

He said: 'It isn't very warm, is it? If you want to talk about something we'd better go somewhere where it's warmer. Alternatively, you'd better come inside.'

She said: 'I want to talk about Lionel. It was perfectly right what you said. I have seen him. I saw him down here, in the neighbourhood, four days ago.'

He grinned at her. He said:

'Now we're getting somewhere. Come in . . . you'll die of cold there.'

He switched on the main bedroom light, closed the door behind her, snapped on the electric fire, pulled a big chair in front of it, indicated that she should sit in it. He took the eiderdown from his bed and wrapped it round her.

She said gravely: 'One never knows with you. One

never knows whether you're being really kind or whether your apparent kindness is merely put on.'

'What does it matter?' asked Callaghan.

He went to the wardrobe, opened it, produced a bottle of Canadian rye. He poured out a stiff dose, added a little water and gave it to her.

'Drink it,' he said. 'You'll feel better. And don't worry. This is not the first move in an attempted seduction.'

She took the glass.

'I'm not worrying about that,' she said. 'I doubt if you're human enough to want to seduce anybody.'

'You'd be surprised,' said Callaghan. 'But for the moment we'll skip the seduction. Let's get down to hard tacks.' He drew up a chair and sat on the other side of the fire. He lit a fresh cigarette, drew the smoke down into his lungs with obvious pleasure.

She looked at him sombrely. Then, in spite of herself, she produced a small smile.

'You're an odd person,' she said. 'You always seem to be enjoying yourself. It's after four o'clock and you are delighted with that cigarette. I believe you're delighted with this awful business . . . with everything. . . .'

Callaghan said: 'Why not? What's the good of being otherwise. I like this cigarette. Another thing, I don't know any other profession which enables a man to have clandestine meetings with an extremely attractive young woman dressed in eau-de-nil pyjamas at four o'clock in the morning.'

She looked into the fire.

'I've got to talk to you,' she said. 'It's come to this that . . .'

Callaghan said: 'If you don't mind I'd rather you didn't talk. I'd rather you answered some questions. You'll find that process much easier than just talking.'

'Very well,' she said. 'I'll do that. May I have a cigarette?'

He gave her one, lit it. He said:

'I'm going to indulge in a little more "inspired guessing." Any time I slip up you can interrupt.'

She nodded. He noticed that her fingers had ceased to tremble. He said:

'To-night, after I'd finished talking to your mother, you and she had a conversation. She told you that I'd suggested that Lionel, having disappeared, having been in love with Doria Varette, having been seen about with her, associated with her, would be, automatically, a first-class suspect for her murder. That is, unless the police could find someone else who looked a better suspect.

'She told you she agreed with the suggestion. She agreed with it because Milta and or Sabine Haragos, who did not like Doria Varette, and had tried to get Lionel to give her up and settle down to serious writing, also believed that it was Doria Varette who started him on drugs. She believed that he might have lost his head and killed her. It's a tough line of thought, but such things happen.

'I imagine that this shocked you a little. It shocked you rather more because you'd seen Lionel recently. Possibly Lionel had said something to you, indicated something which confirmed this line of thought. You decided that it was necessary for you to go off at once and see if you could learn something else – something important in this matter – from Milta and Sabine Haragos or from one of them.

'So you went off. You did that? Right?'

She nodded.

'That is more or less correct,' she said. 'I went to see Sabine.'

'All right,' said Callaghan. 'Now I want you to tell me exactly what happened when you went to see Sabine. Don't miss anything out. No matter how small or unimportant it may seem.'

'I went to see Sabine,' she said. She was still looking at the fire. 'I was rather frightened. I was frightened for Lionel and all of us. I believed that what mother had suggested to me was right. I believed it possible, especially having regard to Lionel's attitude when I saw him. He said . . .'

Callaghan interrupted.

'I don't want to know what he said. I want you to go on telling me what happened *to-night*.'

'The Haragos live at a place called Vale Cottage,' said Leonore. 'It's quite a place – not far from here. Sabine was in bed. She got up and talked to me. She was very kind, very sympathetic. You see, she's very interested in Lionel. She's one of the few decent women he's ever known. I told her about you. I told her what my mother thought. I told her that we were going to pay you a thousand pounds to find Lionel, but that you were too clever to think anything else but that we wanted you to find a way out of this for him, *if* he'd done it. We thought you might be able to find some way of protecting him. We thought you might be able to find evidence to show that if he'd killed her he wasn't really responsible.' She shrugged her shoulders. 'I suppose it all sounds rather idiotic,' she said. 'But that's what I told Sabine.'

Callaghan nodded.

'And what was her attitude?' he asked. 'What did Sabine think?'

'She agreed with everything,' said Leonore. 'She said she thought we'd done the right thing. She thought that you were quite clever and a little unscrupulous. She thought that if any one could find a way out for Lionel you'd be the person to do it. She said we ought to leave it to you. She said she believed that it was more than possible that Lionel had killed Doria Varette. She said that he'd told Milta once that he'd probably kill her.'

Callaghan said: 'Do you think he killed Varette?'

She nodded miserably.

'Yes,' she said very softly 'I'm afraid I do.'

Callaghan asked: 'Did you tell Sabine that you'd seen Lionel four days ago?'

She shook her head.

'I've told nobody that,' she said. 'Only you. I might have told Sabine, but, in the circumstances, I couldn't.'

'In what circumstances?' asked Callaghan.

'Lionel sent me a note here,' she said. 'A typewritten note, so that no one should recognize his handwriting. I received it five days ago. He asked me to meet him at an old summer-house, a place right at the end of the woodland on the west side of the estate. The place is in ruins, but he was fond of it because he used to write poetry there in the old days.

'I met him next day. He looked awful. He asked me for some money. I gave it to him. He told me that he was in a bad jam, that some woman was driving him mad. I asked him who it was. He said I wouldn't know her, but that her name was Varette. He said that he'd got to make up his mind about things pretty quickly, that he hoped somehow to be able to straighten things out.

'I asked him to give me his confidence, to tell me everything. But he wouldn't say anything else. We smoked a cigarette together, and he gave me his last manuscript – a book of poems. He was fearfully pleased with it. He said it was the best thing he'd ever done. He said that I was to keep it and not give it to any one until he'd cleared up this business and could return to more or less normal life.

'I talked to him about the book because he seemed happier when he spoke about that. I asked might I not give it to Sabine to read. She'd helped him with it – she's a clever woman – and she'd practically arranged to get it published. He said I wasn't to give it to any one. That he didn't want it published until he'd settled this business with Doria Varette. He made me promise that I wouldn't show it to any one until he gave me permission. Then he went off. He said he'd get in touch with me as soon as he could, that I was to say nothing about having seen him, that Mummy would believe that he'd gone off on one of his usual jags. Then he went away.'

Callaghan asked: 'Why did this conversation prevent you from telling Sabine you'd seen Lionel?'

'Sabine talked about the book,' said Leonore. 'She said that she'd arranged the publication, and that one of the best ways to make Lionel reappear was for it to be announced. She said that if we could get something in the newspapers saying that the book was going to be published Lionel would turn up. She said, jokingly, that he was a poet first and last, and that when he saw that, he'd just *have* to know more about it. She said he'd have to turn the manuscript over to the publisher, because he had the only copy.'

'I see,' said Callaghan. 'So you couldn't tell her that you'd seen him. Because if you did you'd have to tell her that he'd given you the manuscript, and then she'd probably want to give it to the publishers. And you'd promised Lionel to stick to it until he'd got his disagreement with Varette cleared up.'

'Yes,' she said. 'That is what I thought.'

There was a silence. Then he said:

'You shouldn't drink so much. Either that or you're smoking too much. You've been as nervous as a kitten to-night.'

'I've drunk nothing to-night,' she said. 'Nothing at all. I'm not particularly fond of drinking. I've smoked too much though, and Sabine's cigarettes are so fearfully strong. She smokes all the time. I smoked a lot because I was worried.'

She got up.

'I've told you all I know,' she said. 'I've answered your questions. I hope I've done some good. It's all a terrible, awful mess. . . .'

Callaghan stubbed out his cigarette. He got up and stood looking at her. He was smiling.

'Go to bed and don't worry,' he said. 'Nothing is as bad as it looks. It could always be worse.'

He took her by the arm, piloted her to the door.

'What you need is sleep. And don't worry. Besides which' – he grinned at her mischievously – 'don't forget you've got an unscrupulous detective working for you. . . .'

He leaned up against the door-post.

She was moving away, down the corridor. She stopped suddenly, turned towards him. She said:

'That's the kindest thing you've said to me, up to the moment. I suppose you know that I've rather disliked you.'

Callaghan said: 'Well, I guessed that too. I never mind being disliked by any one who's as beautiful as you are. The only thing that would annoy me would be complete disinterest.'

She frowned. She said:

'I see . . . the more they dislike the harder they fall. Is that it?'

Callaghan said: 'I wouldn't know about that. . . .'

She put out her hand. The gesture was sudden and almost involuntary. She said quickly:

'It's funny but I don't think I dislike you at all. I think I trust you. I've got to trust somebody, haven't I. I've *got* to.'

Callaghan saw the tears well up in her eyes. She turned her head away. She did not move her hand. He said:

'Take it easy. . . .'

Then, quite suddenly, neither of them knowing how, she was in his arms. She said, quickly and softly:

'You've got to help us. You've got to help Lionel. If you don't, God knows what he will do. You've got to help somehow . . . please. . . .'

The grandfather clock downstairs struck five. Its wheezy notes sounded through the house. She drew away from Callaghan, stood leaning against the corridor wall. She looked at him. Her eyes were grave. She looked at him for a long time as if she was trying to see into his mind.

Callaghan produced a cigarette. The flame of his lighter illuminated the angle of his jaw.

She smiled wryly. She said:

'I wonder . . .' She stopped speaking, shrugged her shoulders.

'What are you wondering?' asked Callaghan.

'I suppose it's a foolish thought anyhow,' she said. 'I was wondering whether it is part of the Callaghan technique to spend valuable time – time which might be spent in sleeping – in kissing the daughters of clients in cold corridors at five o'clock in the morning. Or are you trying to discover something? Perhaps that was it. Last time you kissed me it was to find out if I'd really been drinking a lot. . . .'

He grinned at her amiably. She thought, believing as she did so that the wish was father to it, that his inevitable grin was reassuring. He said:

'When I kissed you in the taxi, that, I think, was purely a matter of professional inquiry. But this' – he considered a moment – then: 'I think this effort would come under the heading of professional entertainment.'

'And therefore chargeable against income tax,' she said. 'Mr Callaghan must even make a profit out of his kissing.'

He shook his head.

'You're wrong,' he said. 'I never charge kissing against income tax. The right tax would be entertainment tax. I don't think I mind paying it a bit.'

She looked away. She said:

'I'm going to bed now. I think you've tried to be kind for once. And we must forget about this. . . . It seems rather silly, doesn't it? But I hope you meant it. . . .'

Callaghan turned and flicked his cigarette into the fireplace. He said:

'I always mean it. When I kiss a woman I always mean it like hell. Let me show you. . . .'

He showed her.

8

Meet Mr Maninway

Callaghan came down the wide staircase. He was whistling softly to himself. The tune was still 'It Was Good While It Lasted.' Callaghan, who did not know the words that went with the tune, wondered *what* was good while *what* lasted. He made up his mind to find out – when he had time.

The main doors of the house were open. Across the broad hallway Callaghan could see the April sun shining on the lawn, tinting the rhododendron bushes. The sight was cheerful. He wondered why people lived in cities, then concluded that the people who lived in the country were probably bored with it. He thought it was an easy matter to become bored with anything. He thought he was bored with Lionel. He wondered if it would be possible to become bored with Leonore. The thought intrigued him. He made up his mind to consider the subject further – when he had time.

As he arrived at the bottom of the stairs she came into the hall. She said:

'Isn't it a lovely day? I hope you slept well.'

He said: 'It's a marvellous day. I slept very well. Whoever it was wrote *'Oh to be in England now that April's here'* knew what he was talking about.'

She smiled. She said:

'I didn't know that Mr Callaghan appreciated such minor things as poetry.'

'You'd be surprised if you knew some of the minor things that Mr Callaghan appreciates,' he said.

They stood at the top of the entrance steps, looking at the sunshine. After a moment she said:

'Have you got any plan of campaign? Do you know what you're going to do?'

'I haven't any plan of campaign and I don't know what I'm going to do,' Callaghan answered. 'I never have plans of campaign anyway. They never work. Something always happens to upset them. I just follow my nose.'

She nodded.

'Even so you have to point your noise in some direction before you can follow it. It doesn't work by itself . . . does it?'

'Correct,' said Callaghan. 'At the moment I'm pointing it in the direction of the Grasscutter Inn.'

'Lionel liked the Grasscutter,' she said vaguely. 'There was a bairmaid there . . .'

'I know,' said Callaghan. 'She used to listen to Lionel reading his poetry – in the days when he used to read poetry to barmaids.' He lit a cigarette. 'Are you going to stay here for a bit?' he asked.

'I shall be here at Deeplands so long as you want me to be here,' she said. 'I thought I might be of use. If not I can go back to London.'

'Why not stay here?' asked Callaghan.

'Very well,' she said. 'I take it that it's agreed that we trust each other?'

He grinned.

'We might try,' he said. 'If you can find it possible to trust an unscrupulous detective.'

Leonore said: '*I* didn't say you were unscrupulous. Sabine said that.'

'Sabine was dead right,' said Callaghan. 'I am unscrupulous. Why not? You can't mess about with the underneath side of life and wear white kid gloves, you know. Sometimes a lack of scruples makes up for a great deficiency of intellect. Look at Hitler . . .'

She laughed. She said:

'I don't think you're deficient intellectually. I think you're much *too* intelligent . . . you know too much . . .'

'Granted,' said Callaghan. 'That, plus my lack of

scruples, is responsible for my amazing success. I'll tell you about it some time.'

He went off in the direction of the garage. She stood on the top of the steps looking after him, asking herself questions to which there appeared to be no answers.

Nikolls was playing patience in his sitting-room at the Grasscutter. His breakfast tray was pushed to one side. He presented a picture of urgent concentration.

He said: 'This goddam game is terrible. I can't get it out even when I cheat.'

Callaghan sat down in the chintz-covered arm-chair. He said:

'How's the barmaid, Windy? Have you got to a really confidential stage, yet?'

Nikolls grinned.

'Yeah,' he said. 'Last night she told me she reckoned we was made for each other. She's gonna be sorta sore when I take a run-out powder on this dump. I never met with a dame who talked more an' said less than this baby.'

Callaghan nodded. He lit a cigarette.

'So she's gone dry on you,' he said.

'She's said her piece,' said Nikolls. 'She don't know any more. She's the sorta dame who falls for every guy who makes a pass at her. She oughta be called Dandruff. She's always fallin' on some guy's collar.'

He began to stack the cards.

'I was talkin' to her last night about the Haragos pair,' he said. 'They're sorta popular around here. They pay their bills regularly an' don't argue when the tradesmen stick it on a bit. There was a sorta rumour flyin' about one time – about three–four months ago – that Sabine was keen on Lionel. They usta get around together an' look at each other like a pair of love-sick cows. That's all I know – that, an' that Effie's been through on the telephone here. She called through about ten minutes ago. She'd been through to Deeplands an' the butler told her you was out. I said maybe you was on your way down here. She'll be ringin' in five or six minutes.'

Callaghan smoked silently. He was thinking about Leonore. When the telephone bell rang he went over and talked to Effie.

'Mr Maninway came through this morning, Mr Callaghan,' she said. 'When I rang him and told him that you wanted to know something about the Haragos people he said that wouldn't be a very difficult matter. He said that Milta and Sabine Haragos were fairly well known to friends of his. He said he could give me a certain amount of information right away. I suggested that you wouldn't want that. I suggested that he checked carefully on any information he already had and endeavoured to add to it. Mr Maninway asked if I'd any idea as to what you expected to pay him. I said that so far as I knew you didn't expect to pay him anything until you'd assessed the value of his information, but that if he were to work fast I thought you wouldn't be ungenerous. I fancy Mr Maninway is a little hard up.'

'He's always hard up,' said Callaghan. 'When he came through this morning what did he say?'

'Quite a lot,' said Effie. 'First of all he said that the Haragos couple were people of quite good reputation, that they were gamblers and interested in all forms of gambling, but they were most careful about paying their debts; they always paid on time. They have a flat in St John's Wood – in Rufus Court – where the rent is £300 a year. Their reputation with the local tradesmen is good. They have a place in the country – not very far from Taunton – called The Vale. Apparently they bought this place about a year ago.'

'Did Maninway know who they are, where they come from?' asked Callaghan.

'They're White Russians,' said Effie. 'They escaped from Russia in 1923. They managed to bring quite a lot of money with them. They've lived in France and England ever since. Sabine isn't as keen on gambling as Milta. Sabine, Mr Mininway says, is rather an artistic person and interested in books and art generally. She's a sort of partner and reader for a small publishing firm that Milta put some money into, a firm in Curzon Street called the Zayol Press. Milta is inclined to make fun of Sabine's artistic pretensions. Mr Maninway thinks that Milta Haragos is rather stupid – except where gambling is concerned. He is rather an expert at that.'

'How do they spend their time?' asked Callaghan. 'Did Maninway say anything about that?'

'Yes, I've a note about that,' said Effie promptly. 'Sabine goes a lot to parties. She spends lots of time in picture galleries. She does a lot of reading and occasionally helps in the construction of other people's books – books that the Zayol Press propose publishing. Apparently she's very good at that.

'Milta Haragos doesn't do anything very much. He never gets up until midday, Mr Maninway says. He used to go to a club very often – a gambling club – called the Salem Club. This place is near Fitzroy Square, and Mr Maninway says that it originally belonged to and was run by a person called Santos D'Ianazzi. D'Ianazzi had apparently mortgaged the place, and when the time came wasn't able to pay off the mortgage. Milta Haragos paid the mortgage off and took the club over, keeping D'Ianazzi on as manager. Mr Maninway says that D'Ianazzi had made quite a lot of money for Milta Haragos by running games and acting as *croupier* in several places in London and outside. Milta does the financing and D'Ianazzi looks after the games. Mr Maninway said that I was to be careful to let you know that all these games were run perfectly straight and that the people who played at them were of good social standing. Mr Maninway said that he used to play himself and knows that everything was above board.'

'Anything else?' asked Callaghan.

'That's all,' said Effie, 'except that Mr Maninway asked if that was worth fifty pounds to you.'

'Tell him it isn't,' said Callaghan. 'It's worth twenty. He's being overpaid at that. I'll sign a cheque for him when I come up.'

'Very well,' said Effie. 'There's a cheque arrived from Mrs Wilbery. It's for a thousand pounds. Shall I pay it in?'

'Yes,' said Callaghan. 'Pay it in right away. I'll look in and see you some time.'

He hung up, went back to his arm-chair.

Nikolls fumbled in his pocket for a cigarette. He lit it and sat on the end of the sofa, looking at Callaghan.

He said: 'When do we start lookin' for Lionel. Or don't we know where to look?'

'We don't know where to look,' said Callaghan. 'Except we do know that Lionel was down here recently. Leonore Wilbery saw him. He was scared of Varette. He handed over the manuscript of his last book of poetry and made Leonore promise she'd hang on to it until he'd got the Varette business straightened out – whatever it was. Leonore seemed to have the idea that Varette was riding Lionel – riding him hard.'

Nikolls said: 'I gotta theory. Maybe it'll be useful to you to pick holes in.'

Callaghan grinned. He asked:

'Is it one of your intuitive theories? Your intuitive theories are usually lousy.'

'No,' said Nikolls. 'This ain't intuitive. This one's based on facts. Here's the way I look at it. First of all we got information that Sabine Haragos usta be stuck on Lionel. O.K. Well, when a dame's stuck on a guy she always wants to push the mug up in the front rank, don't she? She wants him to amount to somethin'. O.K. Well, this Sabine dame is stuck on art an' poetry an' all that sorta bunk, so she gets Lionel to start in writin' this book. She reckons that she's gonna get the Zayol Press to publish it. She reckons she's gonna share in Lionel's glory. Maybe she even helps Lionel write the book. How'm I doin'?'

'You're doing very well,' said Callaghan. 'Go ahead.'

'All right,' continued Nikolls. 'Well, you gotta take into consideration that this guy Lionel is a punk. We know he's a punk. Varette thought he was a punk. She said he was always gettin' cockeyed an' playin' around with the wrong

149

guys. I reckon that just when Lionel had finished writin' this book, after he'd made all the use of Sabine that he wanted to he meets up with Varette. I reckon he woulda fell for Varette, although by what I can hear about that baby it's goddam strange that she shoulda fell for him. But she does, an' so she gets him away from Sabine.

'O.K. Well, maybe the Varette baby does a little dopin' on the side. Maybe she is fond of coke or somethin'. So she gets a big idea. Lionel has told her about Sabine an' she reckons she ain't gonna let her grab Lionel offa her again, so she starts Lionel doin' a little coke sniffin' too, just to keep him hangin' around.

'I reckon then that Lionel gets goddam sick of the lot of 'em. He's always been a guy who couldn't stick at any-thing or anybody very long. So he takes a run-out on Varette an' Varette gets tough somehow. Maybe she's got some sorta hold over him. Maybe she knows too much about him.

'Lionel makes up his mind that he has had enough of this baby, so he thinks he'll take a run-out on her. But before he does this he comes down here an' hangs around an' fixes up a meetin' with Leonore. He does this because he wants to hand over the poetry manuscript to Leonore. He knows it'll be safe with her, an' he tells her not to let anybody have it because he knows that if she tells Sabine about havin' it Sabine will wanta get busy an' publish it. He reckons this will cause more trouble with Varette so he wants it kept quiet. I reckon Lionel was tired of both these janes. He just wanted to get away from both of 'em, an' have a little peace and quiet. Maybe he has got himself some other dame?

'O.K. Anyhow he hands the poetry over to Leonore an' tells her that Varette is gettin' tough. Then he scrams. I reckon he goes back to town an' Varette finds out – or maybe she runs inta him. I reckon she saw him the day after she met you an' asked you to find him. I reckon she told him so too. I reckon she told him that she'd already got detectives lookin' for him an' I don't think he liked that. I think he got sorta desperate an' lost his temper. So he bumped Varette an' scrammed. That's my theory.'

Callaghan said: 'It's not bad. It could be a lot worse. But people who commit unpremeditated murder don't usually use stilettos.'

Nikolls grinned happily. He opened his large mouth and exhaled a cloud of tobacco smoke with obvious relish.

'Don't they?' he said. 'Well let me tell you somethin'. I told you that this Lionel guy usta read poetry to the frail in the saloon bar downstairs, didn't I? In the old days, I mean. Well, last night this jane tells me about some of the stuff he usta read to her. She remembered one thing. It was about killin' people. The poem said that the dagger was the romantic thing an' that if you was gonna kill anybody the stilleto was the way to do it. The goddam poem was called "Stiletto." An' what d'ya know about that? I reckons my theory is the berries.'

Callaghan said: 'It doesn't answer any of the questions. The questions that need answering. You're remembering all the things that don't matter, forgetting the things that do.'

'Such as what?' demanded Nikolls.

'You're forgetting the beginning of this business,' said Callaghan. 'You're forgetting that it was Gringall who originally threw Varette at us. Why? You're forgetting that Lionel was a weakling, that he'd neither the guts nor the mentality to stand up to women like the Varette or Sabine. That's the reason why he might have killed Varette. Because he hated her, because she made him feel small. People like Lionel are little people. They love in a small way and hate in a little way. Most murderers are mean.

'Then there's Varette. Varette was a beautiful woman. She had personality. She knew how to dress. I wonder what she saw in Lionel? I wonder why she took so much trouble over Lionel? If a man were in love with a woman like Varette and decided to take a walk out on her, I should think she'd let him go. There'd be a lot more men in her life. Why should she worry about a cheap drunk like Lionel? Why?'

'Search me,' said Nikolls. 'I wouldn't know. I wouldn't know because I don't really know anything about Lionel. Maybe if we was to meet up with this bozo he'd look a goddam sight different to what we think he's like.'

Callaghan said: 'You've got something there. Most of the descriptions of Lionel up to date have come from women. And most of these women seem to have been too close to Lionel to be impersonal about him.'

'Sure,' agreed Nikolls. 'That's what *I* think. You remember that book I was readin'. The book about intuitive deduction. O.K. Well, didn't I prove to you that practically every goddam thing a woman says is a helluva lie. . . .'

'That's too sweeping,' said Callaghan. 'A woman has got to tell the truth sometime.'

'Don't you believe it,' said Nikolls. 'I have met up with dames who wouldn't know the truth if they saw it on a plate. A woman is a strange sort of cuss. She just don't play anything the way a guy does. She don't ever take a logical point of view. She spends most of her time sorta kiddin' herself along. I remember a dame I met up with in Layola, Michigan, one time. This dame was so good-lookin' that every time she usta go out they usta turn out the riot squad. She sorta fell for me in a very big way, an' she asked me to give her a fur coat. So I slip this baby five hundred bucks an' tell her to buy herself somethin' good. She takes the jack an' she scrams. When she comes back she has got herself a summer ermine coat that looked like a million dollars. When I ask her how much it cost she says it cost just what I gave her – five hundred bucks. The funny thing is that the dame thought she was tellin' the truth.'

'And didn't it cost that?' asked Callaghan.

'Yeah,' said Nikolls. 'It cost that all right. Five hundred bucks – *a month*. That was a lesson to me, that was. An' I was gonna marry that dame . . . but she wasn't my type. . . .'

'So you didn't marry her?' said Callaghan.

'Yeah, I did . . .' said Nikolls. 'That was how I knew she wasn't my type.'

He picked up the pack of cards, began to shuffle them expertly.

'It would be goddam funny if they hung that Cuban for killin' Varette,' he said. 'That would give me a big laugh. I don't like that guy. I never did like guys who wear pointed shoes.' He began to lay out the cards for patience.

Callaghan got up. He said:

'I'm a little tired of this case. It hasn't any beginning. There isn't any place to start. There's just a lot of people talking about each other all the time. . . .'

'Yeah,' said Nikolls. 'That's how I see it. When they ain't talkin' about each other they're killin' each other. The only thing is it's good for business.'

Callaghan picked up his hat. He said quietly:

'I'm going to London, Windy. You might telephone through to Deeplands and tell Leonore that I shan't be back today. Maybe I'll be back tomorrow. I don't know.'

'O.K.,' said Nikolls.

Callaghan went out. After a minute Nikolls heard the Jaguar start outside.

He got up and stretched. He went over to the telephone, asked the operator for the Deeplands number. He got it, asked for Miss Wilbery.

When she came on the line he said:

'I'm talkin' for Mr Callaghan. He asked me to tell you that he won't be back today. Maybe he'll be back tomorrow. Maybe not.'

She said: 'Isn't that the chauffeur who drove me home from The Dene a few nights ago . . . the one who told me the story about the woman in Iceland?'

Nikolls grinned.

'That's right,' he said. 'It's Nikolls. How did you know?'

Leonore said: 'I remembered the voice. Would it be rude to ask exactly what you're doing down here?'

'No,' said Nikolls, 'it wouldn't. I'm playin' patience an'

cheatin' like hell. I get that way every time I play the goddam game.'

'So you work for Mr Callaghan?' asked Leonore.

'Yeah,' said Nikolls. 'I'm the power behind the scenes. I'm practically the life and soul of Callaghan Investigations.'

She laughed softly.

'I'm sure you are,' she said. 'Tell me, Mr Nikolls, do you think that Mr Callaghan really believes he can find Lionel? Has he discovered anything? Or shouldn't I be asking?'

Nikolls said: 'If I know anything of Slim he's gonna start something. He's gettin' sorta restless. When he gets that way he's liable to do something' definite. My own idea is that he's goin' to start somethin' good an' quick . . somethin' a little tough maybe.'

She said: 'Please tell me where he's gone?'

Nikolls said: 'I wouldn't know. Say, Miss Wilbery, did you every hear the story about the fish that got caught?'

She said she had not.

Nikolls grinned.

'It woulda been O.K. if it had kept its mouth shut,' he said cheerfully. 'Well, so long . . . I'll be seein' you.'

He hung up quickly.

It was half-past five when the house telephone on Effie Thompson's desk rang. She raised her eyebrows, took off the receiver. She said:

'I didn't know you were back, Mr Callaghan. There isn't anything special to report.'

Callaghan asked: 'Who's in the office?'

'Blake's here,' said Effie. 'D'you want him?'

'Telephone down to "Service" and ask them to send me some strong tea,' said Callaghan. 'Tell Blake to get through to Maninway. If Maninway's there I want him to come round here and see me – as soon as he can get there. Let me know what he says.'

She heard the staccato click as Callaghan banged down

the receiver. She smiled a little. She called through the open door to Blake, who was sitting at Callaghan's desk smoking a cigarette.

'Mr Callaghan's upstairs. He's back. You're to get through to Mr Maninway – Mayfair 55674. If Mr Maninway's there you're to tell him that Mr Callaghan wants him to come round here at once. Tell him it's urgent.'

'I got it,' said Blake.

She heard him dialling. She called through on the house telephone to 'Service.' She ordered the tea.

'It must be very strong,' she said. 'And I'd advise you to be quick about it. Mr Callaghan's in a bad temper.'

Callaghan was in his sitting-room, slumped in a leather armchair in front of the fire, when Maninway arrived. A half-empty bottle of Canadian rye and a glass stood on the floor. The fireplace was littered with cigarette ends.

Maininway stood in the doorway smiling. Effie Thompson closed the door gently and disappeared. Callaghan got up, stood in front of the fireplace, looking at Maninway.

Eustace Maninway was very slim, very graceful, very tired-looking. He wore a suit that was just old enough, that bore the hallmarks of Savile Row. His shirt was silk and of a very quiet pattern. Callaghan thought it probably came from Sulka. His silk collar was caught, under a soft crêpe-de-chine tie, with a thin platinum pin. Everything about Maninway reflected a certain *ton*, a certain background.

His eyes were rather large and dark and very pathetic. Quite a lot of old ladies had looked into those eyes and sympathised – before reaching for their cheque books. His hands were very white and the fingers were slim. His cheek-bones stood out from a face that was pale except just under the cheek-bones where there was a slight flush.

Eustace Maninway's mouth was what is usually described as mobile. That means it could smile and look pleasant or frown and look sulky. It could also straighten itself out and look angry, or strong, or merely unpleasant. Mr Maninway could make it do all those things very easily.

Callaghan said: 'Sit down, and have a cigarette.' He indicated the silver box on the table.

Maninway said in a very soft voice: 'Thanks . . . but I'll smoke my own if you don't mind.'

He sat down in the chair opposite Callaghan's. He sat down very slowly, very gracefully, drawing up his immaculate trousers so that his thin knees should not spoil the creases. He produced a thin, white gold case, extracted a Cyprian cigarette, lit it with a gold and platinum lighter. He looked at Callaghan with an expression of tired inquiry.

Callaghan's hand went to his hip pocket. He produced a wallet. He took out two ten pound notes. He said:

'I don't think the information I got was worth twenty pounds.'

Maninway smiled. He said: 'I'm sorry.' He knocked the ash from his cigarette into an ash-tray with a delicate gesture.

Callaghan rustled the two bank-notes between his fingers. After a moment he said:

'You said you wanted fifty pounds. I'd like to pay you fifty pounds. And you'd like fifty pounds, wouldn't you?'

Maninway said yes. He said he would like fifty pounds very much. He indicated that things weren't very good in these days. Callaghan thought dryly that too many of the old ladies were paying heavy income tax for Maninway's liking.

He said: 'All right. I'll pay you fifty if I get what I want from you. It's obvious to me that you've met Milta and Sabine Haragos; that you've met Santos D'Ianazzi – the fellow that Milta Haragos financed over the Salem Club business; that you know most of the people who get around to such gaming parties as are going these days. It's a certainty that you must have met or heard of Lionel Wilbery. It's possible that you've met or heard of a woman called Doria Varette. I want to know everything you can tell me about Wilbery and about Doria Varette. I also want to know what you know about the Salem Club. I want to know who's running it.'

Maninway said: 'I'd like to help if possible. I suppose you couldn't let me know what's behind all this? I mean to say if you could it might help me to try and tell you what you want.'

Callaghan said: 'Lionel Wilbery's people think he's disappeared. They've asked me to find him. That's all there is to it.'

'I see,' said Maninway. He looked at his fingernails. 'I've met Lionel Wilbery,' he said. 'I used to think he wasn't too bad. He was always rather stupid, of course, rather slow in the uptake. I thought he was a person who rather went in for poses. I expect you know what I mean. At one time he was amazingly keen on the ballet, then it was something else, then it was gambling. He was rather a stupid gambler. He lost quite a bit, but I think he used to get money from his mother when he needed it.'

Callaghan nodded.

'Would you like a drink?'

'No, thank you,' said Maninway. 'It's amazingly kind of you, but I've a little trouble with my chest. I don't drink very much. . . .

'It was rather amusing,' Maninway went on, 'when Lionel took to poetry. He'd always dabbled in it of course, but after he'd met Sabine Haragos he became one hundred per cent poet. Before he'd used to dress well – if not elegantly – and be seen at the right places and all that sort of thing, but after he took to writing poetry he changed extraordinarily. He wore very old clothes and didn't go in for shaving very much. In fact he took to looking rather a wreck.'

Callaghan asked: 'Did you meet Doria Varette?'

Maninway nodded.

'Oh, yes,' he said. 'I met her. She and Lionel used to gamble around town. I've met them at several places.

Mostly at the Salem Club. I don't think Miss Varette was much of a gambler. I think that she used to do it to humour Lionel. Latterly he seemed rather impossible. First of all he drank a great deal too much and then he gave that up and I'm afraid he began to dabble a little in drugs. I've heard Doria Varette and Lionel having arguments in corners about that. It seemed the cause of a certain amount of trouble between them. I had an idea she had some sort of pull where Lionel was concerned.'

Callaghan asked: 'What about Milta? Where did Milta come in?'

Maninway shrugged his shoulders.

'Milta Haragos is just a bore,' he said. 'A lady-killer. He's the usual sort of boorish White Russian who had a certain appeal for a certain sort of woman. He's got some money. He gambles. He's a good gambler. I've heard it said that he's helped people out of bad spots once or twice, lent or given them money, when they've been broke. I must say that *I've* never found him particularly generous. When D'Ianazzi went broke at the Salem Club Haragos put up the money to save him. But that wasn't generosity. That was business. And very good business too. The place used to be a little gold mine. There was about two or three thousand changed hands there every night and the *cagnotte* took ten per cent of the stakes. You can work it out for yourself that even if expenses *were* high there was a certain amount of good money in it.'

'Does D'Ianazzi run the Salem Club now?' asked Callaghan.

'Not personally,' said Maninway. 'I believe he supervises the place for Milta Haragos, but there's another fellow – he seems quite a decent sort of chap – a foreigner of some sort who came here from America – named Salkey. At least that's what he's called. He actually runs the place.'

'And they still play there?' asked Callaghan.

'More than ever,' said Maninway with a smile. 'People have got to do something – even if there is a war on.'

Callaghan said: 'You say this Salkey is a decent sort of chap. That means that he's been decent to you. I imagine you've taken people there to play and that Salkey's paid you for your trouble.'

'Something like that,' said Maninway. 'One doesn't like doing that sort of thing of course, but one has to live.'

He produced the thin gold cigarette case, took a fresh cigarette.

Callaghan sat down in his arm-chair. He put out a long arm and raked in the rye bottle. He poured out a good four fingers and drank it neat. He looked sideways at Maninway. He asked:

'What times do they play at the Salem Club?'

'It depends,' said Maninway. 'It depends on who wants to go there and whether there's an air raid on. If there's an alert quite a lot of people go there – especially women. They'd rather do that than sit in a shelter. Gamblers are sensitive people' – he smiled a little deprecatingly – 'they'd rather gamble and take their mind off things. If there's no alert people trickle in there about eleven or twelve o'clock. There's quite a small crowd there by say, one o'clock, and play goes on until about three. They finish, usually, round about four o'clock.'

'I see,' said Callaghan. 'Thanks, Maninway. It's been very interesting.'

Maninway got up. He picked up his hat. He stood, holding his hat by the brim, looking at Callaghan. He was smiling a little. He said:

'I suppose I can touch for that twenty now – or is it to be fifty?'

Callaghan said: 'Fifty, I think. Yes . . . it's going to be worth fifty.'

Maninway sighed.

Callaghan went on: 'But you'll have to earn it, I'm afraid.' He looked at Maninway and smiled.

Maninway said: 'Earn it? I don't understand.'

Callaghan helped himself to another shot of rye. He said evenly:

'Tonight – or rather tomorrow morning – I want you to drop into the Salem Club. Quite casually, you know. Perhaps you'd better ring up first and say you're coming. You might tell Salkey that you're coming and that you want to talk to him. Something that you aren't keen on discussing on the telephone.'

Maninway said: 'I'm fearfully sorry. But I'm engaged tonight.'

Callaghan went on as if he had not heard.

'You'd better arrive there about three o'clock,' he said. 'You'll probably find me there. I shall be playing, I expect. But you won't take any notice of me. You'll make an opportunity to take Salkey on one side. You'll tell him that Santos D'Ianazzi's been pulled in for killing Doria Varette. You'll tell him that the police are very interested in D'Ianazzi, that he hasn't a passport, and that the Cuban Legation don't like him very much and don't seem very concerned about him. They go so far as to say they don't know him.

'Remember all that. That's what you've got to tell Salkey. Have you got that?'

'Yes,' said Maninway. 'But as I was . . .'

Callaghan said: 'By this time I imagine that Salkey will be interested. You will then point out to him that there's somebody playing at the Salem – myself – who has been put in to do a little snooping. You can go so far as to suggest that I'm working on the D'Ianazzi case for one of the Intelligence Sections. That sounds much more frightening these days than Scotland Yard. You can tell Salkey that so far as character is concerned I'm pure poison, that I'm out to get a pinch and that I'm going to frame somebody as an accomplice to D'Ianazzi, and that the idea is that I frame *him*. You can then go home and sleep in peace, and if you like to call in at the office downstairs tomorrow morning Miss Thompson will give you fifty pounds.'

Maninway said easily: 'I'm fearfully sorry, but I don't think I can do what you ask. It isn't really my line of country, you know. I don't do that sort of thing. Really.'

'I know,' said Callaghan. 'I know you don't do that sort of thing. The sort of thing you do is to play tame cat to some discontented woman, and when her husband gets a little bit suspicious you put the screws on her and collect a little money; or you take young women to dubious places of entertainment after they've had a drink or two and then put the screw on *them*. But you're going to do this job, and if you want a good reason I'll give it to you.'

Maninway said: 'I'm always interested in what you say.'

Callaghan said amiably: 'Eighteen months ago Mrs Harveleur asked us to try and find the young man or men who'd lifted her diamond bracelet. She'd been rolled for it. It was the old "Mayfair" technique. A couple of charming young men took her out to supper one night, and afterwards on to some card place. They finished off at one of the young men's flats somewhere in the Clarges Street area. Somebody put some knockout drops in her drink and she passed out. When she woke up next morning her bracelet was gone.

'We found out who'd fixed the business. She instructed us to drop it when we reported that her own nephew, young Vale-Lettersley, was behind the job. The other two lads were both friends of yours, Maninway.'

Maninway said: 'Possibly. But I'm not responsible for my friends.' His smile was still quite charming.

'Granted,' said Callaghan. 'But we know who sold the bracelet. We know who fixed to have the stones cut and re-set. Blooey Stevens did the re-cutting, and you got rid of the bracelet. There isn't any need to argue about it. I don't like arguments. You're either going to do as you're told or you can have what's coming to you. Mrs Harveleur died two months ago, and I think her executors would be interested in the story if we liked to resuscitate it. That bracelet was worth an easy fifteen thousand. But you do just as you like, Maninway.'

Callaghan put his feet up on the mantelpiece. He groped for the rye bottle, found it, poured out another stiff shot. He drank it with obvious pleasure.

Maninway said: 'All right. I think I'll be able to do what you want.'

'Excellent,' said Callaghan. 'You know your piece?'

'I've a good memory,' said Maninway. 'I remember what you said.'

'Good,' said Callaghan. 'And don't make a mistake, will you? I'd hate you to do that.'

'No,' said Maninway. 'I won't make a mistake. I'll call in the morning for the money. Well . . . *au revoir*. . . .'

He went out quietly.

The Chinese clock on the mantelpiece struck seven. Callaghan got out of the arm-chair, went to the telephone. He dialled a Holborn number. When the connection was made he said:

'Is that you, Bale? This is Mr Callaghan. Just get around to the Priory Club and find someone who plays at the Salem Club, near Fitzroy Square. Somebody who's hard up and wants to earn a fiver. It's quite simple. All they have to do is to take me there, introduce me and get out. I don't mind if I lose a tenner or so. You get that?

'Tell whoever it is to meet me at the Zouave Club in Dover Street at twelve o'clock. Tell 'em what I look like. I'll be wearing a dark overcoat and a black hat. . . . All right.'

He hung up and began to undress. He walked about the sitting-room and bedroom, shedding clothes. He was intrigued with a new line of thought.

When he was undressed he walked into the sitting-room, rang down to Service, told them to call him at eleven o'clock. He got into bed, smoked one cigarette, went to sleep.

9

They Get Tough Sometimes

The house telephone began to jangle. Callaghan woke up, yawned, looked at the ceiling. He was annoyed at being awakened. He had been dreaming, a process which seldom occurred to him and was therefore appreciated when the dream was as good as the one he had experienced.

He thought that the business of getting out of bed, of dressing, of going out, talking to people, trying to find out things, was boring.

The house telephone continued to ring. The noise began to get on Callaghan's nerves. He put his arms behind his head and thought about Leonore. He began to smile. He wondered if he would be at all interested in the whereabouts of Lionel Wilbery if it were not for Leonore. He thought he would not. Then he remembered Mrs Wilbery's thousand-pound cheque.

He thought he would.

He leaned out of bed, collected the water carafe from the bed table, threw it at the house telephone. The instrument ricocheted off its table, fell to the floor. But the receiver was still in place. It continued to ring. Callaghan accepted the omen. He got up.

He went into the bathroom, took a warm shower, dressed. He went into the sitting-room, sat in front of the fire, with a bottle of Canadian rye in one hand and a glass in the other. After three stiff doses of the rye he began to feel almost human. He put the bottle and the glass on the floor, his feet on the mantelpiece. He thought about Maninway and his conversation.

People were funny when they tried to tell you things,

thought Callaghan. With the best will in the world they always left out the most important thing, the thing you were trying to get at. Then quite casually, two or three weeks later, when they were not even thinking about it, they would tell you accidentally. He yawned. Life was like that. Nobody ever said what they wanted to say, did what they wanted to do. There were not sufficient *nuances* either in life or language.

At ten minutes to twelve he got up. He put on a dark overcoat, a black soft hat. He went out, began to walk round to the Zouave in Dover Street. On the other side of Berkeley Square he stopped to light a cigarette. When the cigarette was lit he stood for a moment motionless, thinking.

He turned and walked in the direction of Hay Hill. He went into the telephone box at the bottom, rang through to Effie Thompson. He stood in the box yawning. He could hear the ringing noise at the other end. Then, after what seemed a long time, a sleepy voice said hallo.

Callaghan said: 'Is that you, Effie? I'm fearfully sorry to wake you up.'

She said: 'You always are, aren't you? But you always do. What can I do for you?'

Callaghan said: 'There's a place called the Salem Club near Fitzroy Square. I expect you'll find the number in the telephone book. Give me a ring there at half-past four, will you?'

'Very well,' said Effie.

Callaghan went on: 'If by any chance I don't answer the telephone, give me a ring directly you get into the office tomorrow morning.'

'I see,' said Effie.

'If I'm not in the flat,' said Callaghan, 'telephone Nikolls at the Grasscutter. Tell him where I went. He'll know what to do. Have you got that?'

'I've got it,' said Effie.

'When I've rung off,' said Callaghan, 'get through to Grant. You remember Grant?'

Effie said she remembered.

'Tell Grant it's urgent. Tell him he's to get out at once and go and case a place for me. It's the Zayol Press in Curzon Street. He'll find the number in the telephone book. Tell him to go round there and look the place over. When he's done it he's to write a note and leave it with Wilkie, the night porter, at Berkeley Square. He's got to do it at once, and he's got to leave the note so that I get it before five o'clock tomorrow morning. Have you got that?'

Effie said she had got it.

Callaghan said: 'Goodnight, Effie.' He hung up.

He walked round to the Zouave Club in Dover Street.

There was a man leaning against the upstairs bar. He was short, plump and jovial. Callaghan looked at him casually, then ordered a double Bacardi rum. He leaned against the bar, drinking the rum. He thought rum on top of whisky tasted foul.

The man came a little closer. He said:

'Would you be Mr Callaghan?'

'Yes,' said Callaghan. 'Who are you?'

'My name's Welkins,' said the man. 'I'm a friend of Jimmie Bale's. Jimmie said you wanted somebody to take you round to Salkey's place – the Salem Club. He said there'd be a fiver in it. Is that right?'

'That's right,' said Callaghan.

The man went on: 'You're not workin' for the police or anything, are you? I wouldn't like to put Salkey in bad.'

Callaghan said: 'No, I'm not working for the police.'

Welkins said: 'You paying me a fiver is a sort of 'and of justice.'

Callaghan ordered another double Bacardi. He said: 'Is it? Why?'

'You're a private dick, ain't you?' said Welkins. 'Callaghan Investigations, just off Berkeley Square? If I remember rightly you 'ad a case about three years ago. It was through you they pinched a fellow called Philip. Do you remember?'

'I remember,' said Callaghan.

"E was my brother-in-law,' said Welkins, not without a certain pride. "E was a fair bastard, 'e was. The day before they pulled 'im in 'e touched me for a fiver – that's why I said this is the 'and of justice, gettin' that fiver back through you, I mean.'

'It just shows you, doesn't it?' said Callaghan. He finished the rum. 'Come on,' he said. 'Let's go round to Salkey's.'

An air-raid had sounded twenty minutes before. Callaghan remembered what Maninway had said. People – especially women – had trickled in in a continuous stream ever since the first notes of the siren had begun. The women were usually middle-aged, quite well-dressed, looking as if they had got out of bed in a hurry. Callaghan wondered vaguely why middle-aged women should prefer to play cards during an air-raid alert. He wondered why young women did not want to do it. Then he thought that perhaps they had something better to do.

The room was well-furnished, rather spacious. Callaghan thought it was an incongruous place to be in the neighbourhood of Fitzroy Square. There were four tables going – a roulette table, a poker game, a bridge game for high stakes, and on the long green table in the far corner of the room half a dozen men and three women were shooting craps.

Salkey was acting as *croupier* at the roulette table. Salkey looked rather nice, Callaghan thought. He was middle-aged, slim, well dressed in a dinner suit that had been made by a good tailor. His complexion was clear, his eyes bright. An almost permanent smile was set about his rather full lips.

There was quite a crowd round the roulette table. Just in front of Callaghan a woman with slender hips and a not so slender bosom was staking five-pound plaques on a number. She lost sixteen times in succession. Her face was very pale, her eyes too bright. Callaghan wondered whether she had acquired the too ample bosom through suppressed excitement. He considered the problem seriously for some minutes.

The roulette table was doing very well for the bank – zero turned up twice in seven minutes. Callaghan yawned. The next time the wheel spun he put a five-pound note on red. Red came up. Callaghan left his stakes on his winnings. Red came up three times. Callaghan put the forty pounds in his pocket and lit a cigarette. He thought it was funny how you could always win money when you were bored with the game – that you never could when you wanted to win. He walked away from the table, stood in front of the fireplace. The clock on the mantelpiece said it was a quarter to three.

Maninway came in. He came in with a very well turned out, very good-looking woman of about forty. He looked casually round the room, but his eyes swept past Callaghan. There was no recognition in them. He went over to the roulette table.

Callaghan walked across and began to watch the poker game. Ten minutes later, out of the corner of his eye, he saw Salkey hand his *croupier's* rake over to a young man in a grey lounge suit. Then he went out of the room. Maninway went with him. The woman who had come in with Maninway remained behind, went on playing.

A quarter of an hour afterwards Salkey came back and took the roulette game over. Maninway did not appear again.

The four men playing poker finished off the round of jack-pots, began to count their chips. Callaghan, leaning against the wall, smoking, casually interested in the closing of the poker game, was watching Salkey out of the corner of his eye.

The room began to clear. The bridge game was over. Out in the hallway people were putting on their coats. There were only three people left at the roulette table.

When the clock on the mantelpiece struck half-past

three, Salkey closed the game. The remaining players began to cash in their chips. The young man in grey who had deputized as *croupier* during Salkey's absence, came back into the room. He gave Callaghan a vague glance, walked to the roulette table. Callaghan saw Salkey whisper to him. The young man nodded and went out.

The poker four disappeared. The last roulette players, including the lady with the ample bosom, were bidding each other commiserating or congratulatory farewells in the hallway outside. A *post mortem* between two of the bridge players grew fainter as the participants descended the stairs that led to the door on the street level.

Callaghan went over to the fireplace. He stood with his back to the fire. He took out his cigarette case, lit a cigarette. He began to blow smoke rings, watched them sail across the room.

Salkey got up from his chair at the head of the roulette table. He put the box containing the roulette plaques under his arm. He walked slowly across the room towards Callaghan. His smile was as charming as ever.

He said: 'I'd like to be able to make smoke rings like that. It's a thing I've never been able to do.'

Callaghan smiled at him.

'It's one of those things you can either do or you can't,' he said.

Salkey's smile became even more charming. He radiated good will. When he spoke Callaghan noted that his English was almost perfect, that the odd suggestion of an American accent gave a piquancy to his speech.

'It's just on four o'clock,' said Salkey. 'We're closing down now. Come again some time. We shall be glad to see you. I'm glad you won a little tonight.'

'Thanks,' said Callaghan. 'That's very nice of you. But before I go – if you could spare a few minutes, that is – I'd like to talk to you. Nothing important. Just a little thing. . . .'

'Sure,' said Salkey. 'Come upstairs. Let's have a drink.'

Callaghan followed him out of the room, across the

hallway through the curtained passages that led to the curving flight of stairs. They went up. At the top there was a landing, lit by a shaded electric light. There were two doors on the landing – one on each side of the staircase. Salkey opened the one on the left. They went in.

The room was of fair size. A fire burned brightly in the grate. The furniture was comfortable. There was a table with drinks in one corner. On another table was a silver-framed photograph of the lady with the ample bosom.

Salkey indicated an arm-chair. He said:

'Sit down. Make yourself at home. What'll you take?'

Callaghan said a little whisky. Salkey poured a stiff shot, added a splash of soda, carried the glass, and a silver cigarette box, to Callaghan.

Callaghan took the whisky and a cigarette. He threw a quick glance at Salkey. Salkey's face was in complete repose. His smile was still quite static. Callaghan noted with a certain approval the supple co-ordination of muscle when Salkey walked, or handed something.

Salkey went back to the drinks table. He poured himself a long gin, added a little lime, a lot of soda water. He turned and looked at Callaghan. He looked as if he and Callaghan might have been old friends – very old friends. He said cheerfully:

'What can I do for you?'

Callaghan looked at the glowing tip of his cigarette. His attitude was casual.

'It's just a little thing,' he said. 'I'm a private detective – Callaghan Investigations. I'm looking for some young idiot called Lionel Wilbery. I heard that he used to come here and play sometimes. I thought you might know something about him. You might have some odd idea about the sort of place he'd go to if he wanted to disappear for a bit.'

Salkey nodded. He took a cigarette from the silver box and lit it. After a moment he said:

'I remember young Wilbery. That one was sure an idiot. A bum drinker, a bum gambler and a bum where women were concerned. I reckon he didn't really know he was alive – not properly, I mean. He used to come here. When he won he got excited and when he lost he got silly. I had to ask him not to come any more. He caused too much atmosphere – if you know what I mean. I like things to be sort of nice and quiet around here. I don't like any excitement. You know how it is.'

Callaghan nodded.

'I know,' he said. 'When you're running a game like this you want to know your people. You don't want any trouble. There's enough trouble as it is.'

'Sure,' said Salkey genially. He seemed to have forgotten about Lionel Wilbery. 'You know the way it goes,' he went on. 'It's tough enough running a *spieler* like this under the best circumstances. Any time some dame loses enough to really get hurt she's always inclined to go shooting her mouth, and then the police get to hear of it and start snooping around. It's got a bit easier since the war's been on. The police have got plenty to do without hanging round putting the kybosh on every card game that's going – like they used to.'

Callaghan said: 'I know. But I thought you might know something about young Wilbery. He used to come here with a girl named Doria Varette. She was a torch singer – a damn good one too – but you probably know that. Somebody killed Varette the other night. It hasn't been in the newspapers yet – maybe it won't be, but it's true. I heard it because she used to get about with Wilbery, and the police – they knew I'd been commissioned by the family to try to find him – asked me if I'd any ideas about it.'

Salkey said: 'That's too bad – about Miss Varette, I mean. She was a lovely woman. She was the sort of woman that you don't often see around places like this. She sort of took your breath away. Everything about her was right – if you know what I mean.'

Callaghan said patiently: 'I know. You see, there was some sort of connection between a fellow called Santos D'Ianazzi and Doria Varette. I know there was a connection because I was with Varette one night pretty late and D'Ianazzi came round to see her. She didn't want to talk to him. She smacked the door to in his face. So I know there was *some* sort of connection between Miss Varette and D'Ianazzi. I suppose you know Santos D'Ianazzi.'

Salkey flipped the ash off his cigarette. He said pleasantly:

'Sure I know Santos. I don't know much about him, but I know him.' He smiled a little. 'It seems to me that he's the boyo you want if you want to find out about Miss Varette or young Wilbery. He'd know, wouldn't he? Have some whisky.'

Callaghan said thanks. He passed his glass over. Salkey filled it, brought it back to Callaghan.

'I'm sorry to hear about Miss Varette,' he said. 'They don't come like she was – not a lot, I mean. She was a nice piece if ever there was one.'

Callaghan drank some whisky.

'Coming back to D'Ianazzi,' he said. 'I thought you'd know quite a lot about D'Ianazzi. . . .'

Salkey said: 'Why?' He forgot to smile.

'Well,' said Callaghan. 'He owned this place, didn't he? He used to own it in the old days. He used to run it as a *spieler*. Then he went broke – or he was *supposed* to go broke. He'd got the place mortgaged and couldn't pay it off. Somebody called Milta Haragos paid it off and then D'Ianazzi used to get around working for Haragos. I've played at places where D'Ianazzi was head *croupier*, running the place for Haragos.'

'Really,' said Salkey. He seemed politely interested. 'Such as what places?'

'Such as The Dene down in Ashdown Forest,' said Callaghan. 'But that isn't *really* the point.'

He said: 'Just what is the point?'

Callaghan said: 'D'Ianazzi put you in here to run this place. You knew him. You knew Doria Varette. You knew Lionel Wilbery. You knew Milta Haragos. I've got an idea that you know where Lionel Wilbery is. *I* want to know.'

Salkey said: 'Aren't you being just a little unpleasant?'
Callaghan grinned amiably.

'No,' he said. 'I'm not. I'm just being pressing – shall
we say – about this business of Lionel Wilbery.'

Salkey shrugged his shoulders.

'I'd like to help,' he said evenly. 'But I can't. Another
thing,' he continued – he had begun to smile again.
'You're taking it for granted that I know a lot of people
well. Milta Haragos and all these people you talk about.
Aren't you bluffing a little?'

Callaghan said: 'Possibly. All the same I want an
answer. And I'm going to get one.'

'You don't say so,' said Salkey. 'And what makes you
think that?'

'I'll tell you,' said Callaghan. 'The police have pulled in
D'Ianazzi. He's suspected of killing Varette. Whether he
did kill her or not is a question. Personally, I shouldn't be
surprised if he had. He's a nasty bit of work anyway. You
know D'Ianazzi. This place belongs to him. I should imagine that he lived here when he was in these parts and
that you're a sort of manager-caretaker for him when he's
away. So that the police might want to talk to you about
D'Ianazzi. They might want to talk to you about his
movements on the night that Varette was killed. They
might even suggest that you knew something about it;
that you were an accessory "before and after".'

Salkey stubbed his cigarette out. His smile was a little
tight. It seemed to stretch his mouth sideways.

Callaghan inhaled deeply from his cigarette. He sent a
thin stream of tobacco smoke trickling out of one nostril.
He concluded:

'Even if you could alibi yourself out of the D'Ianazzi-
Varette business – there's still the other angle. . . .'

Salkey got up. He went over to the door, opened it.

He called softly: 'Wulfie, come here. . . .'

He went back to his chair and sat down. He was looking
at Callaghan oddly. His eyes – Callaghan noted – were
light blue. He said:

'Go on, Mr Callaghan.'

Callaghan looked at the doorway. A man came in. He was tall and very thin. His face was pasty white and his cheekbones stood out. His arms were very long and hung down by his sides. He walked with a strange circular gait. When he spoke his voice was high and cracked like a eunuch's voice. His lips were made up and his face was powdered.

He said: 'What's the trouble, Carlo?'

Salkey said to Callaghan: 'This is Wilfred. We call him Wulfie. He's a nice fellow if you keep on the right side of him. Wulfie, this is Mr Callaghan. He's sort of interested in us.'

Wulfie smiled at Callaghan. His teeth were small and pointed. The three centre ones were missing. When Callaghan saw the teeth he knew why they called him Wulfie.

Wulfie said: 'Charmed to meet you.' His words were mincing. Like a pansy's.

Salkey said: 'You were talking about the other angle. . . .'

'Oh, yes,' said Callaghan amiably. 'The other angle. The point is that Santos D'Ianazzi is supposed to be a Cuban. He had a passport that was *visèd* by the Cuban Consulate at Naples . . . at least that's what the passport said. D'Ianazzi had lost it. He said somebody took it off him. The interesting thing is the Cuban Legation here say they don't know anything about D'Ianazzi. So it looks to me as if that passport was screwy. It would be rather tough for you boys if the police came to the conclusion – whether you had anything to do with the Varette killing or not – that there might be some more people around here with screwy passports.'

Salkey said: 'All this is silly. First of all, about this Varette killing. I couldn't know anything about that. I was out of town when she was killed. So . . .'

'Were you?' said Callaghan. He began to grin. '*How* did you know *when* Varette was killed. *I* didn't tell you?'

Salkey looked at his fingernails. Wulfie began to smile. He got up from his chair. He went over to the table and picked up the cigarette box with his right hand. His left was in his trousers pocket.

He said: 'Really, Carlo . . . I think we ought to be honest with Mr Callaghan.' He carried the open cigarette box over to Callaghan. He said in his mincing, high-pitched falsetto: 'A cigarette, Mr Callaghan?'

He began to draw his left hand out of his pocket. Callaghan, one hand in the cigarette box, saw, out of the corner of his eye, the shape of the knuckle-duster on Wulfie's knuckles, showing against the soft cloth of the trousers. He lifted up his knee and kicked Wulfie in the stomach.

Wulfie uttered a horrible little shriek. He slithered down on to the carpet. Callaghan stooped, picked up the cigarette box, threw it at Salkey who was going for his hip pocket. The box hit Salkey on the shoulder, knocked him off balance for a second. Just long enough for Callaghan to shoot out of the chair.

Callaghan landed on Salkey just as the pistol showed in his right hand. Callaghan got a grip on the arm, but Salkey brought his knee up. Callaghan gasped, fell sideways, but managed to trip Salkey as he fell. They went down on to the carpet together.

Callaghan was underneath. He had a grip on Salkey's right arm but it wasn't good enough. Salkey had both thumbs on Callaghan's throat. Wulfie, over by the fireplace, began to make a nasty moaning noise. He was drooling saliva from the corners of his mouth. He got up on his hands and knees and began to crawl towards Salkey and Callaghan. He took a long time. Vaguely Callaghan could hear him mouthing obscenities.

Salkey tightened his grip on Callaghan's throat. The room began to go dark. Suddenly the telephone in the hallway began to ring.

The sound was so sudden, so startling, that for a split second Salkey's grip eased a little. Callaghan threw up his knees and twisted sideways. Salkey was thrown clear. Callaghan rolled over on him, smashed his bent elbow joint into Salkey's face. He heard the jaw crack. He rolled away, began to get up on to his knees.

Just behind him was Wulfie. Callaghan looked over his shoulders and saw the skin-tight, white face, with the white saliva drooling about the mouth.

Wulfie was in a bad way. One hand was pressed to his stomach where Callaghan had kicked him. But he was not 'out.' Callaghan thought that Wulfie had all the twisted courage of his type.

He put his weight on his right arm, drew back his left leg, kicked Wulfie in the face. Wulfie squealed like a dog that has been run over, subsided on the carpet.

Callaghan picked up the pistol, put it in his jacket pocket. Salkey was lying on the uninjured side of his face, one hand underneath his broken jaw. He looked vaguely surprised. Callaghan was almost surprised that he was still smiling.

He got up, went into the hallway, took the receiver off the wall telephone, leaned against the wall. The hallway was going round and round. After a minute his head began to clear.

He said: 'Hallo!'

'Hallo,' Effie said. 'Is that Mr Callaghan?'

Callaghan said: 'Yes.'

'I thought your voice sounded a little funny,' she said.

Callaghan said: 'Your voice would sound funny if you'd been doing what I've been doing. Did you get through to Grant?'

'Yes,' said Effie. 'He said he'd go and do that job at once.'

'All right,' said Callaghan. 'That's fine. Thank you very much. Goodnight, Effie. I hope you sleep well.'

'I hope so too,' said Effie. 'There isn't much time left, is there?'

Callaghan hung up the receiver. He went back into the room and stood in the doorway. Wulfie had managed to crawl to the fireplace. He was lying with his head over the fender. He was vomiting.

Salkey had pulled himself over to the opposite wall. He was sitting on the floor with his back against the wall, still supporting his injured jaw with a hand that was bloody.

Callaghan said: 'The trouble with you bastards is you always start something that you can't finish.'

Salkey raised his head and looked at Callaghan. Callaghan had an instantaneous bet with himself that he would smile. He won it. Salkey smiled. The smile was not a very nice smile, but nevertheless it was a smile. He said out of the corner of his mouth:

'One of these days I'm going to get you, Mr Callaghan.'

Callaghan said cheerfully: 'I'll take you six to four you don't. Perhaps you'd like to hear why. Listen . . .'

He went back into the hall, picked up the telephone. He dialled the Scotland Yard number, asked for the Information Room. Then he said:

'Is that the Information Room, Scotland Yard? Never mind who I am. If you like to send a Squad car round to the Salem Club in Fitzroy Square you'll find a couple of nice cases there. One of 'em's a fellow called Wulfie, the other a Carlo Salkey. There's been a little trouble round there. I think you ought to pick 'em up.'

The voice at the other end asked why.

'I think Mr Gringall would like to have a word with them tomorrow morning,' said Callaghan. 'You might tell him that Carlo Salkey has been running the Salem Club for Santos D'Ianazzi, the man he's holding as a suspect in the Varette murder. I think he'd like to hold these two as well.'

The voice said: 'Would Mr Gringall know who you are, by any chance?'

Callaghan grinned.

'When you give him that message,' he said, 'he'll know.'

10

On Rhyme and Reason

Callaghan stood leaning against the pillar box that stands in one corner of Fitzroy Square, looking uncertainly into the darkness. His head ached. The glands of his neck were still throbbing from the impact of Salkey's fingers.

He remained leaning against the pillar box for two or three minutes. The 'All Clear' sounded. For some unknown reason the cheerful note had a tonic effect on Callaghan. He pushed himself away from the pillar box, began to walk towards Berkeley Square. By the time he arrived he felt almost human.

He went into the building, walked along the corridor to the night porter's office. Wilkie, his peaked cap over one eye, was busy studying a handbook of racing form. Callaghan said:

'Good-morning, Wilkie.'

'Good-morning, Mr Callaghan,' said Wilkie. 'Nasty raid tonight, wasn't it? And you look as if you've had a bit of trouble yourself.'

'I have,' said Callaghan. 'Have you a note for me?'

Wilkie said he had. He produced a sealed envelope, handed it to Callaghan.

'A gentleman by the name of Grant left it,' he said. 'He asked me to give you his kind regards.'

Callaghan took the envelope, walked along to the lift. He got out at his apartment floor, opened the door, went in. He threw his hat and overcoat on the settee, walked across to the sideboard, opened a fresh bottle of rye. He put the neck of the bottle in his mouth and drank nearly a quarter of a pint. He stood leaning against the sideboard, holding the bottle by the neck, shuddering. He felt a lot better.

He opened the envelope and read the note from Grant. It said:

'*The Zayol Press isn't really in Curzon Street. It's on the corner of Winter Place and the back end of Shepherd Market. If you go through the courtway out of Curzon Street and turn right, then through Lime Alley, right at the end is a wall. Over that wall is a back yard. On the other side of the back yard is a door painted blue. This door leads to a kitchen which is behind the Zayol Press store-room.*

The door was so easy I did it with a cold chisel while I was there. You only have to turn the handle. On the other side of the kitchen is the door leading to the store-room. I left this alone. There are no burglar alarms and the air-raid wardens aren't interested because there's no one in the place at night.

I wore gloves while I was doing the outside door. I left no prints.'

Callaghan took out his lighter and burned the note. He threw the charred remains into the wastepaper basket, took off his collar and tie, went into the bathroom, washed. He put on a fresh collar and tie, went back into the sitting-room. He put on his overcoat and hat, went downstairs to the office floor. He selected a bunch of spider keys from a drawer in his desk and went out.

Shepherd Market was quiet and very restful to the nerves, thought Callaghan. He took a quick look up and down Curzon Street, moved quickly through the passageway into Shepherd Market, turned into the alley, walked to the end. He put on his gloves, caught the top of the wall, pulled himself up. He dropped down on the other side. A few paces ahead was the blue door.

He pushed it open, went in, closed it quietly behind him. He was in complete darkness. He switched on his electric torch, walked across the kitchen, took the small bunch of spider keys from his pocket. The seventh one opened the door.

He was in the store-room of the Zayol Press. There were no windows. He closed the door, switched on the electric light. The walls were lined with bookshelves, and in one corner were one or two large packing cases. Most of the shelves were filled with books, paper jacketed, all of them new. Callaghan took one or two down, looked at them casually. Mostly they were books of poetry, slim volumes filled with the sort of stuff that young men and women are inclined to write before they reach the age of common sense; the sort of books that get published if one is prepared to pay three-quarters of the cost of publication.

Callaghan replaced the books carefully, crossed the room, tried the door on the other side. It was open. He walked through the little passageway and up the circular flight of iron stairs that led to the floor above. At the top of the iron stairway was another door. Callaghan opened it, went in. It was the first-floor office of the Zayol Press.

The room was small, contained more bookshelves, two desks, a typewriter, a collection of papers. Callaghan began a systematic search. He found nothing that interested him until he started work on the desk. In the lower right-hand drawer he found the rough layout of a jacket intended for a book of poetry. The title was 'Sea Songs,' by Lionel Wilbery.

The inside flap of the jacket bore a rough typewritten blurb containing the usual information that such blurbs give – 'Lionel Wilbery – a coming poet . . . unique rhythm . . . will appeal to all modern minds.' Inside the jacket were two or three typewritten pages. They were poems. Most of them dealt with some angle of the sea. They were the sort of poems that young men who want to write about the sea, write about the sea.

Callaghan read them very carefully. He thought that as a poet Lionel Wilbery was not so bad. He replaced the papers in the drawer, closed it.

He examined the other desk. None of the drawers were locked, and the books inside, which dealt with the business of the Zayol Press gave the usual information that one expected to find in the books of a publishing firm. There was one incongruity. Most of the business seemed to be export.

Callaghan put the books back carefully in their places. His eye was caught by a cupboard in the corner of the room. It was locked. It took him two minutes to open it. Inside were a series of letter files marked alphabetically. Callaghan took out the one labelled 'W.' He looked through it.

There was a letter to Lionel Wilbery dated two months back. It said:

'Dear Mr Wilbery,

I have had a word with Miss Haragos and she says there is no doubt that we shall be pleased, with your consent, to publish your book of poems within the next two months.

There is only one outstanding point, which is that Miss Haragos has suggested some alterations in several of the poems. I am sending you a note of these alterations and hope you will approve.

Miss Haragos tells me she handed the original MS back to you. She suggests you return it as soon as possible.'

The letter was signed by a Bettina Clarke – *'For Zayol Press Ltd.'*

Callaghan put the file back into the cupboard, locked it. He went back to the desk, sat down and lit a cigarette. He remained there until the cigarette was almost finished. He stubbed out the end in the ashtray on the desk, was about to put the stub in his overcoat pocket. Then he grinned and put it in the ashtray. He went out of the office, down the iron steps, through the store-room and the kitchen, out of the blue door. He did not even bother to close the door behind him.

The Chinese clock on the mantelpiece of Callaghan's sitting-room struck six. He heard the chimes vaguely, as if they came from a long way away.

His head ached with a dull steady throbbing, punctuated by the sharper pain of neuralgia. He walked slowly up and down the length of his bedroom, the floor of which was strewn with clothes he had shed. He was dressed only in his undervest and shorts. He held one sock in his hand. He wore the other, and the unfastened suspender dragged behind him as he walked.

His tongue was rough. Callaghan thought about the condition of his mouth. His thought it felt like a rather nasty brown carpet. He sighed, went into the sitting-room.

Daylight, he considered, was a nice change. Looking out of the window, towards Berkeley Square, he could see the sun making a brave effort to appear. He considered it might easily be a nice day, qualified the idea with the thought that it did not matter a damn anyway.

People were fools. When they were not fools they were either entirely idiotic, unintelligent, quite senseless or merely stupid. Some people were.

Salkey was definitely senseless, so was Wulfie. If Salkey had not been stupid at the right moment, if Wulfie had not gone utterly crazy they might have got away with it. And Salkey had accused him, Callaghan, of bluffing!

He began to grin. The thought pleased him. He went over to the sideboard, took out the rye bottle, put the neck in his mouth and took a long swig. The raw liquor made him shudder but the process of shuddering was tangible. He liked it.

And Salkey had accused him of bluffing. . . .

Life was mostly a matter of bluff – so far as a private detective was concerned. Bluff was one of the main items in the stock-in-trade of a private detective. Bluff and an ability to discount the intelligence of other people at the right valuation. Life was a matter of discounting the intelligence of other people, of valuing it, almost as precisely as a bill broker considered the discount value of a bill. A nice smile, thought Callaghan.

He continued that process of thought with a certain satisfaction. He began to think about the people in the Wilbery case, to discount their intelligences or their intelligence – if any.

He took them in order; in the order of their appearance . . .! Characters in the order of their appearance. . . . What a programme! First, Miss Doria

Varette – played by Miss Doria Varette *alias* somebody or other. One would probably never know what lay on the other side of that *alias*. Miss Varette was intelligent enough. Intelligent enough to play her part right up to the time when the ghostly prompter had suggested that it was time that she made her exit. Callaghan thought that she had probably made her exit rather gracefully. Doria Varette had been intelligent enough. . . .

He thought rather sadly that he had possibly let her down. Callaghan Investigations did not like letting their clients down – not unless they wanted to. And he had not wanted to let her down. He apologized mentally.

Enter Mr Gringall. George Henry Porteous Gringall. Chief Detective-Inspector Gringall. Product of the Metropolitan Police Force of the flat heavy boot on the pavement, of the four years as a constable, of the five years as a station Sergeant, the three years as an Inspector – with all the probing into the raw side of life that only a police Inspector knows; of the three years as a Detective-Inspector; of the two years as a Chief Detective-Inspector. And the last step had come over the Riverton case. Callaghan smiled at the thought of the Riverton case. He had helped in that promotion and Gringall had a long memory. Callaghan remembered the Riverton case and Gringall and Thorla Riverton. . . . A hell of a woman Thorla – even if she had not given him a cigarette case! Maybe what she had given him was a trifle more valuable even if slightly less tangible. . . .

And Salkey had said he was bluffing! Callaghan took another swig at the rye bottle and drank a silent toast to the god Bluff. It was because of the god Bluff that Gringall had thrown Doria Varette at Callaghan Investigations, knowing that Callaghan Investigations would catch her as Gringall had meant, because of that ability to bluff that is the main part of the stock-in-trade of a private detective and is no part – because it may not be – of the stock-in-trade of a policeman.

Here's to the art of bluff. The heavy bluff, or the sinister bluff, or the threatening bluff, or the merely suggestive bluff, or the bluff with the crooked elbow behind it.

Enter Mr Santos D'Ianazzi. Clever Mr D'Ianazzi. Cute Santos. Intelligent. Certain that what was behind him was adequate. So certain that he could afford to bluff with a hundred pounds. Walking easily and prettily on his way in his pointed patent shoes, in his beautifully cut suits and his horizontally striped shirts that came from a Paris that could, in those days, specialize in such things. Poor Mr D'Ianazzi. Poor Santos. Who had been sold out by the god of chance in spite of his intelligence. Callaghan had wondered about his exit. . .

Enter Leonore Wilbery. A clear stage for the lady please. She deserves it. Intelligent? As intelligent as is good for a woman who looked like Leonore. Trying hard to use that intelligence, finding it not so good against the 'stings and arrows of outrageous fortune,' throwing it overboard, sacrificing it at the bidding of a couple of *marihuana* cigarettes, and the subconscious groping of a woman for something stronger to lean on. Which was Mr Callaghan, whose speciality was bluff, and on whose ability to use that standard commodity she was now relying.

Up stage please, Leonore . . . make room for the big double turn – Miss Sabine Haragos, Mr Milta Haragos. Hetman of Cossacks Haragos. Big, burly, handsome Milta Haragos. Intelligent? Yes. Clever? Yes . . . damned clever . . . yes. Oh yes . . . damnably clever . . . bloody clever, thought Callaghan. Who dies if the Haragos live? A green, a sinister lime on the double turn please. Thank you, Mr Electrician! And now a steel blue lime on Sabine to bring out the lights of that flat beauty, those slitted eyes, that sinuous grace.

Callaghan put the rye bottle down on the sideboard. He went into the bedroom and put on a dressing-gown. He threw away the dragging suspender, inserted his feet into slippers. He went out of the flat and into the lift.

If you have tears, prepare to shed them now. If you have bluff, prepare to use it now, thought Callaghan.

183

He stopped the lift at the office floor. Walked along the passage, opened the outer door, went in, sat down at Effie Thompson's desk. On one corner, acting as a temporary paper weight, was the book she was reading – a Crime Club book. Callaghan grinned. One of his occasional relaxations was the Crime Club. Where clues were so neat and tidy, where logic was so relentless, where detectives were so apt, where the reader's brain, one step behind that of the author, fitted together the pieces of the jig-saw puzzle that pictured the mystery, only to discover, in the last chapter, that he had foozled with the main piece; that the author had still something up his sleeve.

If only life was like that. Being a private detective meant only too often that one had nothing up one's sleeve except one's arm, which, used only as a last resort, was hardly adequate for bluffing.

Callaghan opened the top right-hand drawer of Effie Thompson's desk, opened the big box of Player's cigarettes which she used to replenish the silver box on his desk, took a cigarette, lit it, put his elbows on the desk top and considered just how much he was going to say – just how little. . . .

He made up his mind, groped for the telephone directory, flipped it open, searched for the number. He found it eventually – G. H. P. Gringall, Riverside Drive, S.W., RIV 67452. He dialled the number, and waited.

He waited a long time. He began to blow smoke rings, ruminating on the scene within Gringall's flat. Gringall would be struggling into a dressing-gown, cursing, wondering who it was wanted him at such an unearthly hour. Then he would guess. He would guess that it would be Callaghan. And he would wonder what it was that Callaghan had to say and just what he, Gringall, would say, if Callaghan said so-and-so or, alternatively, so-and-so.

Gringall's voice said hallo.

Callaghan said: 'Good-morning, Gringall. I suppose they haven't rung you up from the Yard?'

'No,' said Gringall. 'By the same token, what are you doing, ringing me up at this hour? I thought you never got up till lunch time? And why should the Yard have telephoned me?'

'Well,' said Callaghan. 'I called through to them about half-past four this morning. I asked the Information Room to pick up a couple of people at a place called the Salem Club, near Fitzroy Square. I said I thought you'd probably want to talk to these two birds. That's all.'

Gringall said: 'Ah. . . .' There was a pause. Then: 'What two birds, and why?'

'Well . . .' said Callaghan, 'I went along to the Salem Club last night. It seems that Lionel Wilbery used to go there with Doria Varette. The Salem Club is by way of being a *spieler*, see? Quite a good class one. All the usual things, you know, *roulette*, *chemie*, poker . . .'

'I know,' said Gringall.

'I won forty pounds too,' said Callaghan cheerfully. 'Anyhow, while I was there I thought I'd have a word with the boyo who runs the place, a person name of Salkey. This Salkey seemed quite a nice sort of fellow, at first that is. He was nice enough until I began to ask questions.'

'People are always nice until you ask for something,' said Gringall. 'But don't let me interrupt you.'

'I won't if I can help it,' said Callaghan amiably. 'Well, to cut a long story short, I stayed on there after everyone else had gone. Then I had a little talk with this Salkey boyo. He just didn't know anything about anything at all. He said he'd met Lionel and he remembered Varette. He remembered what a hell of a fine woman she was. Beyond that his memory didn't seem to work very well. So I thought I'd have to try and do something to give it a gyp.'

'I see,' said Gringall. 'So you gypped up his memory a bit. Would it be curious to ask you how you did that?'

'I took a bit of a liberty – with you I mean,' said Callaghan. 'Thinking things over I realise I shouldn't have done it, but you know how things are, you sort of get carried away.'

'Like hell you do,' said Gringall. 'The day that something or somebody makes you get carried away I'll eat my hat in Piccadilly Circus.'

Callaghan grinned into the transmitter. He went on:

'Well, anyway, as I said, I took a liberty. I forgot for the moment that I was using a bit of private information that possibly you didn't want divulged. I told this Salkey lad that he'd better gyp up his memory a bit, otherwise the Yard, who were holding Santos D'Ianazzi as a suspect in the Varette murder, might want to ask him some questions.'

'Nice work,' said Gringall. 'How did he react to that one?'

'He didn't seem to mind that one a lot,' said Callaghan. 'He wasn't worrying about any "accessory before and/or after" charge. He'd got a cast-iron alibi. He told me that he was out of town when Varette was killed.'

Callaghan paused, blew a careful smoke ring.

'The joke was,' he said, 'I hadn't told him when Varette was killed.'

'Quite,' said Gringall. 'But on the other hand he might be a lad who's out of town an awful lot. Anyhow, I expect he could suggest that he was. But go on. . . .'

'There was another lad there,' said Callaghan. 'A real, proper boyo, this other lad. A tall, thin, rangy sort of one. A very wiry one. A perfect sweetheart. Used a little make-up too, and had a cupid bow mouth. One of those. With all the nasty temper they usually have too. He didn't like me a lot.'

'I'm not surprised,' said Gringall. 'And what did he do — or didn't he?'

'I was saying,' said Callaghan, 'they didn't seem to be bothering a lot about any connection between Santos D'Ianazzi and themselves – not a lot. So I tried another line. I suggested that Santos hadn't got a passport, that he'd said that somebody had taken it off him. I also said that the Cuban Legation didn't know anything about him. I suggested that possibly, even if he had a Cuban passport, it was a screwy one. That seemed to make 'em think a bit.'

'Did it?' said Gringall. 'Fancy that now. And what gave you the idea that the D'Ianazzi passport might be a fake?'

'Nothing gave me the *idea*,' said Callaghan. 'I know it's a fake. The last visa on the D'Ianazzi passport is that of the Cuban Consulate at Naples. If they don't know anything about him there it's a stone certainty that that visa is a forgery. After all, anybody can make a rubber stamp and do a little faking with a pen, can't they? Or they might even have pinched a rubber stamp from the Cuban Consulate at Naples.'

'Quite,' said Gringall. 'So that's where Santos' passport went to. You've got it.'

'Right,' said Callaghan. 'I've got it. Aren't you shattered with surprise?'

'Like hell I am,' said Gringall. 'I knew you'd got it. Just as I know it was Nikolls who manhandled Santos.'

'No!' Callaghan looked pleased. 'Now that's clever. How did you know that?'

'You invariably hit 'em with your elbow joint,' said Gringall. 'I remember that fellow Piercer. It catches 'em under the jaw an' telescopes one side of the jaw. But somebody had slugged Santos right on the nose – hard, and then on the mouth. The nasal frontal bone's cracked a bit, and he's got four teeth missing. That, I imagine, would be the Nikolls technique. But go on . . . it seems this was a nice sort of party.'

'It was grand fun,' said Callaghan. 'When I got on to the screwy passport angle Wulfie – the little sweetheart – didn't like me a bit. He was going to start something. I was sitting down and had to kick him. Salkey was getting rather forcible too. He was trying to get a gun out. I had to be a bit rough.'

'A bit rough!' said Gringall. 'You're telling me. Why, Salkey's jaw's telescoped. He's in the hospital now, and as for little Wulfie, I doubt if they straightened him out yet. Little Wulfie was still doubled up when they brought him in.'

Callaghan said: 'I thought they hadn't rung you up from the Yard?'

'Ah . . .' said Gringall. 'That was before I knew you were going to talk. You're such a slippery customer, aren't you?'

'Shocking,' agreed Callaghan. 'Unscrupulous too. . . .'

'I know,' said Gringall.

There was a pause. Then Gringall said:

'Are you going to be in London?'

'Not for long,' said Callaghan. 'I've got an idea I'm going to Norton Fitzwarren some time this afternoon. Why?'

'Well,' said Gringall, 'I've got an idea that I shall be somewhere in the neighbourhood of Berkeley Square some time this afternoon. And you might as well have that D'Ianazzi passport waiting for me. I want it. Who the hell do you think you are hanging on to Exhibit "A" like that?'

Callaghan said: 'I'll be glad to see you. But don't be later than, say, four-thirty. Why don't you come to tea?'

'Tea!' Gringall was laughing. 'I didn't know you drank anything else but neat rye round at that spider's web you call an office.'

'We drink tea as a chaser,' said Callaghan. 'We might also give you a piece of cake. And mind you wipe those big feet of yours before you come in.'

Gringall said: 'I'll be with you about four-thirty. Just take care that nobody kills you before *I've* done with you.'

Callaghan sighed.

'Now, who would want to do a thing like that?' he said.

'I know about sixty people who'd stretch your neck with pleasure if they could get away with it,' said Gringall. 'And I don't know that I'm not one of them.'

'I like that,' said Callaghan. 'Who was it brought you that Riverton job on a plate? Who was it that stood by and got nothing while they made you a Chief Detective-Inspector with a room of your own, and all sorts of things?'

Gringall laughed.

'So you got nothing,' he said. 'I like that. You ought to have retired on what the Riverton lawyers paid you for that crooked job. And look at that Vendayne case. The police did all the work and you got about two thousand pounds out of it. Besides which . . .' He stopped suddenly.

'Besides what?' asked Callaghan.

'Oh, nothing,' said Gringall airily. 'By the way, how's Miss Vendayne?'

'She was very well the last time I saw her,' said Callaghan.

Gringall said: 'I think somebody ought to warn these women about going out with private detectives with warped minds like you've got. Unscrupulous too. I can never make out why your women clients get stuck on you. I think it's disgraceful.'

'Don't be jealous,' said Callaghan. 'You can't expect to understand nice women – not with that awful mentality of yours. It even makes *me* shudder. Good-bye, flat-foot. I'll see you at four-thirty – if I remember it.'

He hung up quickly.

Gringall stood, twisting the tasselled cord of his dressing-gown between his fingers. His expression was one of amiable contentment. He walked out of the hallway into the small, tidy kitchen, put the kettle on the gas stove, prepared an early morning tea tray. For the business of being Chief Detective-Inspector, and the ramifications of this case and that, did nothing to affect the habits of George Herbert Porteous Gringall – one of which was the serving of his wife's early morning cup of tea.

Having lit the gas under the kettle, and filled and lit a small, chubby pipe, Gringall went into the sitting-room. He sat down at the telephone table and dialled the Scotland Yard number.

He said: 'This is Mr Gringall. About those two who were brought in from the Salem Club this morning. Just keep 'em on ice for the time being. If they start shouting for a lawyer let 'em have one – or a dozen if they want. They probably won't. They'll probably be canny and silent. When Fields comes in you can tell him that they'll be charged under a Section of the Defence of the Realm Act. I'll see the Assistant Commissioner about that when I arrive. I shall be there at nine o'clock.'

He said good-bye, hung up. He went into the kitchen and stood watching the kettle, drawing on his pipe.

Callaghan stubbed out his cigarette, took a fresh one, lit it, thought that he felt tired.

His headache was gone. A tinge of neuralgia remained to remind him that life is a matter of comparison between having a pain and not having a pain – mental or physical.

He sat looking at the desk, drawing great breaths of tobacco smoke down into his lungs. After a while he leaned across the desk, switched on the dictaphone. He said:

'Effie, directly you get here ring through to Nikolls at the Grasscutter. Tell him to telephone through to Miss Wilbery at Deeplands and ask her to meet him as soon as possible. He is to find out from her whether Milta Haragos is with his sister Sabine at The Vale, or whether he is in town. Miss Wilbery will have to find this out by some means known to herself. But she's to do it un-obtrusively. If Milta Haragos is in London, he'll probably be at the Haragos flat at Rufus Court. Wherever he is Nikolls is to get on to his tail. If he's at Rufus Court Nikolls must get back to London as quickly as he can. That means that Miss Wilbery must get the information by ten o'clock so that Nikolls can get up to London by two o'clock. Nikolls is to get on to Milta Haragos immediately he arrives here so that he can report to me here at four o'clock. That's that.

'Secondly, I'm now going to bed. I want to be called at half-past three with some strong tea. I want my blue pinhead suit pressed. Tell the valet. Also Mr Gringall is calling about four-thirty. When he comes show him into my office and give him some tea if he wants it. Thank you, Effie.'

190

He switched off the dictaphone, locked the office door, walked along to the lift and went up to his flat. He took off his dressing-gown, vest and shorts, put on a pink silk pyjama jacket, got into bed. In three minutes he was asleep.

Callaghan sat at his desk drinking tea. He was cleanly shaved, well-dressed. He wore a blue pinhead suit fresh from the valet's pressing, a pale blue silk shirt and collar, a navy blue tie. He wore a few violets -- extracted from a bunch worn by Effie Thompson – in his button-hole.

The office clock struck four. Nikolls came in. He walked through the outer office, stuck his head round Callaghan's door, grinned, walked across the room, inserted his large body in the big chair opposite Callaghan's desk.

Callaghan threw over a cigarette. Nikolls caught it, put it in his mouth, lit it with a match struck artistically on the seat of his trousers. In order to strike the match he had to lean sideways off the chair. Callaghan wondered why it was necessary to light a cigarette like that.

He said: 'Milta?'

Nikolls grinned.

'It's O.K.,' he said. 'I got tabs on that baby. He's at Rufus Court, an' he's stayin' there. He's got some man-icure jane workin' on him at the moment an' then he's gonna bath an' have the barber in for a haircut. I been workin' fast. I got up here at three. I got the express. Leonore was swell. When I met her this mornin' she did a 'phone call to The Vale an' got the works from Sabine.'

Callaghan said: 'That's all right. But don't lose Haragos. I'm leaving here about five o'clock. I shall be down at Deeplands by about nine tonight.'

Nikolls yawned.

'This case is gettin' me down,' he said. 'I hope I don't have to go down to that Grasscutter dump again. That jane in the saloon bar is after my blood. She's a de-termined baby. She won't take no for an answer. . . .'

'I expect that's the trouble,' said Callaghan. 'I expect you wouldn't take no for an answer in the first place.'

'Well. . . .' Nikolls spread his large palms. 'I gotta get results, ain't I? I gotta find things out. The way to a man's heart is through his belly, an' the way to a woman's information is . . . but let's skip it. All I gotta say is I'm goddam glad to get away an' I hope I don't haveta go back there. If I do I'm gonna stay some other place otherwise that jane is gonna scalp me when I ain't lookin'. That dame has got too much character for me. She reminds me of a baby I usta know in Wyoming. Did I ever tell you about that kiddo?'

Callaghan said: 'No . . . I don't think I heard about the Wyoming one.'

'It was terrible,' said Nikolls. 'I got myself in a jam with some baby in Chicago, an' this baby was the berries, I'm tellin' you. She was sorta fond of love. In fact I christened that dame Muscles because she was in every guy's arms. Every guy she met up with she fell for. But when she met me she fell with such a bump that she thought she'd been bombed.

'O.K. Well, I took a run-out on this doll. I took a run-out when I heard she was lookin' for me with a lovin' smile an' a jack-knife. I went as far away as I could. I went to Wyoming. When I got there I stayed on some farm. The farmer's daughter was one of them babies you read about. She had everything. She was like a picture off the front of a magazine with lots of class an' what it takes. I take one look at this doll an' she practically faints in my arms. This is the effect I have on this dame.

'O.K. Well, there I am. Right in the heart of the ranchin' country, with lovely sunsets, four meals a day, unlimited hooch an' this baby hangin' on my every word. What a dump – everything to hand an' no extras.

'One night I am sittin' on the porch an' I get sorta confidential. I tell this baby about the dame in Chicago. An' before I know where I am she has issued me a smack on the beezer that you could hear out in Honolulu.'

Callaghan said: 'Well, you asked for it. She was jealous of the other woman.'

'Nope,' said Nikolls. 'You got it wrong. The other woman was her sister. She'd written an' told her what some so-an'-so had done to her, an' this dame recognizes me by the description. It just shows you how small the world is, don't it? An' also you should never let your right hand know what you'd like to be doin' with your left. Me – I don't like determined women. I mean to say I don't like women who are determined about the right things at the wrong moment.'

Callaghan said: 'When you pick up Milta again, don't lose him. You'd better keep in touch with the office up till one or two o'clock in the morning. I may be coming back. If Milta decides to go home and go to bed, come back to the office and leave a message on Effie's dictaphone. If that happens you can lay off and go to bed.'

Nikolls heaved himself up.

'O.K.,' he said. He walked to the office door. He turned and said. 'I suppose we haven't got any ideas where Lionel is yet?'

Callaghan shook his head.

'Is it troubling you?' he asked.

'Not much,' said Nikolls. 'Except for that Leonore baby. She's worried sick. She's a nice kid that one.' He looked at Callaghan and grinned. 'She's sorta taken a bend on you, hasn't she?' he said. 'She sorta thinks you got everything that opens and shuts. It just shows you, don't it?'

He closed the door quickly behind him.

Callaghan lit another cigarette. He put his feet on the desk and thought. He was thinking about Lionel Wilbery – which was something he had almost forgotten about.

Gringall stood in the doorway of Callaghan's office, smiling at Callaghan. Callaghan grinned back, took his feet off the desk, indicated the leather arm-chair opposite. Silently, behind the police officer, Effie Thompson closed the office door.

Callaghan said: 'Have you a cigarette? Or are you still faithful to that pipe of yours?'

'I still smoke a pipe,' said Gringall. 'Sometimes I smoke a cigar. Usually when I want to celebrate something.'

He sat down in the arm-chair, unbuttoned his overcoat, put his hat down on the edge of Callaghan's desk.

Effie Thompson came in with a tea-tray. She put it on the desk. On it were the usual things, a chocolate cake, biscuits.

Callaghan said: 'Or there's rye if you want it. We keep that in the desk drawer. Nikolls uses it in the morning.'

Gringall said: 'I'll have tea. It's nice being here. It's a long time since I was in this office.'

Callaghan nodded.

'The last time you were here was during the run of the Riverton case. That's a long time ago.'

Gringall smiled. He began to pour out tea. He said:

'It's amazing how you last. You go on from success to success. One of these fine days somebody's going to crown you with a sandbag and there'll be one private detective the less.'

'You'd be sorry,' said Callaghan. 'What *would* you do without me?'

'The question is what we'd like to do *with* you,' replied Gringall. He cut himself a piece of chocolate cake.

Callaghan said: 'I'm going to Norton Fitzwarren soon after five o'clock. So if you want to talk about something you'd better talk fast. Or perhaps you'd like me to talk?'

Gringall said: 'No, I don't want you to do any talking. You might talk too much and not get away by five o'clock.' He took a large bite of chocolate cake. He said: 'This is a good cake. It's a long time since I've tasted a really fluffy chocolate cake. But then you always did yourself pretty well.' He finished the piece of cake.

Callaghan watched him. Gringall, he thought, ate just as he did everything else. Slowly, concisely, thoroughly. A great many people would assess Gringall's character on that, would sum him up as a slow and ponderous police officer who had attained seniority by the process of being slow and ponderous, concise and thorough. A great many people, thought Callaghan, would be wrong. Gringall was all those things and a lot of other things too. Gringall could produce quite a lot out of a hat if he wanted to. Even a certain brilliancy of thought and execution. Gringall was no fool. Too many people – clever people – had been taken in by that slightly ponderous attitude and recovered when it was too late.

Gringall began to fill his pipe. He said almost casually:

'I suppose you haven't found Lionel yet?'

Callaghan shook his head.

'No,' he said. 'We haven't. To tell you the truth I'd almost forgotten about Lionel. Strange but true. You see there were other interesting personalities besides Lionel.'

'Perhaps you don't want to find him,' said Gringall.

'I do,' said Callaghan. His smile was friendly and open. 'The devil of it is we don't know where to look.'

'Quite,' said Gringall. He looked sympathetic. 'But then,' he went on, 'you'd have some sort of plan, wouldn't you? Otherwise it'd be like looking for a needle in a haystack, wouldn't it?'

'It is like looking for a needle in a haystack,' said Callaghan. 'It's worse. We haven't even got a haystack to look into.' He lit a cigarette slowly, looked at Gringall through the flame of the lighter. 'The trouble was we lost our first client,' he said. 'Miss Varette, I mean. She'd have been a great deal of use to us. She'd have been able to tell us a lot about Lionel. I'm certain that she'd have said a great deal in the letter she'd have sent us with that hundred pounds she promised. But she couldn't send the letter. Somebody decided to kill her first. Which was a great pity.'

Gringall said: 'It's always a pity when somebody gets killed. But it happens. I suppose you were curious when you didn't hear from her?'

'Not for a bit,' said Callaghan. 'Of course I was curious about her. I couldn't quite get an angle on Miss Varette – not at first I mean. Then I came along to see you and then

I got rather mixed up with the Wilbery family. They all decided that they wanted me to look for Lionel. And they've paid some very nice money too.'

'Have they?' said Gringall. 'I think it's amazing the way people pay you money. You never seem to do anything for it either. I suppose it's your fatal charm.'

'Oh, I don't know,' said Callaghan airily. 'We usually pull something out of the bag – in the end.'

'Yes,' said Gringall. 'I know you do.' He drew on his pipe appreciatively.

'But after you'd got mixed up with the Wilbery family,' he went on, 'you must have been curious about Miss Varette?'

'I was,' said Callaghan, 'very curious. I still am.'

Gringall smiled.

'That was why you sent Nikolls to case her place,' he said slowly. 'That was why you went there after Nikolls had told you somebody had finished her off, and that was why you planted that money you'd taken off Santos D'Ianazzi in her stocking top and faked that letter from her to Santos – a letter which gave him a first-class motive for killing her. I suppose you did all those things because you were curious about her?'

Callaghan said: 'It's amazing how you policemen do find out things, isn't it? Supposing all this were true – and I'm not, for one moment, admitting it is – how did you find out?'

Gringall yawned.

'The trouble people took not to leave any fingerprints,' he said. 'All the door-handles and things wiped clean, all except one.' He re-lit his pipe. 'You remember in the Layne case Nikolls made a statement about Susy Layne?'

Callaghan nodded.

'I remembered that statement,' said Gringall. 'The only prints on it were Sergeant Fields' and Nikolls'. When I went to Varette's house – the fingerprint johnny found one print on the electric switch in the hall. . . .'

Callaghan said quietly: 'Nikolls is always so damned careless about light switches.'

'I had an idea,' said Gringall. 'We checked that print with the ones on the Layne statement and they compared very nicely. I knew Nikolls had been around there. I knew he'd been round there when it was dark because he'd used the switch, and so I put two and two together and guessed that you'd been there after he'd told you Varette was killed. I put two and two together and guessed that you had decided to frame Santos D'Ianazzi. I wondered why you'd wanted to do that. D'you think Santos killed her?'

Callaghan said: 'I wouldn't know. I don't even care much. All I know is he kicked me in the stomach. I don't like being kicked in the stomach – not that I like Santos much either.'

'Quite,' said Gringall. 'I think he's not so good too.'

He began to refill his pipe.

'I was wondering where you met D'Ianazzi,' he said.

Callaghan stubbed out his cigarette and lit a fresh one.

'I met him the night I met Varette,' he said. 'I took Varette home. It was as dark as hell. When I was coming out of the *cul-de-sac* Santos went in. I went back and listened. I was interested. I saw Varette slam the door in his face. Obviously she didn't like that bird. I waited for him outside and asked him what he thought he was doing. He told me to lay off and gave me two fifty pound notes to mind my own business.'

Gringall grinned.

'My God!' he said. 'Fancy Santos thinking you'd mind your own business for a hundred pounds!'

'Quite,' said Callaghan. 'It's silly, isn't it?' He blew a smoke ring, watched it sail across the office.

'It was damn' funny,' he said. 'But I met Santos again. I met him the next night. The night of the day I saw you. He was running gambling games at a house in the country. I went there.'

'How?' asked Gringall. 'How did you manage to get there?'

Callaghan said: 'That's my business. It's good enough

for you to know I was there. I was sufficiently interested in Varette to have a showdown with D'Ianazzi. I wanted to know what he was after. He got rough. He was very annoyed with me. I think he'd have finished me off if Nikolls hadn't turned up. Nikolls pasted him properly. Santos is a bad-tempered fellow.'

'I see,' said Gringall. 'I'm beginning to see daylight. You traced a connection between Santos and the Salkey and Wulfie birds at the Salem Club and you had to go along there and stick your nose in. A proper Daniel in the lions' den, aren't you?'

'Yes,' said Callaghan. 'I never mind so long as the lions aren't too big.'

'Well,' said Gringall, 'we've all got to take a chance sometime. By the way, have you got that D'Ianazzi passport handy?'

Callaghan took it from his inside breast pocket. He handed it to Gringall, who pocketed it.

Gringall got up. He stood looking at Callaghan. He looked friendly. He looked very unlike an efficient, a senior police-officer. He said:

'I don't think you're doing so badly. I think that one of these fine days you might even find Lionel Wilbery.'

Callaghan grinned. There was a world of mischief, of understanding, in that grin.

'When I do,' he said. 'What do I do? Do I bring you the pieces?'

Gringall began to put on his gloves.

'That wouldn't help a lot,' he said. 'You can't get pieces to answer questions. You want the entire man – if you can call it a man – all in one piece. You want something you can get to work on. Something that you can make up your mind about and get at.'

Callaghan nodded. He lit another cigarette. He said:

'Before you go, there's just one little thing I'd like to know. Perhaps you'll be able to answer it. Perhaps you won't.'

Gringall said: 'What is it? I suppose it wouldn't be

about that money you took off the Cuban and stuck in Miss Varette's stocking top?'

'That's it,' said Callaghan. He looked at Gringall. He began to smile. 'You're rather like a mind-reader, aren't you?' he asked.

Gringall said: 'Perhaps.' He looked at Callaghan. He went on: 'Maybe I am – maybe you are – maybe we all are . . . what is it they say? Things that are equal to the same thing are equal to each other . . .'

'Do they?' said Callaghan.

'Yes,' said Gringall. 'They do. I suppose you wanted to know where those notes came from originally. I suppose you're going to say that the two thousand that came out of D'Ianazzi's banking account had to go into it from somewhere or other. It was two thousand, you know – but I expect you'd know that. I expect you took the odd hundred, didn't you?'

Callaghan grinned.

'Correct,' he said. 'We'll call that Exhibit "B" if you like. Those notes are earmarked for future reference.'

'It doesn't matter a lot,' said Gringall. 'Anyhow, Varette owed you a hundred, didn't she? But you'd better keep the notes handy just in case. About the other thing, that's not so easy.'

Gringall stopped talking. He walked over to the window and looked out. Callaghan watched his back – a very broad back.

'We know where the money came from originally,' said Gringall. 'But I'm afraid the information isn't going to be a lot of use. We can't use it.' He came back to the desk, stood looking down at Callaghan. 'The devil of being a police-officer,' he went on, 'is that you've got to prove things. You've *got* to prove things. Sometimes you can get away with a half-proof – at a time like this when there's a war on. But when you haven't even got a half-proof, when you've got nothing, you can't do a thing. Sometimes it's damned difficult. You know, you're certain and you can't do anything because you can't prove what you know.'

Callaghan nodded.

'Exactly,' he said. 'I feel the same way about Miss Varette. If she hadn't died, she might have been able to talk about Lionel — quite a bit. But she died, so that's that. She was a nice woman — a beautiful one, a clever woman.'

Gringall said: 'So they tell me. It was a damn' shame that she had to snuff out like that. There has to be a helluva motive for snuffing a good-looking girl like she was.'

'Quite,' said Callaghan. He blew another smoke ring — a beautiful smoke ring. 'I'm not half so curious about her now,' he said. 'Ever since you told me about the prints on the typewriter — about her being a touch typist and using all her fingers to type with, I mean.'

Gringall nodded.

'Well . . . I'll be getting along.'

Callaghan got up. He said:

'It's been nice seeing you. Come in and have some more chocolate cake some time.' He stubbed out his cigarette. 'If and when we find Lionel,' he said, '*if and when*, well . . . if I think that there's anything you ought to know I'll get in touch. But somehow I don't think that you'll have to be bothered. In the meantime I'll remember what you said about things that are equal to each other being equal to the same thing. I think that's rather a nice thought . . . maybe.'

Gringall was at the door. He said:

'Fancy — nice thought in this den of iniquity. I suppose you've a cellar somewhere where you keep the bodies?'

'No,' said Callaghan. 'We keep 'em on the roof. It's nice and cold up there and they're good company for the fire watchers.'

Gringall went out.

Callaghan lit another cigarette. He got up, took his hat and coat from the stand, put them on. Outside the telephone rang. Effie Thompson put her head round the door.

She said: 'It's Nikolls.'

Callaghan took up the receiver. He said:

'Well, Windy?'

Nikolls said: 'I got tabs on this bird – Milta, I mean. There's a woman porter here at Rufus Court – a baby with a helluva hip line. I just been gettin' to work on her, an' did she react or did she?'

Callaghan said: 'What about Milta?'

'Milta's goin' out,' said Nikolls. 'He's goin' out to dinner. He's comin' back some time after one o'clock tonight. He's asked for his fire to be kept in an' some cold supper set out. So I reckon he's on ice for a bit. What do I do now?'

'You can lay off,' said Callaghan. 'And go easy with that woman porter.'

'That's whata I been doin',' said Nikolls. 'This dame is a mine of information. She goes off at eight o'clock tonight an' I'm takin' her to the movies. I reckon once I get this dame in the back row in the dark I'll find out a helluva lot. When I'm workin' on a case nothin' stops me. . . .'

Callaghan said: 'If the woman porter has got any sense she will. I suppose you'll have the nerve to charge up the cinema seats to office expenses?'

'Why not?' said Nikolls. 'If that don't come under "investigation" what the hell does. I'll be seein' you.'

Callaghan hung up. He went into the outer office.

He said: 'Effie, you can go home. Maybe I shall be back tomorrow. Maybe not. I'm going to Norton Fitzwarren now. You'd better telephone Miss Wilbery and tell her I'm on my way. I ought to make it by nine.'

'Very good,' said Effie. She picked up the telephone.

Callaghan went out. When the door closed behind him, she said to herself:

'Miss Wilbery . . . Miss Leonore Wilbery . . . the beautiful Miss Wilbery . . . damn Miss Wilbery.'

She felt a lot better.

11

Enter Lionel

The Jaguar was doing a steady sixty-five. Callaghan noted with appreciation the moonlight on the long road, drew deeply at his cigarette, thought about Gringall. Gringall was no fool – certainly no fool.

Callaghan thought back through the years, resuscitated in his memory the times he had been up against Gringall on other and perhaps not so important matters. Those had been in the piping times of peace, when murder was merely murder, blackmail merely blackmail; when there were no other strings attached. Callaghan thought that in those days he and Gringall had spent most of their time being 'clever' with each other. He thought that the score was fairly equal. But Gringall was being more clever now than he had ever been before. He was putting it up to Callaghan. He was asking Callaghan to see something through that he, Gringall, could not see through *because* he was a policeman.

Callaghan remembered Gringall's words: 'The devil of being a police-officer,' Gringall had said, 'is that you've got to prove things – you've *got* to *prove* things. Sometimes you can get away with a half-proof, but when you haven't even got a half-proof, when you've got nothing you can't do a thing. Sometimes it's damned difficult. You know, you are certain, and you can't do anything, because you can't prove what you know.' Gringall had said that. Gringall had said something else too. He said that things that are equal to the same thing are equal to each other. Cryptic? Possibly – but Gringall had never under-rated Callaghan's intelligence. Gringall had meant that in this case he and Callaghan were equal to the same thing; that therefore they were equal to each other. And what was the thing that they were both equal to. They were both Englishmen.

Gringall had said nothing, not even the merest hint, about Callaghan's illegal activities in the Wilbery case, about the framing of D'Ianazzi, the stealing of D'Ianazzi's passport. Gringall accepted those things because the commission of those acts was in effect helping him. He knew they were helping him. He knew that Callaghan knew they were helping him.

Right from the start Gringall had made it obvious that Doria Varette was being thrown at Callaghan Investigations, knowing that Callaghan would know that the things that Doria Varette asked Callaghan Investigations to do might in certain circumstances have been done by the police, but in these circumstances – the circumstances of the Wilbery case – it was necessary that someone unofficial should do them because someone unofficial could do things that a policeman could not do. Callaghan hoped he would be able to do those things.

He swung the car off the main road, cut down his speed as he negotiated the secondary road, with its twists and turns, that ran past the great iron gates of Deeplands. The gates were open – a good omen, thought Callaghan.

He put the car in the garage, walked round to the front entrance, pulled the bell-pull. Far in the recesses of the house he heard the jingle of the old-fashioned bell.

When the doors were opened and he went in, Leonore was standing on the other side of the hallway. She was standing beneath a shaded wall lamp. Callaghan, looking quickly at her, thought that the adjective breath-taking was one easily applied to Leonore.

His eyes swept over her. She wore a black velvet dinner frock with tight-fitting sleeves – a frock that lost nothing by the severity of its line. A string of pearls was about her throat. The hall firelight caught the colour of her flesh-coloured silk stockings showing against black satin court shoes. The light from the wall lamp gave a sheen to the green combs which held back her brunette hair.

The butler took Callaghan's things, went away. Leonore came forward. She said:

'There's dinner if you want it. I didn't wait. I thought you might be late.'

'I don't want dinner, thanks,' said Callaghan. 'I want to talk.'

'Very well,' she said. 'Shall we go into the library? I'm having coffee there.'

Callaghan nodded. He lit a cigarette, followed her into the oak-panelled library, watched her as she sat by the side of the fire and began to pour coffee. He asked:

'How's Mrs Wilbery?'

'She's gone away,' said Leonore. 'I sent her away. She's staying with friends. I didn't want her to be here. . . .'

'Why not?' asked Callaghan.

She looked at him. He thought her eyes were a little scared. She said:

'I don't know. I feel awfully worried – rather frightened. All this business about Lionel, which started almost as a sort of bad joke which we had experienced before, which seemed not to matter very much, now seems frightening – rather awful. . . .'

Callaghan noticed that the slim fingers which held the handle of the coffee pot were unsteady, that the pot itself was shaking a little. He smiled wryly.

He said: 'You need a drink.'

'Do you think so?' she said. She smiled suddenly. Callaghan thought that her smile was like the sun coming out. She asked: 'Is that your remedy for being scared?'

'It's a damn' good one,' said Callaghan. 'When in doubt have a drink. If you have enough you either don't care what happens or you acquire sufficient brains to think something out.'

She raised her eyebrows.

'It seems that you haven't been caring what happens,' she said. 'There is a bruise on one side of your face. Have you been in the wars?'

Callaghan said: 'No, I always keep out of wars. When things get really tough I have a habit of disappearing. I got the bruise from a lamp-post in the black-out. Very annoying, the black-out.'

He went to the table. She handed him his coffee cup. He said:

'I want to talk to you about Lionel. I think it's time we begin to be frank about Lionel. I mean by that I don't think it's going to be any good if anybody tries to be clever with anybody else – if you get what I mean.'

She smiled. She said:

'You mean you don't want me to tell you any lies?'

'Correct,' said Callaghan. 'Not only do I want you not to tell me lies, but I'd prefer that you told me the whole truth. Sometimes half the truth is as good as a lie . . . "The whole truth and nothing but the truth."' Callaghan blew a smoke ring. 'Whoever it was that evolved the oath that a witness takes in a court of law knew his groceries, as Nikolls would say.'

She said: 'I like Mr Nikolls. There's something very refreshing about him. He's always cheerful. His humour is quite irresistible.'

Callaghan said: 'You'd be surprised.'

He looked at his watch. Nikolls, he imagined, would be seeing the woman porter home to Rufus Court. He wondered whether she had found Nikolls' humour irresistible.

Leonore said: 'What about Lionel? What is it you wanted to know?'

'Only this,' said Callaghan. 'Do you think when he came to Deeplands three days before Doria Varette was killed, that he came here merely to see you? Do you think he might have come here to see anybody else in the neighbourhood? For instance, do you think he came here to see Mrs Wilbery?'

'I know he didn't come here to see mother,' she said. 'He wanted money. He knew he wouldn't get it from mother. You know, he's had an awful lot from her. She said she wouldn't let him have any more. I think he came here because he was desperate too, because he felt he was sort of hunted. I think he wanted to see me.'

Callaghan said: 'But he thought he'd get money from you, didn't he?'

'He knew I'd give him what I had,' she answered. 'But he knew that wouldn't be much. I hadn't very much to give him. I gave him fifteen pounds. I said I'd try and get some more.'

'What did he say to that?' said Callaghan. 'Did he suggest that he'd come back for more?'

'No,' said Leonore. 'I got the impression that he wasn't coming back here, that he was going somewhere else – that he wanted to get away.'

'But he needed money,' said Callaghan. 'Don't you think it was on the cards that if Lionel wanted money desperately he'd have gone to Milta Haragos for it. After all Milta was a friend of Lionel's. He sympathised with Lionel about the Varette business. Sabine was sorry because of Varette starting Lionel on drugs. Don't you think that if Lionel had wanted to get away from Varette they'd have helped him?'

'Yes,' she said. 'I had the idea – I don't know why – that he would go and see Milta, that Milta would help him. That's why I wasn't worrying about money.'

Callaghan said: 'You and Lionel have always been rather friendly haven't you? Apart from the fact that you're brother and sister. Do you think he'll write to you?'

'I don't know,' she said. 'I don't see why he should. We used to be very good friends in the old days.'

Callaghan asked: 'What was Lionel like in the old days?'

'Quite nice,' she said. 'He was always a little bit odd about poetry. He always believed he was going to be a great poet, but beyond that he used to do the normal things. He played tennis, he played quite a good game of golf, and he and I used to have good times together. We used to go to parties. Then he changed. In the old days when he was away from home he used to write to mother at least once a week. Sometimes he would write to me two or three times in a month, telling me what he was doing, what his hopes – his ambitions – were. Lionel was quite a one for writing letters. When we were children he used to leave notes for me in a place we called our pillar box – a crack in the roof of the old summer-house that used to stand – it's fallen down now – right in the middle of the copse on the far side of the flower garden. But suddenly – and we never discovered the reason – Lionel ceased to be a good correspondent.'

Callaghan said: 'I suppose that was when he took to drinking. I've never known a really consistent drunkard to be a good letter-writer.' He lit a fresh cigarette. 'About this manuscript of his,' he said, 'this last book of poetry, you've got it. Where is it?'

She said: 'It's in the bookcase in my flat in Welbeck Street, but I promised Lionel –'

'I know,' said Callaghan, 'you promised Lionel you wouldn't produce it until he'd cleared all this business up. At the same time it might tell me something about Lionel. I'd like to see it. I'd like to have those poems, to read them.'

She said: 'I gave my word to Lionel.'

'Quite,' said Callaghan grimly. 'You gave your word to Lionel before somebody killed Doria Varette. You're not being very helpful, are you?'

She said: 'If you think it'd help I'll get the manuscript for you. I'll go up to town tomorrow and get it. You know I'd do anything that would help.' She sighed. 'It's rather awful, isn't it?' she said. 'This not being able to find Lionel and this terrible murder hanging over us all like a cloud. I do wish we could get some news of him.'

Callaghan said: 'I shouldn't worry. Lionel will turn up some time. Everybody turns up some time.'

She got up. She stood in front of the fire, looking gravely at him. She said:

'I suppose you have got some plan – otherwise you wouldn't have come down here. What are you going to do?'

Callaghan said: 'I'm not sure, but I think I'm going to have a talk with Sabine.'

'You think that'll help?' she asked.

Callaghan said: 'It might. I'll know when I've had it.'

She nodded. She said:

'I'm going to bed now. I'm tired. I expect I'll see you to-morrow.'

There was a pause. She was about to say something else. She was still looking at him with grave eyes. She stopped herself speaking.

Callaghan said: 'Go to bed and sleep. Don't worry. Nothing is ever quite as bad as we think it's going to be. Good-night.'

She smiled at him. At the doorway she said:

'I hope you didn't want mother for anything. You didn't mind my sending her away?'

'No,' said Callaghan. 'I think it's a good idea.'

She asked quickly: 'Why?'

'I don't know,' said Callaghan. 'But I think it's a good thing sometimes to clear the decks for action, don't you?'

She smiled – a slow sad smile. She said:

'So Mr Callaghan is proposing to go into action?'

He grinned at her.

'Right,' he said. 'This Wilbery business is hanging about too much. Somebody's got to start something. I think I'll start it. Good-night.'

He closed the door softly behind her.

Callaghan sat looking into his bedroom fire. The ash-tray bore the stubs of innumerable cigarettes. He yawned. He remembered suddenly that he had had no breakfast, no lunch, no dinner. Nothing except tea. He came to the conclusion that the amount of rye he had drunk the day before must be responsible for such energy as he had.

He began to think about Sabine. He grinned. Sabine had something else besides looks. Sabine was clever, thought Callaghan. Sabine would be an expert at knowing just how much to say, just how much not to say. He felt a pleasurable anticipation of his interview with her. He thought it might be amusing. He threw the stub of his last cigarette into the fire, undressed, got into bed.

He lay there, his hands folded behind his head, looking up in the darkness, thinking about his conversation with Leonore, thinking about Lionel. His mind came back to her description of Lionel in the old days. Most sisters had pleasurable memories of their brothers – when they were young. Callaghan visualized Leonore and Lionel on the golf course, on the tennis court, at parties, leaving notes for each other in the old summer-house. . . .

The old summer-house – Callaghan swung his leg out of bed, began to dress quickly.

Callaghan walked down the broad path that led across the main lawn at the back of Deeplands. The moon, slowly emerging from behind a bank of clouds, gave him sufficient light to see, vaguely, into the near distance. At the bottom of the lawn, a low wall divided it from what might be the flower gardens. He wished that he had made himself better acquainted with the lay-out of the Wilbery estate.

Callaghan reached the wall, looked over. On the other side was the flower garden, a garden of formal pattern, bisected with paths, a sundial set in the middle. A pleasant place, he thought, when it had the sun on it. The sort of place that women in summer gowns used to take tea in, and talk to the Rector – *that* sort of place.

A cold wind was blowing. It blew in great gusts, heralding rain. Callaghan turned up his coat collar, pulled his soft hat well down over his eyes, decided he could not be bothered to find the gate, scrambled over the wall. He took the main path across the wide garden. On the other side, at the end of the flower beds, sloping down towards the little rivulet that lay a mile to the west, was a small wood. A path ran through it. Callaghan, safe in the darkness of the trees, lit a cigarette before continuing on his careful walk.

It was very quiet. There was no sound except that of the wind in the trees. He compared the quiet of this part of the country with the noises of the town – the war noises – the drone of high-flying bombers, the roar of anti-aircraft guns, the swish of incendiaries.

The world was a hell of a place, thought Callaghan, a hell of a place. Wars and rumours of wars. Yet underneath the great battles that were raging over the surface of the earth, were the smaller battles, the sort of guerilla warfare in which he, Callaghan, was engaged at that moment; the sort of guerilla warfare in which, for once, he, the 'private investigator' – that title which covered such a multitude of activities, cleverness, slickness – and Gringall, the police-officer, found themselves for once allies.

The trees began to thin out. Callaghan came to a little clearing. On the other side two separate paths ran through the coppice. This, he thought, was the sort of place in which children would play. He crossed the clearing took the path on the left. It was a narrow path and the thick bushes and shrubs bounding it pressed against him, damping his clothes.

He came out on the other side of the coppice. Here was another small clearing sloping down sharply on the left of him and more gradually to the right. Half-way down the slope was a thick plantation. A little path ran through it. He followed the path. Twenty yards down he found what he was looking for.

The summer-house, built, he imagined, by Victorian hands, stood, surrounded by shrubs and bushes. Three or four wooden steps, worn and mildewed, led up to it. One end of the wooden roof, farthest from him, too heavy for the rotten wooden supports, had half fallen. One side of it hung precariously.

He went up the steps, stood inside the mouldy structure. It smelt of damp and rotten wood, the scent mixing with the clean smells of earth and dewy plants that came from the outside. He switched on his torch, shading it with his hand to keep the light within a small circle. He directed the light against the good end of the roof. He saw that, in the corner, where one support had pulled away from its neighbour, was a black space. He crossed over and put up his hand, feeling in the cavity. There was nothing, but as he withdrew his hand his fingers encountered something that felt like a window cord.

Callaghan got a grip of the cord and pulled. From inside the hole came a tinny noise; then, as he pulled harder a box came out. He caught it as it fell.

It was a small tin box of the size used, years ago, for the packing of a hundred cigarettes. It was rusty and dented. There was sufficient of the lettering on the lid to enable him to decipher the remains of the words 'Ogdens Guinea Gold.' He grinned. He remembered smoking Ogdens Guinea Gold when he was a boy – in those far-off days when a cigarette surreptitiously smoked was an adventure.

He pulled at the lid. The box opened easily. Inside was an envelope.

Callaghan stood in the middle of the uneven wooden floor of the summer-house, the opened tin box in his right hand, in his left the torch with its shaded light falling directly on the envelope. On the envelope were scrawled the words: 'To Leo.' He smiled. Within that envelope, possibly, was the ending – or the beginning – of the Wilbery case.

He took the letter out of the tin box, put the box on the floor. He moved to the corner of the summer-house, stood in the apex of the triangle formed by the two good walls. He took the piece of notepaper out of the unsealed envelope. He read:

'It's no good, Leo dear. It just isn't any good. Life can be such a mess, can't it? In spite of us or because of us, I don't know which. I'm in a hell of a jam. Varette has been riding me like hell, putting on the screw until I can't stand it any longer. I don't know what I can do. I shall see Varette. I shall do the best I can. In any event I've got to find some way to finish this fearful business off – even if it brings disgrace on you and the family. I've got to do it.
                                                    'Lionel.'

Callaghan put the note back in the envelope. He put the envelope in his pocket. He pushed the tin box with its cord back into the old-time post-box of the Wilbery children. He put his torch back in his pocket, went out of the summer-house. He walked round the edge of the broken-down veranda, stood on the far side, his hands in his pockets, thinking about Lionel.

That was the sort of note that Lionel would write. That was Lionel that was. Callaghan's lip curled. Lionel Wilbery, near poet, near drunkard, near dope-fiend, near everything. The weak thing pretending to be strong, hoping all the time against hope, rather like Wilkins Micawber, that something would turn up, or somebody would turn up, somebody who might undo all the lousiness, the rottenness that Lionel had started – the rottenness that once started, could not be finished.

Callaghan threw his cigarette stub away, took out his cigarette case. As he stood, lighting the cigarette, his head bent forward towards his cupped hands about the flame of the lighter, a sudden gust of wind blew off his hat.

He went after it. He took two steps forward, slipped and half-fell, half-rolled, down the shallow gully, which was hidden by the thick bushes on its edge.

The gully was wet and muddy from recent rain. Callaghan retrieved his hat ruefully, cursed comprehensively, looking at the soiled black felt in the uncertain half light of the moon. He cleaned it with his handkerchief as best he could, prepared to climb back to the summer-house.

He took one step, caught his foot and fell. He got up quickly, fumbled for his torch, flashed it on the thing he had fallen over.

Callaghan whistled softly. He stood looking at what remained of Lionel Wilbery. He knew it was Lionel. There was no mistaking that. That body lying there – a nasty enough sight – *had* to be that of Lionel.

Callaghan sighed. It was an odd sort of sigh. Then he began to grin – a little ruefully. Callaghan Investigations had, once more, brought a case to a successful conclusion. Callaghan Investigations had found Lionel Wilbery. . . .

He drew on his cigarette, filling his lungs with the tobacco smoke. So this was the method selected by Lionel to 'finish this fearful business off.' And the finish was definite – very definite. As definite as suicide always is.

Lionel had killed himself. There was no doubt of that. Looking at what remained of the long, rather thin face, Callaghan wondered what last hopelessness had driven Lionel to this end. Having got such money as he could from Leonore, having failed to 'go away' to wherever it was he had planned to go, he had come to this. Callaghan thought that something must have prevented Lionel from getting away. Money probably. And that would mean that he had been unsuccessful with Milta. Milta had been stern. Milta had refused the money.

The body lay on its side half doubled up. Behind the head was a rotten tree stump. Callaghan could reconstruct the final scene easily enough. Lionel had left the note in the children's 'pillar-box' in the summer-house. But when he had left it he had not been without hope. There was still a chance. He would see Varette. He would try something there. Probably afterwards he had seen Milta and Milta had refused to help. Lionel had come back to Deeplands. He had come back possibly to see Leonore once again. Or possibly merely to spend his last moments at the summer-house – the place where he had once known happiness. Then he had come down into the gully, into the thick bushes, had sat on the ground, leaning against the old tree stump. Then he had shot himself.

And that was that.

Callaghan put his handkerchief on the ground by the side of Lionel and knelt on it. He put on his gloves. He began to search through the pockets. There was nothing.

He got up and stood, the light from the torch shining through his fingers.

The pistol was still gripped in Lionel's right hand. He had shot himself through the right side of the head. Just behind the temple. Callaghan put his gloved hand underneath the head and moved it a little. There was no exit hole for the bullet. So the bullet was still in the head.

Very gently Callaghan moved the head back to its original position. Then he started on the grisly business of getting the pistol out of Lionel's right hand. The spasm of death had loosed the grip on the butt a little, but the hand and fingers were stiff in *rigor mortis*. It took ten minutes work to get the pistol free.

He looked at it. It was a .28 Spanish automatic. Callaghan slipped out the ammunition clip and examined it. There were nine cartridges left in the clip, which took ten. Lionel had used one on himself. The rest of the ammunition was intact. Callaghan smiled a little.

He sat down on the tree stump with his back to the body. He picked up his damp and muddy handkerchief, and with a fairly clean corner of it began to clean the butt of the pistol, to remove Lionel's fingerprints. When he had finished he sat, looking into the darkness in front of him. He was grinning. He was beginning to get an idea . . . a whole lot of ideas . . . excellent ideas.

He got up. Walking carefully he moved away from the body along the gully. He put his feet carefully on the ground, making his footmarks as light as possible. He worked his way out of the gully and into the wood at the top. He switched on the torch, shading it carefully with his fingers. He began to search.

After five minutes he found what he was looking for. A short, broken branch of a tree, an excellent natural club. The very thing that a man, about to be attacked, might pick up for his defence.

The moon had gone in. The wind had dropped. It began to rain. A storm was coming. The thought pleased Callaghan. Sufficient rain would turn the bottom of the gully into a morass of mud, would obliterate every mark of his descent and footsteps.

He returned to the body. He crouched by the side of it, forced the end of the broken branch into and between the

214

stiff fingers of the right hand, the hand that had held the pistol.

He straightened up, put his torch into his pocket, walked out of the gully. The rain was beginning to descend in torrents. Callaghan, his overcoat soaked, walked quickly past the summer-house, through the coppice, through the flower garden, climbed over the wall, crossed the lawn, slipped into the house by the side entrance.

He went quickly and quietly to his room. He hung up his wet overcoat in the wardrobe, changed his lounge suit for another, put on fresh shoes. He put the damp clothes, the muddy shoes into a drawer and locked it. He took out a dark blue raincoat, put on his wet hat and went quietly down to the hall.

He stood there listening. There was not a sound. Deeplands was as quiet as a grave . . . as Lionel's grave – which was a gully. Callaghan went out quietly by the side door.

He walked round to the garage, pulled open the door, started up the Jaguar. He backed out on to the drive, swung the car round, drove down the drive on to the road.

Callaghan brought the Jaguar to a standstill at the telephone box on the main Taunton road. He went into the box, fumbled for sixpences and pennies, dialled 'Operator,' asked for the telephone number of Rufus Court, St John's Wood.

He smoked nearly a whole cigarette while he was waiting for the number, hoping that there would be no *blitz* in London at that moment to hold up telephone communication.

The operator said: 'Here's your number.'

Callaghan dropped the cigarette stub from his mouth. He said: 'Is that the night porter at Rufus Court?'

A hearty voice replied: 'Yeah . . . it is . . . sort of. . . . What can I do for you?'

Callaghan grinned. It was Nikolls!

He said: 'So you went back with the woman porter?'

'Yeah,' said Nikolls. 'What do you think? Anyway, you'd be wrong. I been hangin' around here because Milta is back. He rang down here an' told the porter he was expecting a telephone call. I stuck around to plug in on it. The calls have gotta go through the switchboard down here, see? A swell setting. So I told the girlfriend to take an hour off an' I'd look after things. She's a honey,' said Nikolls. 'She'd do anything for me . . . well . . . practically anything.'

'All right,' said Callaghan. 'Well, you may stay there. There's going to be a call coming through to Milta. The call will be from Sabine Haragos. She'll telephone Milta after I've seen her.'

'When you gonna see her?' asked Nikolls.

'I'm going there now,' said Callaghan. 'I'm talking from a box on the Taunton road. Do you know where The Vale is?'

'Yeah,' said Nikolls. 'You can't miss it. Go back an' get on the Deeplands road. Go right past Deeplands an' take the first on the right. Half a mile along you come to The Vale. It's the only house an' it's white. A nice place.'

'Thanks,' said Callaghan. He looked at his wrist-watch. 'It's just before twelve,' he said. 'I'm probably coming back to town to-night. With luck I'll get away pretty soon. I ought to be in London by about three-thirty. Stay where you are until three o'clock and then go back to the office and wait for me. Have you got that?'

'I got it,' said Nikolls. 'It sounds as if somethin' is happenin'. Maybe we're gonna find Lionel.'

'You never know,' said Callaghan.

He hung up.

Callaghan turned into the driveway that led to the front door of The Vale.

The Vale, modestly described as a cottage, was a low rambling house, set in fair-sized grounds, standing back from the road. The house had atmosphere. Callaghan thought with a grin that Sabine – the artistic Sabine – had probably had the choosing of it.

He rang the bell and waited. The rain had stopped. The moon was coming up. Callaghan was glad that he would have the light of it for his drive back to London.

Two or three minutes went past. He rang the bell again. Eventually he heard the noise of a chain being taken off the door and the door unlocked. Then it opened. He found himself looking at a little old woman whose face reminded him of a wizened apple.

He said: 'My name's Callaghan. It's very urgent that I should see Miss Haragos.'

The old woman said: 'She's in bed. I don't think she'd want to see anyone.'

'Maybe you don't,' said Callaghan cheerfully. 'All the same, I'm going to see her – one way or another. So you'd better get a ripple on.'

The old woman muttered something under her breath. She turned away and disappeared into the dark recesses of the hall. Callaghan followed her, closed the door behind him.

He stood in the darkness for a minute or two, then produced his torch. He switched it on, found an electric switch, turned the hall light on. He sat down on a carved chair, lit a cigarette.

After a while the old woman reappeared. She said:

'Miss Haragos is coming down. She says, will you wait?' Callaghan nodded. She went away.

He looked about him. The hall was large, furnished in good taste. Most of the furniture was old and the walls were decorated with trophies of one sort or another. On the wall opposite Callaghan there hung the high fur red-topped cap of a Cossack officer. He could see that the badge on the front – the old Imperial Russian Eagle – had been recently polished. Under the cap two Cossack knouts were suspended on the wall. Callaghan thought they were appropriate indications.

Sabine came down the wide stairway. Her flat,

beautiful face was relaxed and smiling. She wore a long red silk Chinese coat embroidered with gold dragons. Her Medusa-like hair was tied with a red ribbon. Beneath the Chinese coat her long peach satin nightgown trailed over red satin sandals. He noted that her toe nails were painted gold to-night instead of the red lacquer of their last meeting.

She stepped off the bottom stair. She walked across the hall-way with one hand outstretched. Callaghan thought that Sabine was good . . . damned good.

She said: 'So-o eet ees Mister Callagha-an. . . . The clever Callagha-an. The onscroopulous Callagha-an . . . steel looking for our poor Lionel. . . .'

She held out her hand, Callaghan took it. He thought it was cold and felt rather like a damp fish. Her fingers glittered with rings. He wondered whether she had put them on for his benefit or whether she went to bed in them.

He said amiably: 'I want to talk to you. I shan't keep you long. And I haven't much time, because I've a lot to do tonight.'

'Co-ome thees wa-ay,' said Sabine.

She led the way to a room off the hall. Callaghan followed her. The room was still warm and the embers in the fireplace were not yet dead.

She stood in front of the fireplace. She smiled at him. It was a long, slow smile. Callaghan thought she looked like a very attractive devil. He thought that under different circumstances Sabine might have been interesting, if dangerous, to know.

She said: 'Alwa-ays, when you talk to me you ha-ave to go somewhere else – to do something else. I should like to talk to you – a lo-ong talk . . . one da-ay.'

Callaghan said: 'Maybe you'll get the chance, Sabine. In the meantime I want you to tell me where Milta is. I've got to see him. I want to talk to him about Lionel.'

'Milta ees in London,' she said. 'At the fla-at in Rufus Court. He will like to see you. He likes you. He will tell you anything you wa-ant to know.'

'Excellent,' said Callaghan.

They stood, looking at each other. She said:

'Well . . . my friend . . .?'

Callaghan said: 'There's going to be a lot of trouble when we do find Lionel. There's going to be a lot of trouble about that book of poetry he wrote – the one you tried so hard to get.'

She shrugged her shoulders.

'I did not try so ha-ard, my friend,' she said. 'Why should I? I was interested in the book. I was gla-ad to help for eet to be published. Beyond that . . .' She shrugged her shoulders again.

'You're a damned liar,' said Callaghan pleasantly. 'And you know it, Sabine. And you know I know it. And you know I can't prove it. You wanted that book like the devil. Lionel pulled a fast one on you when he wouldn't hand it over unless Milta gave him some money – enough money to make a getaway. But Milta wanted the book first, and he didn't know where it was. Neither of you knew until Leonore came here the other night and you got her to talk.'

Sabine smiled.

'You spik so strangely, my friend,' she said. 'I don' understa-and when you say *got* her to ta-alk. . . .'

'She was nervous and upset,' said Callaghan. 'You gave her *marihuana* cigarettes. Women always talk when they smoke reefers – especially when they're not used to them. I saw her afterwards, looking like nothing on earth and on the verge of hysterics. But let's skip that. It doesn't matter. She wouldn't give you the book and didn't tell you where it was.'

Sabine said: 'I thought you wa-anted to ta-alk about Lionel. What ees eet you wa-ant to know. You seem to know everything. . . .'

'I know a lot,' said Callaghan. 'But there are one or two things I don't know. But they don't really matter. I've been wise to you for some time, Sabine.'

'A-ah,' said Sabine gently. 'Wise Callagha-an . . .

onscroopulous Callagha-an. Tell me, my friend, how a-are you wise to me?'

Callaghan grinned.

'You knew Leonore would bring me along to see you,' said Callaghan. 'You knew that when they thought that Lionel had really disappeared they'd fix for me to see you. Because you were his friend. And you were all ready for me, weren't you? Right through this case one thing has stuck out a mile. Every bit of information that showed that Varette was the person who started Lionel on drugs came from you. *You* told me. *You* told Leonore. Why? The answer is easy. *You* started Lionel on drugs.'

She looked dreamy. She said:

'Did I? Pliz tell me why I do tha-at?'

Callaghan laughed.

'You wouldn't know, would you?' he said.

He took out his cigarette case. Extracted a cigarette, lit it.

'The game is up, Sabine,' he said. 'You and Milta were on a good wicket. You'd never have been caught out except for one thing – just an odd chance. When I came out to The Dene, I ran into Santos D'Ianazzi. That wouldn't have meant a thing to me except that I'd met him the night before. I met him outside Doria Varette's flat. He'd gone round there in the black-out to see her. He was probably going to finish her off that night. But she was too quick for him. She slammed the door in his face, and when he came out he found me waiting for him. If I hadn't met D'Ianazzi then you might have got away with all this. In spite of the fact that you've been suspect for some time.'

Sabine smiled.

'Suspect . . . what ees tha-at?' she said softly. 'Een thees country you ha-ave to prove things, my friend.'

'You're telling me,' said Callaghan. 'That's what the police were up against. They couldn't prove a thing, not one goddam thing. D'Ianazzi murdered Varette on your or Milta's instructions. She *had* to be murdered. Because

Lionel had told her. So she had to be put out of the way quick before she could talk. If we could only have laid hands on D'Ianazzi, things would have been up with you. But he got away. You've been lucky, Sabine.'

She said: 'I do not oondersta-and you, my friend. I do-on't know wha-at you a-are talking about. . . .'

Callaghan grinned to himself. Sabine was congratulating herself on the fact that D'Ianazzi had got away, that there was still no evidence. He said, lying glibly:

'I'm prepared to do a deal with you and Milta, Sabine. If you like to let me know where Lionel is we'll hang all this on to him. We might even hang the Varette murder on to him.'

She said: 'Lionel keeled Varette. I am sure of tha-at. He ha-ated her. Lionel wa-as nevaire any good. He ca-ame to Deeplands and go-ot money from his sister. He ca-ame here and tried to get money from Milta. When Milta would not give him any he told Milta that he would keel himself. He said he would shoot himself. Milta to-old us afterwards. He to-old every one. All the serva-ant here – who are Engleesh – can pro-ove tha-at Milta to-old us tha-at Lionel had said he would keel himself. But of course he did not. Lionel did not have the courage to do that.'

Marvellous, thought Callaghan. So Lionel had told Milta that he would kill himself. And Milta had told Sabine and others that Lionel had intended to do this. Excellent, thought Callaghan.

He said: 'Where do you think Lionel is now?'

Sabine shrugged her shoulders.

'He will be in hiding with so-ome wo-oman,' she said. 'Alwa-ays so-ome wo-oman will try and look after Lionel. He was like tha-at. I tried to look after heem. . . . I don't know where he ees. I don't care. Why should I?'

Callaghan said: 'Quite. Well, I'll go and see Milta – some time tomorrow afternoon or evening. Perhaps he can help me.'

'Perha-aps,' said Sabine. 'But when you ta-alk to heem,

be more po-olite tha-an you ha-ave to me. He has a queek temper. He would thra-ash you eef you are rude to heem.'

'Quite,' said Callaghan. He grinned at her. 'I'll handle him with kid gloves,' he said.

She yawned. She said:

'I am tired and I am bored. I do not wa-ant to ta-alk any more.'

Callaghan said: 'All right. Don't let's talk any more. Goodbye, Sabine.'

She smiled. It was a sarcastic smile.

'Why not *au revoir*?' she asked.

'Because it's not going to be *au revoir*,' said Callaghan. 'I shan't see you again. I shan't have the chance. The net's closing in, Sabine. And you'll look like a cold wet fish struggling at the bottom of it. A painted flat-faced fish. Your time's nearly up, Sabine.'

She yawned again.

'Who says so-o?' she asked.

'I do,' said Callaghan. He threw his cigarette into the fireplace, turned and walked out of the room. She heard the front door slam.

Sabine walked to the table and took a cigarette from a box. It was a thin, brown cigarette. She lit it, drew the smoke down into her lungs. She went to the telephone on the other side of the room. She asked for a Primrose-London number. She waited, smoking coolly.

When she got her number she began to talk. She talked quickly and quietly in Russian.

All the time she was smiling.

12

The Eleventh Commandment

The Jaguar ate up the road. The speedometer was reg-
istering a steady sixty-five. Once or twice on taut corners
the car had skidded sickeningly on the wet road surface.
But Callaghan did not notice. His eyes were glued on the
road ahead. Between his lips a dead cigarette tasted like
dead cigarettes taste. He did not notice that either. His
mind was busy with the eleventh commandment.

'Thou shalt not be found out.' A nice commandment. A
good commandment for all those people who specialized
in breaking the other ten. A first-class commandment for
people like Milta Haragos. And Milta was a specialist on
the eleventh commandment. Milta, knowing what he was
going to do, knowing what he was up against, had prepared the ground for action, had prepared his plan of
campaign, as carefully as any wise general. Milta had
known what he was up against. He had assessed the
values of the M.I. Departments, of the Special Branch, of
people like Gringall.

But one thing he had not prepared for – one person. He
had not prepared for Doria Varette. He had not believed
that the M.I. Departments, the Special Branch, the
Gringalls of life, had ammunition like Doria Varette – the
woman who had been 'put in' to get next to Lionel Wilbery.

Callaghan imagined the scene of the 'putting in' of
Doria Varette. Gringall, sitting at his desk, drawing fruit
on the blotting pad. On the other side of the desk, sitting
in the big leather arm-chair – the best bit of furniture in
Gringall's room – would be Varette. Varette, who was
beautiful, and who had that indefinable something that
gets over with any man, that something which makes a

man who likes blondes fall for a brunette. Varette had allure and knew how to use it.

And Varette had been 'put in.' Had agreed to be put in. Had agreed to take a chance. Well, she had taken the chance. And she had seen the job through. Even although she did not know that she had seen it through. Whether she knew it or not, it was because of her that what would happen to Milta, to Sabine, to D'Ianazzi, to Salkey and Wulfie, *would* happen. Through her and the 'unscrupulous' Mr Callaghan – with Chief Detective-Inspector Gringall hovering placidly in the background, marshalling his forces, putting in Varette and then, at the crucial moment, when something had to be done quickly, when guerilla tactics had to be used, throwing Varette at Callaghan, 'putting in' Callaghan as a reinforcement for Varette.

But Milta was a specialist in the eleventh commandment. Milta knew that unless D'Ianazzi talked he was safe. Possibly D'Ianazzi was not able to talk, possibly D'Ianazzi did not know enough to talk. Maybe the pointed-toe Santos had been merely a hewer of wood and a drawer of water, a professional thug put in and paid to do a killing when it was required.

Gringall had traced the notes that Callaghan had planted on Doria Varette, the notes that Nikolls had taken from the unconscious Cuban. Those notes had come from Milta. It was obvious that this was what Gringall had meant. But even this fact constituted no proof. Milta had been financing D'Ianazzi. Milta was the man who was financing D'Ianazzi at The Dene, at the Salem Club and probably at other places. That, Milta would say, in his loud and hearty voice, was the explanation of the two thousand pounds. He would laugh at the suggestion that the money was the consideration for the killing of Varette – which in fact it was.

Callaghan began to think about Doria Varette as a woman. She was a beauty, he thought. It was not right that she should be lying under the earth with her beauty food for worms. The stiletto was not a meet end for a woman who looked like Varette.

But she had taken the chance. She had done her part of the job, and he, Callaghan, would carry it on to its logical conclusion.

Its logical conclusion. . . . Callaghan grinned as he swerved the Jaguar round a bend. He knew what that logical conclusion was. Milta must die. . . . Milta, and possibly Sabine, must die. They must die because Varette had died. And because there was no proof, they must die for something they had not done. A grim jest, thought Callaghan. One that suited his mood at the moment. A delightful idea that, the idea of Milta dying for something he had not done.

He reduced the speed of the Jaguar. He spat the dead cigarette from between his lips, fumbled for another with one hand, found it, lit it. He settled back in the driving seat and pushed the accelerator down hard.

His mind was made up.

Nikolls was lying back in Callaghan's chair. His feet were on Callaghan's desk. A Lucky Strike drooped from between his lips. On the floor, by his side, was the remains of the bottle of Canadian rye, extracted from Callaghan's desk drawer.

The office clock said three-twenty when Callaghan came in. Nikolls moved his feet. He got up ponderously. He said:

'Jeez . . . but you musta got a ripple on. You musta done sixty most of the way!'

'I did,' said Callaghan. He put his hand out for the bottle. He took a long swig, put the bottle down on the desk. He lit a cigarette. Nikolls noticed that his eyes were rimmed with the dark patches of fatigue.

'Listen,' said Callaghan. 'You go out and find Willie the Lace. And don't come back without him. He used to live somewhere in the New Cut. You'll find his address on Effie's card index. You go out and get him. Bring him back here quick. Keep him here until I get back. Have you got that?'

Nikolls said: 'O.K.' He put on his hat. He went out. He moved as quickly and as quietly as big men can – when they want to.

Callaghan went round the desk, sat down in his chair. He lit a cigarette and blew smoke rings. His mouth was dry and acid. He was tired as death.

He got up, went into the outer office. He opened the cabinet in the corner, took out a bottle of eau-de-cologne used by Effie Thompson. He poured it over his hands, rubbed it into his thick hair. The spirit stung his scalp, brought a feeling of freshness.

He went out of the office, down in the lift, out to the Jaguar. He got in, drove slowly round to Welbeck Street.

He stopped the car outside Leonore Wilbery's apartment block. He pushed open the main doors, walked along the passage. He rang the bell marked 'Night Porter' and waited.

After nearly ten minutes the lift came up from the basement. The porter got out. Callaghan looked at him. He was a broad-shouldered man of forty-five. On his coat were four medal ribbons.

Callaghan said: 'My name's Callaghan. I've been sent here by Miss Leonore Wilbery. She lives here, doesn't she?'

'Yes,' said the night porter. 'No. 9 . . . on the first floor.'

Callaghan went on: 'She's asked me to get a book from her bookcase. She wants me to take it to her at Deeplands. I'm going there tomorrow.'

The night porter shook his head. He said decisively: 'I'm sorry, sir, I couldn't let anything go out of Miss Wilbery's flat without authority from her. If you could get her to telephone me or –'

Callaghan said: 'I don't want to argue about it. The matter's urgent. Are you going to let me have the book?'

The night porter began: 'I'm sorry, sir . . .' He stopped abruptly when Callaghan hit him under the jaw. He subsided on the floor by the lift entrance.

Callaghan dragged him into the lift. He went up to the first floor. He stopped the lift, opened the gates, pulled the inert night porter into the passageway. He took off the man's key chain, walked along to No. 9, opened the door, went in. He came out three minutes later. Under his arm was Lionel Wilbery's manuscript.

The night porter was beginning to stir. His eyelids were flicking a little. Callaghan flashed his electric torch on the man's eyes. After a minute they opened. Callaghan smacked the night porter gently across the face – two or three times. He said:

'I'm sorry about this. But I had to have that book. You'll find it's quite all right. I'll get my office to send you round a couple of pounds some time tomorrow. Good-night.'

He got into the lift. Went downstairs.

He drove back to the office.

The office clock said it was four-fifteen. Nikolls came into the office with another man. Callaghan was asleep, with his feet on his desk. He woke up when they came in.

The man behind Nikolls was a short, slim man. He was about five feet four in height. He had a thin, clever, attractive, clean-shaven face. He was well-dressed. A small diamond tie-pin glittered in an expensive tie. His hands were encased in expensive gloves. He carried a black Homburg hat in his hand, and his sleek black hair was pomaded.

Nikolls said: 'I got him. I was damn' lucky. He was goin' away tomorrow.'

Willie the Lace smiled at Callaghan. He showed a nice set of teeth that were studded with platinum stoppings.

Willie the Lace was in the front rank of forgers. He was an expert penman. He had served, in all, fifteen years of his life in prison. Willie the Lace's bank notes had given more trouble to the Bank of England and the police than those of any other expert. He was a supreme craftsman. He was very proud of it.

Callaghan fished out his wallet. He took from it two

fifty-pound notes. They were the two fifty-pound notes that Santos D'Ianazzi had given him on the occasion of their first meeting. He said:

'There's a hundred pounds in this job, Willie. And no strings. You'll never be pulled in for what you're going to do now. I give you my word. You're as safe as houses. And it's an easy job.'

Willie the Lace shrugged his shoulders. He said:

'A hundred's a hundred . . . hey? Dough don't come too easy these days. People ain't flashin' money like they used to. If you say it's all right, it's all right. What's the job?'

Callaghan put his hand in his pocket. He brought out the letter 'To Leo' – the letter he had taken from the tin box in the summer-house at Deeplands. He opened the envelope and took out the sheet of note-paper. He laid it on the desk. Willie the Lace came behind him, looked over his shoulder.

They read Lionel Wilbery's letter to his sister together:

'It's no good, Leo dear. It just isn't any good. Life can be such a mess, can't it? In spite of us or because of us – I don't know which. I'm in a hell of a jam. Varette has been riding me like hell, putting on the screw until I can't stand it any longer. I don't know what I can do. I shall see Varette. I shall do the best I can. In any event I've got to find some way to finish this fearful business off – even if it brings disgrace on you and the family. I've got to do it.
                                                        'Lionel.'

Callaghan said: 'The name "Varette" is mentioned twice in this letter, Willie. I want it taken out. When you've taken it out in the two places you put another word in its place. A word of the same number of letters. Another name – "Haragos."'

'I see,' said Willie the Lace. 'It's got to read: "Haragos has been riding me like hell" in the one place, and in the other place it's got to read: "I shall see Haragos." Is that it . . . hey?'

'That's it,' said Callaghan.

'That's easy,' said Willie. 'I could fake that handwritin' with my backside. It's like a kid's handwritin'. It's a cinch . . . hey?'

Callaghan said: 'Get busy.'

Willie the Lace took off his overcoat. He drew off his expensive gloves. His hands were very white, very well-kept. His fingers were very long and supple. Callaghan got out of his chair. Willie the Lace sat down and took a neat leather case out of his pocket. He opened the case, put it on the desk before him. It contained seven pens, a little folder containing nine nibs – all manufactured by Willie – three bottles of graded isinglass, a little bottle of acid.

He pulled Callaghan's desk lamp closer. He took a small camel-hair brush from the case, dipped it in water from one bottle, acid from another. He put the brush down on the desk and began to rub his hands. He rubbed them until they were warm. He took the acid-dipped brush and started work. Callaghan and Nikolls watched him. They watched the delicate sensitive fingers wielding the brush, using it like a pen, taking out the ink that spelt 'Varette.' They watched the writing disappear; they watched Willie use an isinglass brush to re-surface the paper. They watched him select a nib, select one of sixteen little pills that, mixed with water, made the ink that matched that used by Lionel. They watched him take a piece of Callaghan's note-paper and write the word 'Haragos.' He went on writing the word until nobody – not even Lionel, thought Callaghan – could have known that Lionel had not written it.

Willie the Lace – his hundred pounds in his pocket – had gone away. Callaghan said:

'Did you listen-in on the call from Sabine? Did she come through?'

'Yeah,' said Nikolls. 'She called through all right, but it wasn't any good. She was speakin' some foreign language. An' he never said a thing except a word here an' there.'

'It doesn't matter,' said Callaghan. 'Get on the line to Gringall. I'll give you his number. I want to speak to him. It'a urgent.'

Nikolls went into the outer office. Callaghan could hear him dialling. He lit a cigarette. Leaned his elbows on the desk, rested his head on his hands. The cigarette smoke went into his eyes, making them smart. He cursed, threw the cigarette into the fireplace.

Two or three minutes passed. Then he heard Nikolls talking. Nikolls came into the office. He said:

'He's on the line.'

Callaghan picked up his telephone. He said:

'Gringall, is that you? This is Callaghan. I'm in London. Listen to this: Listen carefully. You've got the Haragos where you want 'em. It's easy.'

Gringall said: 'Is it? How is it easy?'

Callaghan said: 'I've got the book of poems. I don't suppose it's any good to you. I don't suppose anyone on earth could work out the code. But that doesn't matter. You've got 'em on something else. Milta killed Lionel.'

Gringall said: 'The devil he did. It sounds as if you've got something. Tell me some more.'

Callaghan said: 'Leonore Wilbery told me that when she and Lionel were kids they used to leave notes for each other in a summer-house at Deeplands. I took a look. Lionel left a note for her a day or so ago, probably the *next* day after he'd been down there to see her and try and raise money. I've got the note. In it he says that Haragos has been riding him like hell, that he's got to do something, that he's going to see Haragos again. He went to see Haragos. They had a row about something. I think that Lionel threatened that he was going to blow the works and tell the truth – for once. Haragos, after that interview told Sabine, and let the servants know, that Lionel had said he was going to commit suicide. That was a plant. Haragos had made up his mind to finish Lionel.

'After I'd found the note I slipped down a gully at Deeplands – in the ground. I fell over what's left of

Lionel. He'd been shot at close range. He'd got a piece of tree in one hand. It looks to me as if Haragos, having started the rumour that Lionel was going to commit suicide, had waited for him. He knew he'd go back to Deeplands and he knew the way he'd go. Lionel had picked up the piece of tree to try and defend himself when he saw that Milta was going to get tough.'

Gringall said: 'Nice work, Slim . . . nice work . . . If we could hang a murder charge on Haragos. . . . Did you see anything that looked like evidence?'

Callaghan paused as if he were thinking.

'There's a bullet hole in Lionel's head,' he said. 'There's no exit hole. That's all, I think. . . . It was pretty wet in the gully.'

Gringall said: 'Perhaps we can find the gun. Perhaps Haragos has got the gun. But I expect he'd get rid of it.'

'He'll try,' said Callaghan. 'I've had Nikolls planted round at Haragos' place. Sabine came through with a frenzied telephone call in Russian. Maybe Milta will get the wind up and do something silly.'

'I doubt that,' said Gringall. 'That bird's as cool as an ice-house. . . .'

'Why don't you pick him up?' said Callaghan. 'Why don't you pick him up and tell him that Salkey and Wulfie, to save their own skins, have blown the gaff, that they've admitted that D'Ianazzi killed Varette; that they've admitted that D'Ianazzi killed Varette on Milta's instructions; that the two thousand that came off D'Ianazzi came from Milta. Why don't you try that one on him . . .?'

Gringall said: 'I'm a police officer. I can't do that sort of thing.'

Callaghan said: '*I'm* not a police-officer and *I* can. I'm going round to see Milta. It's nearly five o'clock now. Give me a break until five-thirty and then pull him in.'

Gringall said: 'You've got your nerve. All right. I'm going to get a rush call through to the Somersetshire Constabulary. I'll get the Chief Constable to send out right away to Deeplands and check on the fact that Wilbery's body's there – where you say it is. I'm going to take your word that you've got that letter from Lionel to his sister saying that Haragos is riding him; that he's going to see Haragos again. That's good enough for an arrest on suspicion. Who knows . . . we might find the gun. Perhaps Milta hasn't got rid of it. He doesn't know that Lionel's been found anyway. You go and see Haragos and try your bluff. I'll be along at five-thirty, but for God's sake be careful.'

Callaghan grinned into the telephone.

'Why?' he asked. 'You don't mean to tell me that you'd give a damn if Milta finished me off too?'

Gringall said: 'Believe it or not I wouldn't like it. You've been such a damned nuisance during the past two or three years I might even miss you.'

'Thank you for nothing,' said Callaghan. 'I'll be seeing you.'

He hung up.

Nikolls lit a Lucky Strike. He struck the match on the seat of his trousers. He said:

'So we finally found Lionel?'

Callaghan nodded. He said:

'You don't think that Milta would have taken a run-out? You think he'll still be there?'

'Sure,' said Nikolls. 'He had a meal waitin' for him at one o'clock. He sent the tray down on the service lift. Then he rang down to the night porter – my girlfriend – an' said he wanted to be called at eleven o'clock tomorrow; that he was goin' down to the country for two days.'

Callaghan asked: 'When he sent the tray down on the service lift, what was on it?'

'Just the tray,' said Nikolls, 'an' the day's newspapers. Milta has a lot of newspapers. He sent them down too.'

'What happened to them?' asked Callaghan.

'My girlfriend chucked 'em in the ash-can,' said Nikolls. 'All the bits of food that come down on the service lifts at

Rufus Court go inta one ash-can for pig-food an' everything else goes inta the ordinary dustbins. They're collected every day.'

Callaghan grinned.

'That's excellent,' he said. He put his hand in his pocket
and brought out the .28 Spanish automatic, the gun with
which Lionel had shot himself. He said: 'You come along
with me to Rufus Court. I'm going to see Milta.
Somehow . . . I don't care how, you get at that dustbin.
You get hold of the newspapers that Milta sent down. Put
this gun inside the roll of newspapers and put it in the
ash-can. Right at the bottom somewhere. D'you think you
can do that?'

'I'll do it,' said Nikolls. 'Don't worry. What are we
doin'? Hangin' something on Milta?'

Callaghan said: 'We're being the hand of Justice for
once. We're being Retribution. We're being all sorts of
things. . . .'

Nikolls grinned.

'That suits me,' he said. 'I been everything else so I
might as well be the hand of Justice for once.'

He put out his hand and took the pistol gingerly. He
covered it with his handkerchief.

'Oughtn't this to have Milta's fingerprints on it?' he
asked.

Callaghan shook his head.

'No,' he said. 'Milta would have cleaned them off . . .
but it doesn't matter. The ammunition's in the clip . . .
they'll check up with the bullet that's in Lionel's head.
They'll find the bullet came from that gun.'

'The gun that Milta's gettin' rid of,' said Nikolls. 'I get
it.' He put the pistol in his pocket.

'Come on,' said Callaghan. 'Gringall will be there at
five-thirty. We've got to work fast. I'll drop you off near
Rufus Court. Can you get in by the tradesmen's entrance?'

'That's O.K.,' said Nikolls. 'I got a good excuse for goin'
back there . . .' He grinned at Callaghan. "An don't worry

about that gun,' he said. 'I'll plant it in the main ash-can – the big one that the Borough Council people clean out – the one that goes straight to the incinerator. The cops are sure to search that . . .'

Callaghan stood in front of the door of Milta's flat waiting. When he heard the sound of it being opened he felt, for the first time in the Wilbery case, a slight feeling of excitement.

Milta stood in the hallway. He was in pyjamas and a dressing-gown. He looked surprised. He said in his hearty voice:

'So . . . it is my friend Mr Callaghan. So Mr Callaghan is still looking for Lionel. I hope you find him. Come in.'

Callaghan went in. He went into the sitting-room – a large well-furnished room. Milta closed the front door, came after him. He got a box of cigarettes, produced a bottle of vodka and two glasses from the sideboard. Callaghan was standing in front of the fireplace. He said:

'I don't want a drink. I don't want a cigarette. I just want to talk to you.'

'Why not?' said Milta. 'I like hearing people talk.'

Callaghan said: 'You think I've come here to do a deal with you about Lionel. I expect Sabine told you that all I wanted to do was to find Lionel. I expect she told you I thought I'd make a lot of money if I could find Lionel, because the family would probably want me to find evidence of some sort that might save Lionel from being tried for killing Doria Varette.' He smiled at Milta. 'The joke is,' he said, 'I don't have to worry. Lionel didn't kill Varette. We know who killed Varette.'

Milta poured himself a glass of vodka. He drank it at one gulp. He smacked his lips. He looked at Callaghan happily, lit a cigarette.

'What do I care?' he said. 'What does it matter to me who killed thees Varette woman?'

Callaghan said: 'It's no good bluffing, Milta. We know D'Ianazzi killed Varette. We know D'Ianazzi did it on your orders. We know you paid D'Ianazzi two thousand pounds for killing Varette.'

'Beautiful,' said Milta heartily. 'What imagination. So you know all these things. Pah! You make me laugh.'

Callaghan said: 'We'll make you laugh before we're done with you. Maybe you've heard of two birds called Salkey – a reputed American – and his friend Wulfie – the pansy boy. They're under arrest. They've talked to save their own skins. They've said that D'Ianazzi killed Varette.'

Milta shrugged his shoulders.

'What do I care what they say?' he said. 'They may know that D'Ianazzi killed Varette, but *I* don't know what D'Ianazzi did. I gave D'Ianazzi money. Well . . .' he spreads his hands. 'I've been giving D'Ianazzi money for the last two years. D'Ianazzi was employed by me. He ran games for me. Maybe that is a crime in England but it is not a very beeg crime like murder. If D'Ianazzi killed Varette I suppose you will hang him. So –' he shrugged his shoulders, spread his hands again.

'You're pretty certain of yourself, aren't you, Haragos?' said Callaghan. 'That means you know D'Ianazzi won't talk. I can understand that. Maybe D'Ianazzi's not so black as we think he is. Maybe D'Ianazzi's not a Cuban. Maybe he's an Italian who came to this country to do espionage work; who came to this country with a passport faked by his Government, with a Cuban visa on it. But he's been working for you. He's been working for you on the other business.'

Milta poured another glass of vodka.

'So there is another business,' he said. 'How interestin'. You get better every moment, my friend Callaghan. Tell me about the other business.'

'You wouldn't know, would you?' said Callaghan. 'You wouldn't know about the Zayol Press, in which Sabine – your delightful sister – took such an interest. Marvellous idea that,' said Callaghan, 'publishing books of poetry for export, books in which the authors were assisted by

Sabine. Sabine reconstructed the poems, and in her reconstruction the information you and she wanted to get out of this country was shown in code. You could even have a code message running through three different books, and there probably isn't an expert in the world who could decipher it.

'Most of the authors, I imagine,' Callaghan went on, 'didn't even know what was going on. But one did. Lionel Wilbery did.'

Milta drew a deep breath of cigarette smoke. He began to smile.

'You got that poor weak bastard where you wanted him,' said Callaghan. 'Sabine got him so soaked in drugs he'd have done anything. You used the gaming houses run by D'Ianazzi as centres for picking up information.

'Then the Special Branch here put Varette in. Varette gave Lionel a chance. She told him she was wise to him. She gave him a chance of working for his country instead of working against it. Maybe he tried for a couple of days. Then Sabine got those long fingers of hers on Lionel again and Varette had to be put out of the way.'

Milta said: 'Mos' interesting. Marvellous! All you have got to do, my friend, is to prove it.'

Callaghan grinned. He looked like a devil.

'We can't prove it,' he said. 'We're not even going to try. D'Ianazzi won't talk because, whatever he may be, he believes he's dying for his country. That's why you know D'Ianazzi won't talk. With D'Ianazzi hanged you'd be safe, excepting for one other person. If we found Lionel Wilbery *he* might talk. But you're not worrying about Lionel Wilbery.'

Milta said: 'For once you're correct, my friend. I don't think you'll ever find our leetle Lionel. I think our Lionel is dead. I think he found things a leetle too hot for him. He tol' me he was going to kill himself.'

Callaghan said: 'That's what you say. That's what you told Sabine. That's what you let the servants at The Vale hear – that Lionel was going to commit suicide. So that you could kill him and get away with *that*.'

Milta said: 'My friend, you are mad.'

'Not very,' said Callaghan. 'Lionel went to see you after he'd seen his sister at Deeplands. You were at The Vale – everyone knew you were there. Lionel went to you for money. You wouldn't give it to him. He went off. You said he was going to commit suicide. You said he'd told you that, but he hadn't. He wrote a note to his sister. In that note he said you were riding him like hell, that he was going to see you again. He did see you again. We know where that meeting took place, Milta. We know what you did. You killed Lionel.'

Milta said: 'So that's your story.' He laughed heartily. 'You prove that, my friend. You try and make that story stick.'

Callaghan said: 'I've made it stick. By God, I have!'

There was a ring at the door. Then a knock – a peremptory knock. Callaghan walked across the sitting-room into the hall-way. He said:

'I'm glad you had that meal last night, Milta. I'm glad you sent yesterday's newspapers down on the tray.' He laughed. 'You'll never know what else you sent down wrapped up in those newspapers to go into the dustbin, Milta,' he said.

Milta shrugged his shoulders. Callaghan opened the door. Gringall and two plain clothes men came in.

13

You Never Know With Women

Leonore Wilbery stood in the flower garden at Deeplands. The April sun was shining brightly, the wind had dropped. It was a nice day. She breathed in the clean air deeply.

Callaghan came across the lawn. He came through the gateway in the low wall between the lawn and the flower garden. He said:

'That was Chief Detective-Inspector Gringall of the Special Branch on the telephone. They've found the gun and they've matched the bullets. The bullet that killed Lionel was fired from that gun. The case against Milta is cut and dried. He'll hang. I don't know what they'll do with Sabine.'

She looked at him. She said:

'So Lionel wasn't so bad, after all. Have you told mother about it – all of it?'

Callaghan nodded.

'Yes,' he said. 'She was glad to know at last he'd done his duty by his country. She was glad to know that he died because he told Milta he was going up to London to tell the truth, to tell the truth about the lot of them, including himself; that he was going to take his medicine.

'I told her that that's what he meant by the words, "even if it brings disgrace on the family."'

Leonore nodded. She began to walk across the flower garden. Callaghan went with her. They walked through the coppice. They stood looking at the old summer-house twenty yards away. Leonore said:

'You're rather a marvellous person, aren't you?'

Callaghan grinned.

'No,' he said, 'merely unscrupulous.'

'Oddly enough,' said Leonore, 'I meant that. But marvellously unscrupulous. I know the truth about Lionel.'

Callaghan said: 'What the hell?'

Leonore said: 'Why do you think I told you about the summer-house? Why do you think I told you about our leaving letters there for each other in the old days? I knew you'd go there and look. I found that letter from Lionel hours before. I put it back so that you should find it.'

Callaghan said: 'Well, I'll be damned.'

She went on: 'But you didn't find all the letter. There were two pages to that letter. I left you the second one. The first page told me the truth. The first page told me what Lionel had been doing, how if he'd been any sort of a man and confessed earlier he might have saved Varette's life.

'I know Lionel killed himself, although I never knew, when I was reading that letter, that that poor boy was lying so near to where I was.'

Callaghan said: 'That's all right. Lionel's better where he is. He's done one good thing anyway. The Haragos couple won't operate any more. Lionel helped a bit in any event.'

She nodded.

'I suppose he did,' she said.

They turned and began to walk back towards the flower garden. Callaghan said:

'You'll forget all this. Somebody said that time heals everything. Well, it does. Life for Lionel would have been a long string of misadventures. He's better off where he is. You'll be happier too in the long run, so will your mother. There's always something good in everything.'

She smiled. She said:

'I believe you're right. But then I'm afraid I believe everything you say, even if you are . . .' her eyes were mischievous – 'unscrupulous.'

Callaghan grinned. He said:

'I like telling the truth when I can. When I tell a lie I do it like hell.'

She said: 'There are other things too that, when you do them, you do like hell, aren't there, Mr Callaghan?'

He said: 'Yes. You're remembering what I told you about kissing women. Well, that's the truth. Let me show you.'

In the shadow of the little wood he showed her.